Return to
Das Kaiser Haus

by

Alexandria May
Ausman

Copyright © 2024 by Alexandria May Ausman

Book cover illustration by Alexandria May Ausman
Editor: Jon M. Ausman

Library of Congress Control Number: 2024900368

ISBN: 978-1-963335-07-1 (ebook)
ISBN: 978-1-963335-06-4 (paperback)

Published By:
Ausman & Cousins LLC
1700 North Monroe Street
Suite 11, Box 284
Tallahassee, Florida 32303-0501

For author interviews: ausman@embarqmail.com

Das Kaiser Haus Series

The Rise of the Priceless (Chapters 1 to 10)
Metal Illness (Chapters 11 to 19)
Jonas the Vampire (Chapters 20 to 29)
Prince of the Elders (Chapters 30 to 40)
Leo's Lamb (Chapters 41 to 50)
Mastermind Malfred (Chapters 51 to 58)
Priceless Lost (Chapters 59 to 67)
Broken Silver (Chapters 68 to 74)

The Collar King Series

Return to Das Kaiser Haus (Chapters 1 to 7)
Felicity's Child (coming soon)

The Psycho Series

Cemetery Kid (Chapters 1 to 20)
Stop Calling Me Psycho (Chapters 21 to 33)
Motor-Psycho (Chapters 34 to 44)
Delusion of the Collar and the Key (Chapters 45 to 53)
Brutality's Prisoner (Chapters 54 to 64)
Aesthetic Akathisia (Chapters 65 to 74)
Metallic Burden (Chapters 75 to 83)

27 Masters Series

Book 1 Characters: Return to Das Kaiser Haus

Abelard: a deceased silver trainee
Altergott, Dr.: a psychiatrist
Agnette: mother of Christian Axel
Anna: a psychiatric nurse
Annette: a Haus black collar
Audrey: a Haus Femdom
Barnum: a deceased Elder of the Haus
Ben: a deceased silver trainee
Bladrick: an Elder of the Haus
Britta: a silver Haus submissive
Briton: a deceased House doctor
Bruno: a low level Haus Dominant
Brutus: a Haus trainee
Byron: a Haus Dominant
Casper: an alias assigned to Malfred
Chenowith: a deceased child molester
Christian: the anger and lust shard
Christian Axel: a Haus submissive, the Priceless
Claus: an Elder of the Haus
Cora: a FemDom of the Haus, the Fur Queen
Debbie: Meine Liebe's sexual psychopathic and sadistic
mother
Der Goldene Hund: the Voice or the Boss shard; the
Conscious shard
Der Makellos: German Shepherd named "The
Unblemished"
Drexel: a deceased Elder of the Haus
Egon: Haus seduction Master and trainer

Felicity: a lamb
Fiona: a Haus Dominant
Friedrick: a Haus Dominant, friend of Byron
Fritz: a young Haus Dominant
Geraldine: a deceased silver trainee
Gerard: a sadistic stepfather to Christian Axel
Gregor: a Haus trainee
Gretta: a Haus FemDom, the Silk Queen
Hedy: a young Haus FemDom
Ivan: captain of the Russian Guard
Jakob: a Haus Dominant
Jonas: an Elder of the Haus
Justus: a High-born Dominant, son of Xavier
Karsten: a Haus FemDom
Kilian: a Haus Dominant, psychiatric rehabilitation counselor
Kloe: Marc's big sister, the name of Marc's lamb
Leo: an Elder of the Haus
Louis: a low level Haus Dominant
Lukas: a Voter
Mad Max: the sadistic shard of Maximillian, aka the Heart and Judgment
Mad Maxx: husband of Meine Liebe; a Haus Dominant
Mad Maxx: the masochistic shard, aka the Brain and Guilt
Magnus: a first floor Haus Dominant
Malfred: a Haus Dominant
Marc: a Haus silver trainee to Karsten
Matz: a first floor Haus Dominant, a loan shark
Max: the Soul shard
Maximillian: the submissive name given to Christian by Peter

Maximillian: the seductive shard, aka the Libido
Maxximillian: the submissive adopted by the Elders
Meine Liebe: submissive and spouse of Mad Maxx
Milo: a deceased seduction Haus trainer
Neil: a Haus door guard
Nelda: a low level Haus FemDom, spouse of Louis
Olaf: Haus black collar door guard
Oswin: a first floor Dominant
Peter: a Dominant of Der Kaiser Haus; best trainer of submissives
Rolf: a Haus Dominant
Roland: a first floor Haus Dominant
Ryker: a deceased Haus trainee
Taube: a shard of Maxximillian
Tamina: a Haus silver collar
Thema: a nurse at a psychiatric hospital
Toby: a Haus door guard
Vagnar, Dr.: a clinical psychiatrist
Valitin: a first-floor Haus Dominant
Vebber: the Black Collar Mistress
Vilber: Haus black collar door guard
Xavier: deceased Fur King of the Haus

Preface

In book one of the Collar King, the ex-Priceless pleasure submissive has broken his collar. The newly minted Master Mad Maxximillian intends to fulfil every contract, vow, and promise he made while trapped in the guise of the disturbed pleasure submissive called Maximillian. He understands he cannot call himself a Dominant until he concludes all his unfinished business. No one in the House should've been surprised by this strict adherence to his personal code. They knew the Priceless had always been a man of his word.

However, despite all he has endured in his fight to regain his dignity, he has managed to get nowhere at all. His brief moment of freedom was interrupted by a most unexpected event. Though the young man had broken the bonds that kept him on his knees. He'd given up everything just to regain his dignity and his freedom. That included his sanity.

Free of his cruel Masters at last, he finds himself trapped in a nightmare world where the devil is a woman, the righteous starve to death at a feast, and the fires of hell are stoked by the souls of the innocent.

Mad Maxx has grown into a very disturbed and confused young man. He discovered that escaping from his metal was the easy part.

Terrified and unsure, he learns that his new life of choice comes with responsibilities he was never trained to handle.

The reality he broke with to survive has now become a deadly pit of quicksand. The more he struggles to get to solid ground the lower he sinks.

If he doesn't get out of this trap soon, he will drown on dry land.

Language in italics is a conversation between the adult male Master Mad Maxx and his female submissive Meine Liebe.

Chapter 1: Buried

I swung the sacred bolt cutters and marched down the crowded hallway without a single thought in my head but getting out of the front door. Maximillian and I took the wheel and despite our grief at losing our honorable brother Shard Taube, the mood within was joyful. We had suffered much humiliation, pain, fear, and loss just to get our right to walk out of the hell hole forever.

I could hear the Elders and Voters yelling behind me (which further upset the already panicking mob all around). I heard every fucking word they said, but I ignored their feeble attempts to continue their control over me.

Master Jonas growled out, "Maximillian you halt right this minute boy. You'd better listen to you husband, or you will be sorry."

Master Leo sounded frightened as he pled with me, "Please Maximillian. Stop and come back to speak with us, honey. We need to discuss what you need to do now that you are a Dominant."

Master Peter's voice joined in the buzz of chatter and yelps coming from everyone (or so it seemed), "Maximillian. You turn your ass around this minute. You and I have business to discuss. Did you forget we have a contract? I demand you grant me an audience right now."

Master Baldrick's laugher rang out into the hall as he yelled, "Ah, run boy! Run as far as you can. I hope you do make it to freedom. You earned it, no doubt but you better hurry up Mad Maxx. The Guard are on their way to try and stop you."

I lifted my left hand that held the broken bat collar and without even looking back at them. I lifted my middle finger to flip my ex-Masters the bird. I didn't care about any of them. I wasn't going to take any more of their shit. It was time for me to leave and try to find Annette.

It was my plan that I would find that beautiful girl. Then the two of us would run away to the green fields at the foot of majestic mountains. I knew that in that magical world things like special services, thudding and collars were fantasy, not brutal reality. I could almost hear the baby lambs and smell her fine cooking on the stove in our humble cottage.

Well, that was my plan anyway. It would turn out that Master Mad Maxx's luck was not much better than that idiot submissive Maximillian's was. Sometimes I must wonder if maybe I was born under a bad star. I am merely too immature to control that nasty temper of mine (*as you are aware My Liebe. Again, I apologize for raping you that first time we formally met…Yikes. that sounded just awful how I said that. Never mind. We can deal with my dishonor another day. Of that you can be sure.*).

Back when I broke my metal, I was even more easily set off into fury than I am today. I suppose the stress of it all kind of assured that the historic rise to Dominance of the first Priceless collar was sure to be an event to remember (*and believe me I wish everyone could forget it!*).

There I was rounding the last corner of the hallway that led right to the House door. Dominants, black, and silver collars alike scattered like cockroaches. They were all trying to get the hell out of my way. Behind me, the powerful men and woman of that place gave chase, but it was useless. They couldn't even get close to me due to the enormous number of residents that choked the halls like the clogged arteries of the old man. I was so far ahead of them by that time, it was impossible to capture me.

Then I heard Jonas yell out, "Olaf, Vilber, stop Mad Maxx! Don't allow him to leave or I'll have your heads for it."

I smiled wickedly as I saw the two brutes backing into the walls behind them. It was not the sight of me coming with speed that worried them. It was that most of the House residents were on my heels in mass. I imagine seeing all those people really scared the shit out of the usually arrogant big men.

It was at this point I recalled I owed those two a service return. I had promised them that I would kill them for betraying their vows to me during the reign of Peter. I decided that moment was good as any to keep my word to the black collar brutes. I had sworn that the day I became a Dominant I would murder them, then bury them outside the House doors.

I suppose that Olaf and Vilber either forgotten that promise, or they assumed that like them I merely say words without intending to see my oaths through. I say that because as I approached them, neither man put up a stance of aggression. Nor did they seem to be ready for a battle.

Too bad for them, because I was already lifting my only weapon, the sacred bolt cutters. I believed that would be the most fitting way to end their terror on the helpless silvers of Kaiser Haus.

I jumped onto Olaf first with the fury of the late Spring tempest. I imagine it took him more than five minutes before he realized the boy he had aided to abuse, assault and even raped twice had sent him to his doom. I swung the bolt cutters with a screech of intense thrill. Then I hit him right in the temple. He wilted and fell to the floor with a loud thud.

I quickly turned my attentions to his partner Vilber. He'd broken my heart when I realized he hated me as badly as his brother did. Vilber was simply better at keeping it to himself. As you recall, I discovered his true feelings too late. His cruelly turning me over to Fritz that day resulted in my terrible situation of seeking a contract with the Voters. I had thought of Vilber often during those five months of suffering nightmares beyond comprehension in the closet from hell.

I again used the bolt cutters like a baseball bat. The heavy metal smashed into his neck sending him to his knees. Vilber never offered a defensive attempt to stop me even after seeing me cut Olaf down moments earlier.

Without hesitation I hit him again on the head like I had Olaf. He wailed then fell face first onto the floor. I turned around moving rapidly and slammed the sharp end of the cutters into the unconscious Olaf's eyes. That move killed him instantly.

I laughed maniacally and yelled out, "I never could stand your spooky eyes Olaf. I am glad to have finally put them out. Now I never have to see them glaring at me anymore. Guess you were always right. You should have killed me when you had the chance, cocksucker."

I then returned to the unconscious Vilber. I rolled the silent, still man to his back. Then with a burst of incredible strength I did the same to him as I did to his brutish brother. He was sent on his way to hell the second that pointy mouthed tool collided with his brains via his eye's sockets.

I stepped back from the fresh corpses, panting, and sweating but feeling much relieved to have these two dealt with at last. I was so busy smiting my enemies I forgot there was an audience of everyone watching my personal vendetta play out.

The screams, gasps, and chatter of disbelief over the bloody scene they had witnessed tore me away from my moment of victorious glory. I turned around to realize there were hundreds of eyes all focused on me, the dead door guards, and the blood drenched bolt cutters in my hand.

I shrugged then yelled at them angrily, "I am a man of my word. You can suck my cock if you don't agree that I am! Someone had better turn off that fucking radio! Listen to me, you sonofabitches. Bring me Felicity or else I'll burn this House to the ground. Actually, I am going to anyway, but if you don't give me my lamb I will kill everyone that tries to escape when those flames start licking the walls! Do you motherfuckers hear me? I want those three-year-old little boys the perverts are raping and the four others silver collars you sent to the dungeon. The ones that failed the Dominance testing. You'd better bring them to me right now. I am a Dominant now! I want those children. You don't want them, and I won't let you injure them anymore. They are welcome to come live with me Mad Maxx! Are you listening? We are leaving and then I am calling the cops! Every one of you child molesting, perverted, rapist, criminal scumbags are going to rot in prison for all the horrible things you've done!"

I shook the bolt cutters at them. Olaf and Vilber's blood splattered off the tool like crimson rain. With a collective shudder the crowd backed away. It was then Jonas stepped forward from the gathered mass.

He glared at me as he growled, "Stop this insanity Maximillian. Do you want to be sent to the yard. No one not even a Dominant is permitted to go around killing anyone they wish. You'd better put down the bolt cutters and come with me. You obviously need some rest. There's simply too much stress on your little shoulders."

I interrupted him angrily, "You'd better shut the fuck up, Vampire! All you ever do is spout lies! If I were you, I'd get around to turning into a bat. The Guard may be coming, but if they are, you are the one they will be hauling away, you sodomite! You cannot touch me anymore. I say no to you, and you, and you (I was pointing out all the cocksuckers that ever raped me, but I finally quit because it was going to take all day). All of you will keep your nasty hands off me! In the meantime, I am going to bury these assholes outside by the front door just like I said I was going to do. While I do that you better get me those kids and Felicity. I am warning you. It's not going to take long to get this trash into the ground. After that, everyone here is toast!"

I turned around and opened the door. I propped it open with a fancy table that the brutes used at sit at when they were bored. It was lucky for me that there was a shovel stored in a closet close by. I'd seen the guards put it in there many times over the years. I knew that it was the very same one the Guard had used to bury poor Ryker. I fetched it quickly, while noting that the crowd was shrinking rapidly.

I found out later (much later) that after I struck down Olaf and Vilber, then began threatening everyone. Many low-born Dominants in the mob ran for their lives. Most headed for the sanctuary of their apartments, but others hauled ass out the back door. I suppose they were interested in beginning a long 'vacation' away from the House. You know, just until things cooled down a little, or should I say I calmed down a bit. I suppose several people were aware I may come knocking, looking to settle a score. It goes without saying that there were dozens that most definitely had it coming for taking liberties with me without my consent.

The truth was, I was finished with taken out my vengeance one monster at a time. I had no intension of hunting down low-borns, Voter, Elders, or other black collars. The plan was to bury the sonofabitches that had plagued me for almost three years, then head out to those greener pastures I've told you about.

Once I had that shovel that was the last sight for many a hapless silver collar, I dragged both the corpses out onto the porch. It was an overcast day, and there was no doubt at some point it was going to start raining. I had hoped to see the sun, blue skies and fluffy clouds for the first time with my free eyes, but as usual I was just going to have to settle for less.

Despite the somber weather and darkened view, I cannot say I could recall a more beautiful day than that late morning was to me. If it had been raining frogs and brimstones, I likely would still remember it with awe and thrill.

After all, I was a freeman at last. Everything seemed brighter, more gorgeous, and perfect. That was because this time, I could enjoy it at my leisure. I marveled at the scenery for a moment then took off my hat, rolled up the sleeves of my long jacket and went to work digging graves for the door Guards.

The workouts with Friedrick, Rolf and Byron had paid off. Not only was I able to murder Olaf and Vilber with ease but carving out a hole to store them in was a breeze as well. The unusual wet summer made the ground easy to work with. I sang a song from Leo's records in English as I worked, then whistled several tunes from the Classical composers of centuries long past.

I don't know how much time went by, but I had one grave dug. It was shallow because what the fuck did I care if the grounds dogs dug them up? Good enough for them to be dinner for the hounds. I was pushing Olaf's battered corpse into the hole when I saw Leo come out onto the porch. He was walking slowly and with an expression of fear on his face.

I stopped my task to wipe the sweat from the boy's brow, "What do you want Leo? I hope you've come to help me dig."

He swiveled his head all around then came down the steps (but kept a safe distance from me holding that shovel), "No my little rabbit. I came out to see if you would let me take the sacred bolt cutters back to the Hall of Records where they belong. You know the next batch of silver's hoping for Dominance selection will be needing them."

I chuckled at that, "Leo, do not come out here to spew bullshit to me. I believe I have plenty of fertilizer for the grass already without your addition (I pointed at the cooling corpses). If you want them, be my guest. I do not intend to ever set foot back in that hell hole. Eventually, someone would have to retrieve the tool. May as well be you, ja?" I went back to digging no longer interested in what the schwuler was up to.

Leo picked up the discarded cutters that were lying in a pool of blood as he said, "My little rabbit, you certainly have made a mess of things. I would ask you to trust me like you once did. Please listen to me. Jonas was not lying. The Guard will come for you soon. This was a public killing. However, if you come back inside with me to our home, I can protect you from their rough treatment. Please Christian Axel, you must listen."

I threw down the shovel with irritation then turned around and spit back at him, "I must not do anything anymore Leo! I am a free man. I broke that fucking collar and you saw it with your own eyes. Take the cutters if you want, but then get out of my sight before I forget that I love you. I told you I am leaving and I'm never coming back. You, nor Jonas or any of his fleas can stop me. I am waiting for Felicity. You promised to get her back if I broke my metal. I also want those others that failed that bullshit you fuckers call a fair collar selection. Everything I was ever told about it was horse shit. I am free and they are not only because the entire Elder and Voter leadership was fucking me. Those poor little kids didn't have a chance and you know it! You'd better get them and let them go Leo. I swear to fucking God, If you don't do as I say then I'll kill every Dominant in this HOUSE. At least those that the police don't arrest. And for the love of God turn down that fucking radio dammit!"

Leo frowned then looked at his boots as he replied, "Honey, you do not understand your situation. The Voters and Elders are not going to let you just walk away. You need professional help for your psychosis, and they believe you are a danger to their continued safety from authorities. That is not a good thing. Everyone hears you telling them that you intend to report their crimes to outsiders. That is a betrayal of the oath you have sworn to the House, my little rabbit. We can change the hellish nightmare that goes on in this community together but doing it the way you threaten. Oh, my love, that kind of attitude will get you put to the yard. Do you want to feed the worms with these two brutes? That's gonna happen if you don't listen to me. In fact, just a few moments ago Cora and Gretta demanded a meeting. They want to the House leaders to order you shot. Please, if you ever loved me, my little rabbit, I beg this favor from you. Just come back inside to our home. Hey, did you know, Der Makellos is asking about you?"

I smiled as I thought of our beautiful hound and said, "Ah, he is? Well, you can tell him about the good news for me. I was going to write him a letter, but since you are here, you can give him a message. Tell Der Makellos the minute I find an apartment out there in the brutal world, I will send for him. First, I need to find a job. Then I'll buy a car, save some money and get a wife. Once I have all that I can take care of him properly. Until then, please keep him safe for me Leo." I picked back up the shovel and went back to my task of digging graves.

Leo stood their sighing for several minutes, but eventually went back inside. He took the bloody cutters with him. I chuckled as I imagined my children playing with Der Makellos. I knew he would love our family and defend us from all attackers.

I began to whistle again feeling another burst of happiness coming over me. I began to imagine coming home from my job as a doctor. I would kiss my wife and many children, and we would all play with Der Makellos. Life was beyond sweet for that moment. Well, at least it was inside my head.

Outside in the real world, things were growing as foreboding as the darkening skies. I noticed that a couple of black collar brutes were showing up in the parking lot. They were driving off in the numerous stretched limos and black cars that belonged to the House. They would leave separate, then come back in one, then take another.

By the time I threw Olaf and Vilber into their final resting spots, that parking area was empty of vehicles of any kind. I found that a bit odd. I wondered if the Dominants of the House had finally taken me seriously. I assumed they were all running for their lives (since I was burning down that motherfucking place you know). It made sense. Why else would the leaders suddenly remove all the cars? I decided not to worry about it as I finished shoveling dirt over the last corpse.

The next task on my pressing agenda was to engage in the tradition all submissive that break their silver collar are expected to do. According to the House law, I couldn't call myself officially Dominant until I'd made the metal that bound me to a Master disappear.

So, I stealthily (in old submissive high protocol on my toes) snuck off into a private spot in the House yard. I dug a small deep hole in a shady spot far from prying eyes. When the hole was of sufficient depth I dropped in my broken collar, leash and all. I watched it drop into the gaping wound in mother earth's bosom. I said no words, nor did I express any emotions as I filled in that ugly blemish on that perfect landscape. I'd made sure to hide the evidence of its location best as possible. This must be done to guarantee no one would ever find it nor lay eyes on that abomination. It is a symbolic way of forgetting the indignity I'd suffered on my knees.

I threw the shovel against the wall with a loud yell of 'hell yes." It was done, and now I was truly free. I decided to rest for a moment. Digging those holes to bury enemies and a Priceless bat collar really took it out of me! I sat down on the porch steps to catch my breath for a moment, while I peered out across the empty parking. It was then I noticed not a single bird, or insect was making a sound.

I perked my ears trying to hear anything other than the noise of the rising wind rattling the leaves in the trees. I realized the signs indicated a storm was coming. I stood up and craned my head all around. I was looking for the quickest route to the road. I'd hoped to be in town before sunset. I, however, had no idea how far I would have to travel, nor which direction to get there.

I shrugged and smiled at the Maximillian shard as I said, "Well at least it is warm. I suppose the rain won't be so bad when there is no chance of it freezing."

Maximillian chuckled and replied, "Yes, I am with you brother. Let's just start walking. Sooner or later there should be a town or village. We can look for work first thing in the morning. Tonight, we can sleep in the woods, ditch or alleyway. Matters not. Anywhere but here sounds like Heaven to me."

I laughed as I began walking toward the parking lot, "Ah I am in agreement with you Maximillian. Better watch out brutal world! Mad Maxximillian is coming to join you." Maximillian laughed, and even the ailing Max shard joined in the mirth for a moment.

With an expression of surprise Maximillian yelled out suddenly, "Hey! Do you know what brother? I am now officially retired! Isn't that the best thing you've ever heard?" He danced around like a fool.

I shook my head and growled in reply, "Well maybe you won't need to suck anymore cocks schwuler boy, but as a Dominant there is more work to do than ever. You better pull your weight, or I will personally kick your ass. Perhaps you can learn to do something useful and honest with that mouth of yours for a change. For starters you could try to sweet talk our way into employment."

He nodded as he said with a wicked grin, "That would be my pleasure for a change!" I was laughing over his statement when suddenly his expression became confused.

16

He pointed in the distance wildly as he yelled out, "Hey, what the fuck? Look at that Mad Max! I can see Christian coming this way. He looks frightened too! Oh my God, what is that sound?" I tracked his finger just in time to see our lust/anger shard running toward us with all the speed he could muster.

Behind him was a huge white van that was wailing. I had heard that sound before on Leo's television. I recalled this is the noise the police officer, and ambulance vehicles made when they are coming to haul someone away. As the siren grew louder, I trembled in terror as I realized they were coming for me!

I took off running toward the backyard of the House when the white and red ambulance pulled into the empty parking lot. Chrisian had caught up and jumped into the boy as we ran for the playground. I heard men demanding that I halt, from the open windows of the ambulance.

Suddenly four big men wearing all white jumped out of and started heading right for me. I was hoping we could lose them in the wooded area behind the swing set. I should have run in another direction but at that moment I was beyond frightened. It was the only plan to lose them I could produce on a dime like that.

I fled at full throttle while Chrisian screamed those men were gaining on us. I never imagined in a million years someone from outside the House would be chasing me across the grounds. Had you told me such a thing was possible I would have laughed and accused you of hallucinations. This, however, was really happening, and not a symptom of a psychotic break.

I came alongside the House ready to take that left turn to the swing set when I immediately came to a screeching halt. Standing in my path were six huge Russian brutes. I recognized them immediately as members of the Haus Guard. I let out a wail and turned around to run back the way I had come.

A scream escaped me when I saw the men in white were blocking that route of escape. There wasn't anywhere left to run but back into the House. Without out hesitation, I headed toward the door. The Guard and men in white closed in around me. No doubt they assumed I was trapped. They were wrong.

I speed off with all the vigor a boy of fifteen possesses. My pursuers growled out in irritation as they also resumed the chase. I hurriedly turned the handle, desperate to get inside to safety but to my horror discovered it was locked.

I cast a quick glance back toward the attackers closing in on me. Pure fear pumped through my veins as I used my own body as a battering ram. To my surprised when I smacked into that motherfucker with all my might, it caved. Avoiding a near spill right to my face, I managed to rapidly slip inside that dark, dusty, horror once more.

The thought of Leo's offer was the only thing on my mind. I was no longer so picky about the company I kept. I'd decided to take him up on his most generous invite to hang out with him in his apartment. Dominants, black and silver collars panicked in their attempts to get out of my way while I made a Bline right for the main staircase.

Behind me the Russian brutes and white clad outsiders came piling thru the door. The first fellow through the door spotted me attempting my wild flight up the steps. He yelled for the others to follow him. Within seconds the entire lot of them were back to giving chase.

I managed to outrun them all the way to the fourth floor. I'm ashamed to admit it, but I was screaming for help the entire way. It was there that I saw Kilian standing on the platform. Even from a distance I could see he was wide eyed in terror upon witnessing this strange scene.

I yelled out to him, "Help Kilian! These men are going to kill me! I need to get Leo. Mercy please! Tell Felicity to call the police."

Kilian nodded as he shouted back, "Come with me Mad Maxx! I can hide you from them. Hurry up dammit! They are gaining on you!" He motioned for me to follow him.

I ran toward him through the fourth-floor hallway nearly out of my mind in fear. The men behind me didn't break off their chase. It was clear they had every intention of catching me at any cost. I wailed out in terror when I turned around and saw they were closing in.

Before I could turn back to focus on what was in front of me, a strange pain filled my head. The world began to spin, stopping me dead in my tracks. A swoon overtook me while ringing filled my ears, and color splotches robbed me of sight. Confusion overtook me and my knees buckled. That caused me to collapse onto my back right there on the carpeted hallway floor.

Above me the faces of the Guard brutes and the men in white filled my field of vision. I moaned in pain as my head began pounding. It was then that I finally realized someone had hit me with something other than a fist. The men in white took hold of my arms and legs. They held me still despite my strong efforts to struggle against them.

The Russians back away but watched as the four men in white coats spoke to each other excitedly. One of them said that though I had been captured I needed to be sedated. I tried to speak to them, but fear had robbed me of my tongue. I wildly looked about for aid of any kind. I saw Kilian lean into the wall observing the situation.

In pure desperation I screamed to the Voter, "Please Kilian, mercy! Call Leo! Call Jonas! Call anyone! These men are going to kill me! Help me and I'll pay you any price for it!"

He smiled and shook his head while showing me a 'billy club' that he held in his hand, "Oh they are not going to kill you Maxx. Jonas and Leo are not going to help you little fool. They called these men on you. Now you mind them and be sweet or else they'll use worse than this nightstick on that touched head of yours. I'll see you soon boy, real soon. Enjoy your vacation." He walked off humming a tune appearing quite thrilled over my predicament.

I wailed at the brute in white that held my left arm to the floor, "That man just hit me with a weapon. Are you going to let him get away? Why are you bothering me? There are criminals all around you. I am not the one you want. These people who live in this House kill children and rape the little three-year-old boys. They also murder lambs and there is a Vampire living among them. Please listen to me. Did you hear that? That DJ just told you. Aren't you listening? He said this House is full of the fleas. Help me burn it down. Felicity, please help me! Someone, anyone help me. I've broken my collar dammit! You cannot do this to a Dominant! Who the fuck do you people think you are?" I began to wriggle, struggle and even tried to bite the brutes.

The one holding my legs told another of them to take his place. I watched that brute reach into his jacket pocket and pull out a syringe. I screamed in terror as he popped off the top then pulled my breeches down until he'd exposed my left hip.

Even Christian joined in adding strength to the boy while we gave all we had to try to stopping him from jabbing that poison into my muscle tissue. It was of no use. The man's three buddies tightened their hold. The moment he felt I was subdued enough to force his shot into the flesh he popped me with his needle. I screamed bloody murder than began weeping loudly as he injected that shit into my veins.

Within moments, I felt my strength leaving me. I watched the men as they cautiously let me go. I tried to get off the floor so I could run away but I discovered the medication had done its job. It had even robbed me of the ability to speak. I gasped while two of them lifted me into the air like a hammock. We all went back down the stairs with the team holding my nearly paralyzed flesh hostage in their grips.

Everything was moving slowly, and I felt fatigued to the point of nodding off despite the seriousness of the situation. The last thing I can clearly recall is the four in white lifting me onto a white gurney. One of them strapped me to it while the others thanked the Russian brutes 'for helping them capture the patient without serious incident.'

Just before the darkness of unconsciousness came for me, I wondered, 'who this fellow named patient was, and why did the Guard need to help these weirdos take him down. I decided he must have been one damned big and scary guy if it took all those brutes to do it. I made up my mind I would find out where Patient lived in the House and get a closer look at him. Well, right after I got a little nap.'

I dreamed that Ryker hadn't been killed and Annette was my wife. He came to visit us in our little cottage. We all had a wonderful time while eating Annette's amazing sausage and sauerkraut dinners. In my dreams, Ryker was a happy man, but not as full of joy as me. I had it all. The fields of green, the lambs, the loyal hound, and the sunshine. It was so bright, I needed to cover my eyes before it blinded me.

I opened them when I realized my arms were not working. I groaned as that painful glare felt as if it were going to sear my head in half. There was a middle-aged man with greying hair shining a penlight into my face. He grimaced and pushed back his heavy glasses. I noticed right away he was wearing a white coat and was speaking to a heavy-set woman sitting at a desk (also dressed in white with greying locks). I slowly understood that she was writing everything he said down on a piece of paper.

My throat was dry as the desert, but I managed to say, "Who are you? Where am I? Call Leo, or the police. I have been kidnapped. Please, you must get help. They are going to kill those little children in the dungeons. You cannot let them do that. Those kids didn't do anything wrong. You must stop them from hurting the innocent. Just ask Felicity. Where is she? The lamb will tell you all about the nightmares in the House. You can trust her because she never tells a lie." The man just stared at me for a moment then he reached for my chest without replying to me.

I moaned as he began unbuttoning my blouse. I thought, well you know what I thought. I struggled in a panic, doing all I could to prevent him from stripping me down. I told him he couldn't force sex on me because I broke my metal fair and square. I reminded him that he couldn't just do as he pleased and touch a Dominant without permission.

Try as I might, I was bound to a gurney bed by my arms and legs. I couldn't prevent him from taking any liberty he wanted from me. I closed my eyes and began to weep when he got my shirt open then went for my breeches.

In a pathetic tone I whimpered to him, "Please don't do this to me. I told you I've broke my collar. If you don't believe me, you can ask the Elders or call Gretta. At least tell me why I've been auctioned. I don't want you to have sex with me. Sir, I beg your mercy." I sobbed even harder after saying that feeling more helpless than I ever had before.

This unexpected horror was confusing me. The only explanation I could come up with (at that time) was that someone had double crossed me. I assumed the House had sold me off and this man was with the circuit.

Well, I need not tell you just how horrified, desperate, and sickened I was at this most heinous idea. In my mind, all was lost, even though I distinctly remembered I had passed the collar selection, or did I? I couldn't be sure. My mind and memory had been playing tricks on me for quite some time by then.

The man gasped and grumbled as he stripped me down. The woman with him took off my clothing when he got them mostly pulled down (to avoid having to unstrap me from the gurney). She appeared upset and kept staring at my naked flesh wide eyed as if in shock.

The man then said to her in a gruff tone, "Thema, please remain professional and remove your expression of distress immediately. This boy has obviously been through serious trauma based on what we can see on his skin. He needs no further stress, nor horrified voyeurs to his pain."

The woman called Thema nodded as she replied, "Yes, Doctor Vagner. I apologize for my lack of candor. I will return to my note taking." She shot me a look of pity then when to sit back down after dropping my destroyed clothing next to her desk.

The man called Doctor Vagner cleared his throat then looked at me as he said, "Try to calm yourself Maximillian. No one here is going to harm you. We are here to help your confusion. I am Dr. Wagner the head Psychiatrist here at the hospital. You are suffering from a psychotic break caused by a disease called schizophrenia. I can see you have been badly treated by someone in your short life. Here at the Heslach Institute we strive to provide you with the latest in medical treatments in a peaceful stress-free environment. I would like to ask you a couple of questions if you would be so kind to attempt to answer them for me?"

I was still weeping heavily but feeling a little bit of hope that maybe this wasn't as bad as it seemed, "Are you telling me this is a hospital outside of the Kaiser Haus? Is that is why you all wear white doctor coats? Do you intend to force me to give you special services?"

He narrowed his eyes and replied, "Yes, this is a hospital, and I am your doctor. What does the term special services mean? Does that phrase have some meaning of importance to you?"

I nodded assuming he was funning me as I responded, "Yes sir, I should say it does. Is this a trick? Well, if you try to make me give you service, you may get away with it for a little while. But I swear the second I get out of these restraints. I'll come looking for my service return. You are not permitted to force my favors now that I am a Dominant. I want to speak to Felicity. Where is my lamb? You better get her for me immediately. If you dare to lay a finger on me she will end your days on Earth, schwuler pig." I spit at him.

He backed up then flashed a look of anxiety at that woman called Thema as he said in a shaky tone, "Maximillian please! There is no need to be rude, and the word, schwuler is most offensive. I must ask you nicely not to use it again."

Tears were streaming down my cheeks as I replied, "Ah, does it bother you that I call you what you are? Okay, you're right. I apologize for hurting your feelings. I will use words that are more comforting to your tender ears, you child molesting, rapist, kidnapping, motherfucker! You see doctor, I am not an unreasonable fellow. I am willing to avoid all the vulgar words that upset your gentle sensibilities. Even though you didn't even offer me the decency of asking the female to leave before you go stripping me down. I wonder when you rape will you ask her to join in at some point? I suppose I should thank you for the mercy of the beautiful distraction of her wiles. You pervert! You'd better let me go or you will be more than a little sorry for it."

Thema grabbed her chest and gasped which drew Dr. Wagner's attention as he growled out, "Thema, I asked you to remain professional. Please leave Maximillian and me. I would like to speak with him without a shocked audience. I will thank you to wait until I ask you to return to this room." She nodded then exited immediately without saying a word.

I craned my neck around to see the room was stark white with blood pressure machines, and other medical tools. I wondered why this fellow felt the need to go all out just to meet his sick fetishes. I told you I've never understood Dominants, not in all my days.

Doctor Wagner pushed his glasses back onto his face and looked at his boots appearing uncomfortable suddenly as he sheepishly said, "I need to examine you Maximillian. Based on what you are saying and the conditions you are in, I must assume the worst. Before I do that, I would like to ask you directly, am I going to find you have been sexually molested? If so, is the person who did that grievous crime to you the same one that all these scars and wounds on your skin. Or is there more than one offender?"

I sobbed and laughed at the same time as I yelled out, "Is this a joke? How dare you pretend to act as if you don't know about the way everyone has misused me and stolen my dignity! If you are serious than I must ask where the fuck have you been Mister Rip Van Winkle. Shit, I was the Priceless collar, for fucks sake! The real question is who's cock have I've not sucked or been fucked by? I must suppose you get turned on by forcing me to say that I am a whore. Well, there you go. So, get on with your rape, will you? I want to make it to town before dark and you are wasting my time. As for my scars. You know God damned well that Gerard cut me to shit. Of course, then there is that Vampire husband of mine. He's been drinking my blood for years. The rest of this horror on my skin, well take your pick. That one is from the statute fucker and that one from my vicious lover, Xavier the child killer. Oh, and those came from Barium's hooks. I hung on those for a bit before the door Guard I murdered went to tell the old Dungeon Master Bladrick that their fun with me was getting out of hand. Did you know he pushed that fucker right off the banister. I wonder if Casper saw that too. That bank robing ghost raped me by the magic blue water with his buddies. Most of them got shot for that, but Casper floated right up to the sixth floor. As usual I got an ass full of blood over that bullshit. I remember that was the day I bit off my mothers' fingers. Hey, is this shit going to be on the exam? Did I pass that collar selection test or not? If I did then I demand you let me go! I don't want you fucking me but if that's what it's going to take to get out of here, then I beg of you get to it! I really need to be on my way."

Doctor Wagner rubbed his forehead then walked to the door and whispered to Thema that was in the hallway, "You need to call in Doctor Altergott. We have a severe case of ritual child abuse with a most disturbed young man. Also, tell the orderly on staff to get the rubber room ready. This boy is going to need complete quiet in a safe space for a very long time, I think. Thank you, nurse." He closed the door then went to Thema's desk and took a seat.

28

I growled at him, "Are you going to call the police Doctor Wagner? You should report that House business to them. If you hurry, then the poor little silvers in the dungeons will live to see the sunrise. I am supposed to be in the Great Hall to share a beer with one of them. You know that guy that was ahead of me in line? Well, I am a man of my word, and I cannot let him down. I swore to be there. Why are you not helping them? They molest, rape, and murder children in the Kaiser House Mister. Didn't you hear the DJ? He just told you I am not lying. The Vampire told lies about my having schizophrenia to steal my father's metal. He is a sodomite that has done many horrors to me. Go ahead and call him. Ask him if he denies he is a flea right out of a hairy bat's fur."

Doctor Wagner shook his head and sighed as he pulled out a syringe. I watched in pure terror as he injected the needle into a small bottle, he had collected from a metal cabinet in the room. I shuddered and wailed louder as he held it to the light and tapped out the air bubbles. Then he approached slowly while I struggled helplessly held down to the table

I screamed out as he stabbed me with his sedative, "Please don't do this! I told you I won't fight your lustful interest. I just want to go home! I'm begging you for mercy! Someone, anyone, please help me! Felicity, where are you? I need you!"

I of course, do not recall most of the next several hours. To be really honest, I don't remember most of the next couple of weeks. All that comes to my memory when I try to pull up anything from this missing time in my life is the color white and the smell of rubbing alcohol with many needle sticks into my hips.

When that fog in my recollections lifted, I found myself restrained in strait jacket that was leashed to a fucking rubberized wall. I had no idea how long I'd been stuck like that. The only other thing in the room was a bed (also made of rubber material), and a hole in the floor. I quickly discovered the hole was there for my piss to roll down whenever I wet myself. That tended to happen often thanks to the lack of regular check-ups made by the hospital staff. I couldn't attend to my nature calls without their assistance.

It was starting to slowly dawn on me that someone had mistakenly thought I was psychotic. This was a real hospital and some pleasure room owned by a Dominant with a fetish for medical play (In case you didn't know Meine Liebe, medical play is a BSDM term for playing doctor grown up style).

I must have begged those doctors and nurses a thousand times to call the police on the House and her residents. Everyone ignored my pleas. It was clear they all assumed the things I told them about the House were merely the ravings and rantings of a 'madman.' I admit that I wept constantly, both day and night, those first few weeks.

The biggest reason for that unmanly behavior was because I'd suffered so much to break my metal. Only to be taken hostage in yet another type of prison. It seemed no matter what I did or how hard I fought, I was always going to be trapped in some cell all alone. First Gerard's barn, then on to the dungeons, followed by my Masters beds and now the Mental Hospital.

Sadly, by this time, I had become an expert at enduring long-term bondage, isolation, and pain. It seemed all I ever did was chase my tail. I never went anywhere but in a circle.

The other reason for all that sobbing was, well, everything. I cried for days over failing to rescue the other Dominant candidates from being sent to off to their doom. Of course, I had no idea at that time that Britta was spared. That is if you could call a lifetime of enforced servitude such a thing.

I was inconsolable, believing that it was my fault many of the people around me while I wore a collar had found their graves. It was obvious to me that I'd squandered their sacrifices by allowing myself to be captured. All I could do is wish I'd successfully drank bleach, jumped from a banister, gotten shot in the yard, or even slit my own throat rather than to have gambled life without the heavy silver would be better.

Christian, Maximillian, Max, and me all were beyond despaired. None of us could find a reason to continue with our struggles. Most days, we didn't even bother to speak. Not even to each other. I'd completely stopped attempting to communicate with the nurses, doctors and other staff too.

By the end of the third week in that rubber room cell from hell, all I did was sit in a corner quietly staring at nothing while wishing for death.

Things were looking grim for your Master. One day melted into another endlessly without space or meaning. I began to refuse the meals the aides tried to feed me hoping that eventually I would starve to death. I assumed that the grave was my only hope for real freedom since nothing else had seemed to work.

The doctors responded by giving me more pills and increasing my injections. I'd become numb from all the side effects of that nasty shit. I thought it ironic that I'd been mislabeled as schizophrenic when in truth, it was everyone around me that was insane.

I mean after all, when you think on it, the House was full of vampires, Masters, children wearing silver or black collars, child molesters, statue fuckers, door and yard guards, oh you know. The list goes on and on. It seemed to me if that shit is not crazy nothing else is. Oddly, it appeared I was the only motherfucker that seemed to think this crap was right out of a funny farm ballad. I admit I had given up. Day after day nothing but white walls, depressing memories, and horrific nightmares.

Then maybe four weeks after I got hijacked from the fourth floor Maximillian, Christian, Max and I were sitting quietly in the wheel room when a familiar voice rang out, "Oh, my God. How long did I sleep? Why is Christian here? Shit, are we killing someone today? Please tell me if the Vampire or Malfred is the target this time. Hey, wait a minute! Where is Taube?" Mad Maxx our intelligence shard, yawned and stretched out his legs as if merely awaking from an afternoon nap instead of the nearly six months he'd been catatonic.

Christian growled out, "Well, I will be damned. It lives. Welcome back Sleeping Beauty. You know I thought it would take the kiss of a Prince to wake up the damsel, but clearly I was mistaken." He chuckled at his bad attempt at humor.

I stood up then asked in a shocked tone, "Brother, are you feeling alright? Tell me something. What is the last thing you remember?"

He stood up and groaned as he held his back then replied, "First of all, I confess. I couldn't handle the pressure and I chickened out. I last thing I recall is that Malfred was forcing himself on us and then then things started to get out of hand. Did you say Taube is resting?"

Maximillian shook his head and replied, "No, he isn't. A lot of things have happened since you went catatonic. One of the biggest caused our dearest brother Taube to shatter."

He gasped then whispered, "What? Oh no, but why? What the hell could have happened bad enough to send Taube to dust?"

I replied flatly, "He sacrificed himself to save us, Mad Maxx. The day we broke our collar, it required him to run the wheel solo. It was too much for him, hell any of us, to manage alone."

Mad Maxx's eyes went wide as a triumphant smile spread across his face, "Wait a second! Are you saying we were judged Dominant during the collar selection? Oh my God, that is glorious news! But if that happened then why are you all sitting around depressed and doing nothing? Well, fuck that. We should go out and celebrate our good fortune immediately. Wait, you better not be funning with me Mad Max."

I shook my head as I said glumly, "I am not, brother. I would let you take the wheel to prove the boy's neck isn't adored with metal, but you'll just have to take my word for it. The arms and hands are useless to us."

His smile melted to a frown as he said, "What do you mean? Did the boy get into an accident and become quadriplegic or something? Is that why you are all so glum despite our being free?"

Christian scoffed a reply, "Are we free? If so, that is news to me. Is this the unrestricted lifestyle you were told breaking our collar assured? If so, then I hope you realize we have been ripped off. We are just as much in a prison as we have ever been. Don't believe me? Go ahead, look for yourself."

Mad Maxx took the wheel then narrowed his eyes then said in a confused tone, "Where the hell are we?"

Maximillian snorted in reply, "In a locked rubber room at a mental institution wearing a strait jacket."

He sighed as he said, "Okay, got it. So, how long have we been here and who sent us. Oh, I know, it was Leo, right?"

I shook my head as I responded, "At first, we thought he had, but now we suspect Jonas did this shit. He took guardianship of the boy just before we broke the collar. He obviously wanted the legal power to keep us from escaping his nasty claws. We think it is still possible that Leo could be partly responsible. But I would like to ask him before we all start assuming this mess is his cruel work alone."

Mad Maxx gasped, "The Vampire did what? Oh, holy hell! Okay, I am listening. You boys better catch me up on everything I have missed. Shit! Next you will be telling me that Malfred is our buddy and Peter has confessed his fatherly love for us."

Maximillian appeared shocked as he stared at Mad Maxx and said, "Yeah, I hate to break this to you, but actually you are right on the money, brother. I think you'd better sit down. This story is going to take a minute to tell." Mad Maxx sat down with a shocked expression on his face.

I sat there listening to Maximillian spew out the entire story of how much we had endured over the last nine months to Mad Maxx. Hearing it all in one sitting was more than a little troubling. I leaned back into the back wall shuddering as I realized that the resulting nervous breakdown we'd suffered was not only possible but probable!

Hell, I even decided we didn't have schizophrenia. Obviously, our symptoms were trauma driven and our psychiatrist had it all wrong. This was simply a misunderstanding. He didn't know the truth about the evils we had suffered since birth.

If somehow, we could convince these people that we were not a raving lunatic, then surely, they wouldn't deny our reactions were completely normal given such extreme circumstances. I even believed it was likely that once we'd proved ourselves sane, the kindly doctors would call the authorities on the criminals that had done this to us.

I smiled with renewed vigor with the idea that with a bit of luck I might manage to get the House shut down. All I had to do was make these hospital outsiders take my reports of the happenings within that place seriously. From that moment forward, I began to do all I could to get the hospital staff to see that I was not the mentally ill patient they had mistaken me to be.

I realized that it was going to take some work, because of my incredibly rude behavior since my arrival. My first step was to immediately curb the worst of my bad habits. For example, I started to quietly comply with the aids by eating the nasty meals they offered to me. I even did it without spitting it back onto them.

"Okay, I admit I had been a bit of an ass to all the medical staff up until this point in my story. I also had

begun to understand that I had murdered Vilber and Olaf publicly. Looking back on that situation I should have been expecting retribution over that. No doubt I had more than earned the punishment I was getting.

However, in my defense those two black collar brutes were abusing their station. There were too many occasions in which Olaf and Vilber had aided in seriously harming, even killing the children cursed to wear a silver collar. I was far from the first kid they'd injured. They even admitted Xavier had ordered them to murder boys and girls after that monster had tired of playing his sick games with them. Do you remember Meine Liebe, that story I told you of the night Olaf sexually assaulted me after I'd been rendered helpless by Drexel's paralytic drug cocktail?

Well, the way I saw it, putting them out of business was only a crime in that of all evil people living in the House, they were no worse than many others. It goes without saying that I should have killed all the rotten child molesters and murderers in that place.

Still, I believe my anger at the doctors in the mental hospital was justified. They had no right to lock me away in a cell, chained to a wall in a Goddamned strait jacket! I had just spent seven years in a prison even though I was innocent of any crimes (well, in the beginning anyway). It seemed most unfair that after spending all that time suffering like I had, there should have been at least a bit of consideration for the time I'd already served. That is, if incarceration as punishment was their intention.

Overdoing the cruelty in the sentencing of the victim while allowing the guilty to run free to create new Mad Maxxes was unfair. You be warned Meine Liebe. That is the reality of the brutal world outside your own prison walls. The victim is often viewed with contempt because many will believe you willingly submitted. I've seen it repeatedly. Many of the guilty are given excuses for their crimes. The more violent, bizarre, brutal, inhuman, and terrible the situation you suffer the more likely society will write you off as a liar which will allow the freedom for the monster to harm others.

It was the ONLY time I ever broke a vow in my entire life, and I did it for Geraldine, Ryker, Ben, Abelard, Tamina, Milo, Annette, all her sisters and brothers still struggling, as well as all the children buried without care in the lush green yard surrounding that House.

I beg you to listen closely to what I tell you in the story of those nineteen months when your Master was held hostage in that hospital. Pay attention to what those well-meaning normals did and didn't do when faced with the evidence that I was telling the TRUTH about a nightmare that existed as their neighbors: A story of a House of perverted pleasures that was fueled by the blood and bones of the forgotten children. All of them, souls that the brutal world had thrown away, just like Christian Axel and you Meine Liebe. There are legions of names erased from the planet out there that suffered unbelievable tortures, but no one ever will ever care, mourn nor even know about them.

I have been told that the Earth is too damned big for it to matter that much that a random child, or adult is kidnapped then sold away to be used till there is nothing left of them. That makes me ask myself was Christian Axel or my little Meine Liebe not important enough to deserve a life without such torment. What about my sweet Annette or even the brute Ben?

It was during this time (when I finally had time to reflect on the life, I had led without always being raped, beaten, or forced to serve someone.) that these deep issues plagued my traumatized mind. I had to look hard look at the journey I had taken, and the good and bad decisions I made. I was at the crossroads that every man or woman must come to eventually.

The question that kept cycling back into my consciousness was, 'now that I had survived, what do I do with the life I had struggled to hold on to?'

As I sat there in that padded cell in my fifteenth summer, the sweet boy with big dreams of fixing the broken was long gone. He had been replaced by the scarred-up shell of a nothing, that teetered on madness and had spent three years shattering some of the broken souls I had sworn to aid. This caused me great shame and dishonor of the worst kind. I feared I had become just like the cruel, sadistic, twisted, predatory motherfuckers that I had been tormenting me all my life.

That realization Meine Leibe changed Christian Axel AKA Mad Maxximillian for all time. I was many things

39

(most too foul to admit ta), but I was going to be damned if I would grow into a man nor more fit to be allowed to walk above the ninth ring of hell then fucking JONAS or ANY OF those MONSTERS.

Ah, I am on a rant my poor demonseed wife. I apologize. what the hell was I thing to try to get into such a deep subject with you. You are barely making it from one day to the next at this moment. These soul-searching issues can wait till your mind is better capable of managing such things. Let's get back to where I left off. Your Master maybe is the nutball so many claim him to be, yes? He ruffled my hair making me giggle.

My Master sighed then cleared his throat and continued on with his story.

It took many days for the staff that attended me in that rubberized cell to finally relax their guard. My hellion behaviors had calmed to that of the peaceful lamb most unexpectedly I suppose (or so they thought so, I overheard them saying so many times hahaha). Several of the aides told me they thought it was a ploy to get them to get close enough for me to injure them (they would say that as they kept out of my leash reach as much as possible when they came to feed, bath or aid me in relieving myself).

They would figure out in another few days, I was indeed a changed man. I no longer fought, rejected nor gave them so much as an evil glance, not even once. This good behavior began to pay off. About six weeks after I was brought to that hospital sedated to stupid thanks to my fighting them, I was finally removed from the leash in the wall and strait jacket.

At first, they left me in that rubber room. It was pretty clear (even to this idiot Master or yours) the doctor wanted to see if I was going to attack a staff member or try to harm myself before he would consider allowing me into a proper room.

Another week (maybe more) passed without me showing any signs of aggression toward anyone. I was sitting in the corner playing cards with my brothers in the wheel room when Dr. Wagner came into the rubber room. I was pretty shocked to see the man. I had not been visited by him since he stripped me down on that gurney bed when I first arrived.

He had that nurse Thema with him. I stood up and cast my eyes to the floor doing my best to appear submissive. I wrung the boy's hand with nervousness wondering what the hell was this meeting all about. I confess I was more than a little frightened at what he may decide to do with the killer Mad Maxx.

Dr. Wagner smiled at me, "Well Maximillian you are looking much better than when you first arrived. I have been hearing good reports from the staff that you are complying with them without a quarrel. I am most happy to hear it. I have come to witness this positive change in you with my own eyes. I am most pleased with what I see. I think shortly we can move you to a bed with a better view, yes?"

I kept my eyes low, "Uhm, excuse my ignorance honorable Doctor but when will I be permitted to leave this fine establishment?"

He chuckled at my high protocol address to him, "Ah, well, not for some time just yet, but you keep behaving yourself you'll be released back to your father in no time. Maybe you will be home before the winter holidays."

I looked up at him with a startle, "Huh? Released to my father? What do you mean the winter holidays? I don't understand. I have no father and is it not still the month of June? Have I been here long?" I looked to that nurse Thema as she looked away from my questioning gaze.

The doctor frowned, "It is now August, Maximillian, so the winter holidays are not as far as you seem to recall. You are still suffering many symptoms of the acute cycle such as memory loss. that is clearly evident since you do not even recall you own kinsmen."

I shook my head, "Are you refereeing to Peter Schmitz? The man never claimed me on paper…wait…has he done so since I broke my metal, I mean since I came to the hospital?" I caught the error before I fucked up and scared this doctor away. I needed the information he was sharing (August. REALLY? YIKES.).

Doctor Wagner shot a confused look at Thema that appeared just as uneasy, "Uhm Maximillian your father's name is Jonas Weiss. I have never heard him mention a contest of your paternity. He has made it clear that he is your father and holds your Guardianship papers."

I groaned and wrung my hands faster, "Ah, okay I understand. I had forgotten that he tricked, I mean married my mother. I must ask, have you met my, uhm, father? I mean have you seen him in the flesh?" I shot a look up at him with an evil smile.

The doctor nodded, "Yes, I have weekly meetings with him Maximillian. He is most concerned about your good treatment and progress. I admit at first his appearance was unusual, but the man proved to be a most caring, attending man for his son."

I snorted then chuckled bitterly, "You bet that freak is. Nothing like having the thing of your darkest desires forever held hostage in your bed to keep you worried for his continued good health. Listen to me please. Jonas has managed to fool you, other authorities, and my REAL parents to obtain full LEGAL control of me. I swear to your honorable doctor I have no quarrel with you over his pulling the wool over your eyes. Hell, he fooled me too, but I am only a foolish boy. I would have thought better of one in your high status. Did you bother to notice he DOESN'T LOOK A FUCKING THING LIKE ME? Doctor Wagner, he is a perverted child molester that paid off the judges to say that I am incapable of looking after myself. If you check on my statement you will find that this year a man called Peter Schmidt also filed to claim guardianship. That man, Peter. He is my truthful sire."

Doctor Wagner nodded at Thema, "Nurse, can you please leave us a moment. I will be alright, I think. Maximillian seems calm enough. Thank you, Thema." The woman opened the door and stepped out leaving me and this man alone.

He stared at me with an expression of curiosity, "Tell me something Maximillian. When you arrived, I had to give you a full examination to determine any injury or health problems. The findings of that examination showed long term and extensive damage to your bones, flesh and many healed head injuries. Your dental exam also demonstrated to me a young man that has endured many horrible accidents or perhaps purposeful beatings. I would even go so far as to call the things that your x-rays and observable scars tell me indicate you have been tortured, not once but many times in your short fifteen years. That aside, my investigation also determined something even more disturbing. I asked Thema to leave to grant you some dignity because I want to know the name of the man or men that have sexually abused you so badly that the damage was visible without a scope. Am I to understand that you are alleging that your father, Jonas, is the criminal that has done all these abominations to you?"

I nodded, "You are correct to assume that is what I am telling you. Jonas is only one of the perverts that molested me and worse over the last three years. I want to tell you something. Please listen to me this time. There is a place, a House, I mean a mansion. I was held hostage there for the last seven years. In this House, the wealthy come to have their ways with the innocent children that are purchased, stolen, or tricked into serving for those perverts' sick pleasures. These poor children are forced to do the sex with the adults and if they refuse, they are shot by the Russians

44

hired to keep them from getting away. The rich people eventually kill all these victims of the human trafficking and get new ones to rape. The cycle goes on and on. I am only alive because this man that calls himself my father and Guardian thinks I have some magical powers in my blood."

That Doctor Wagner's eyes were wide, and his mouth hung open, he blinked when I went silent then said, "Uhm that is quite the story Maximillian, but I won't deny such a thing could be possible. It would certainly explain the extent of your grievous injuries and condition, but I must ask, why would magic in your blood matter to your father, Jonas?"

I sighed, "You will not believe this, but that man believes himself to be a real vampire. He believes that the demons that can give him eternal life live in my blood. You see, he drinks my blood twice a month and forces his intercourse on me after he does that. He does this in the hopes he can stay young forever. Stop calling that beast my father. He is a pervert that thank God has no honest kinship to me other than the accursed perversions he has forced upon me for the last three years. If you really think I am being honest I must beg of you honorable doctor please get help for the children that still suffer in the Kaiser House walls." I fell to my knees into prostrate hoping this reverent behavior would convince him to call the police and help my lost brothers and sisters.

Doctor Wagner gasped, "Please get off the floor Maximillian. I am not the King of Germany or any country. I will call the proper authorities and ask them to check into your story without your needing to humiliate yourself over it."

I sat up with an excited smile, "You mean it. You will call the police, honestly? Oh, thank you so much Doctor Wagner! I swear to you I will find a way to pay you back somehow for your kindness."

He chuckled, "That won't be necessary Maximillian. If there is such a place where little children are harmed it would be my duty and pleasure to make sure it is shut down. My payback would be the safe return of these children to society and the arrest and punishment of those that did harm to them and to you. Now tell me where this Kaiser House is located. I want to make the calls to shut this place down immediately." He smiled as he took out his pencil ready to write down the address that I didn't have, fuck!

I stared at the floor feeling the tears well in my eyes, "I uhm, don't know where this House is located other than Germany. It may be in the east behind the wall. They blindfolded me and all these years were careful to keep the address and location a secret from me. Your men picked me up from this House. They chased me right up to the fourth floor of the mansion. Your orderlies shot me up with sedatives then carried me to the hospital in their ambulance. They know where the House is. There should be records of it from the day they brought me here."

The doctor shook his head, "No Maximillian. You were transferred here from a small country hospital by ambulance. There is no record of the country's medical workers, our orderlies, or staff from that hospital that indicates you were captured in a place like the one you have described to me. I think you are hallucinating the whole thing. How could an ambulance staff bring you to a hospital without noticing or even questioning why a scarred, psychotic young man would be in a mansion such as you describe?"

I wrung my hands harder worried I had somehow hallucinated that horror show, "I am not lying. Someone must have been driving that fucking ambulance. They had sirens and everything. I swear it. I won't argue about this with you. It is not important how I got here but please can you call the police anyway? Tell them to check records around the country. Surely the trained professional undercover agents can find discover the address of Kaiser House even without my knowing it."

The doctor took off his glasses and frowned, "Okay, sure Maximillian. I can call the West German government and tell them that a teenaged schizophrenic patient of mine is claiming there is a large group of wealthy Germans abusing and murdering children through a human trafficking ring somewhere within our borders or perhaps in a neighboring country."

I wept quietly realizing he was being sarcastic and never believed me in the first place (I am such a fool), "I beg of you to at least try to find someone that will listen to me. I would never lie about such a horror. I am telling you

47

the truth. I need to speak with someone with the authority to end their criminal behavior."

Doctor Wagner nodded, "I know you believe you are being truthful Maximillian. I don't doubt it all seems very real to you, and sadly it is something no phone call will make go away. I must tell you that your father Jonas warned us about this recurrent delusion of a House that abuses children that you have. He told me and the authorities that your mother Agnette kidnapped you at the age of eight and ran away with you to Denmark. He reported that only this last winter he managed to locate you and bring you home with him. He reported the horrid condition he found you in back in January to the proper authorities and they have been looking for your mother. They are interested in forcing her to answer for the crimes against you. It is all in the court documents that Jonas had turned over to the hospital when he admitted you to our care. He confesses that he attempted to treat your deep psychotic symptoms from his home but that this June you began to show signs of aggression. Maximillian, I can see with great sadness in my heart that you have been most severely tortured, molested and abused in every way. I have treated many with mental illness in my career and some have horrible tales to tell of their lives. That said, it never stops hurting when I meet a tormented soul so young and hear his pain call out to me. There is no cure for the disease that eats at your sanity, and I think after what I have witnessed on your flesh you likely acquired your illness honestly. There are not many that would not go mad from such harsh treatment as you most definitely have suffered.

Maybe there is some comfort in living in a world of fantasy when coming to grips with such a brutal reality would be so horrifying. I doubt that few would be capable of tolerating it without going mad."

I covered my face with my hands and while sobbing loudly replied, "You knew the whole time what I was going to tell you. That blasted vampire Jonas already inoculated you. You didn't believe a fucking word I said. Yet, you let me go on pretending to care when actually you think of me as a madman that raves of conspiracies and far-fetched fantastic stories. That is fine, have it your way. I will speak no more to you or any of your fleas of the that truthful situation going on in Kaiser House. When I am free of this hospital, I'll take care of that hell hole as I should have from the beginning. When the smoke clears and the flames die down. They will dig up the yard and find the mass graves of those poor people that no one ever missed. A few corpses laying there will be fresh thanks to your lack of making that phone call I've asked you to make. Then you will see I wasn't crazy! You will have to live with the guilt that you let more children die."

Doctor Wagner frowned at me as he said, "Okay Maximillian as you say. I can see you will be with us a long time. this delusion of yours is well engrained. It will be difficult to break it but eventually you will see that you are in error. There is no Kaiser House and your Mother is the one to blame for the deplorable condition of your flesh and mind."

I nodded, "Yes. On that we both agree. Agnette did this to me, but she had a lot of help. If you are done making fun of me and calling me a liar, I would kindly ask you to leave me in peace. As you see you have upset me, and I don't think that is the proper protocol for a good psychiatrist."

He smiled at that, "Well at least you finally understand I am your psychiatrist, and you are my patient in this mental hospital ward. We are here to help you get better."

I nodded then lowered my hands to glare at him, "I believe you think that, Doctor. Seems to me that delusion of yours is deeply ingrained and seems impossible to break it. Perhaps you should increase your own medications and lock yourself up until you come back to your senses. I do not have schizophrenia and I am not delusional. The Kaiser House is real."

Doctor Wagner sighed, "Alright that is enough for today. I will leave as you have asked me to do. Before I go, I brought you something your Uncle Leo asked me to give to you. He said that he promised it to you if you behaved yourself. I am not too thrilled about how this meeting went but you have shown a vast improvement, by not throwing as many fits and calming your aggression toward the staff. So, I think you are ready to have your prize." He reached into his coat and pulled out Felicity.

Chapter 2: Mending the Mind and Breaking the Heart

Doctor Wagner held out Felicity allowing me to see that my lamb toy was somehow magically uninjured. I couldn't believe my eyes. I knew I'd seen Jakob pull a lump of nothing out of the bleach bucket in the hell closet.

Yet there she was, just as perfect and beautiful as she ever had been. I wanted so badly to take her from the doctor's grip, but I was afraid of him to be honest. He didn't believe my story, and I was certain he worked for Jonas at the very least. I thought it possible he was under the employ of that entire House of monsters.

Either way, this had to be a trick. I sat there wringing my hands while keeping my gaze to the floor unsure what to do.

Doctor Wagner scoffed aloud. "Your Uncle Leo said you would be joyous to have this toy back in your possession. He told me that this was something you desired immensely. Am I to assume his belief was in error?"

I shook my head. "What do you want in trade for Felicity? I take nothing from you without knowing the price I will have to pay for it."

He appeared startled by my answer. "Huh? You think I want money to give you this toy your Uncle told me belonged to you already? So, this is the Felicity you have been demanding? I am surprised. I assumed that you were speaking of a girlfriend or even an imaginary friend. I didn't expect this whole time you were seeking your toy lamb. I will be damned." He turned Felicity in his hand with awe as if she were something he had never viewed before.

I looked up angerly. "Stop fucking around with me doctor. What the hell do you want so you give me my Felicity. You know I have no money. I think candor is rude in this case. You wave about something you know I want then act the innocent. Well? Name it. You want the special services no doubt, but how many times must I endure your foul interests before you allow me to hold my lamb?"

Doctor Wagner shot a look of fear at me. "Special services? I recall you have used those words before. I don't remember what you said it means. It assumed it was a neologism (***symptom of schizophrenia where the suffer makes up words that only they can define**).

I stood up feeling the fury rise within me. "I don't know how to do what you are asking, this neologism thing. What kind of fucked up fetish is that. Freak, schwuler, whatever. You tell me what you want, and I will decide if I will give it to you for my Felicity. You be warned though. I will kill you for putting me in this position of humiliation. That lamb is mine. I paid for her already. You have no right to demand anything more for what belongs to me, but I am at the disadvantage. You perverted cocksucker. Get on with this. You are making me angry."

Doctor Wagner began to back up as I took a step towards him ready to beat him to death over his holding my lamb hostage. "You halt right there, Maximillian. You come any closer and I call the orderlies and have you back in that straitjacket, leashed to a wall. I mean it."

I stopped walking but continued my aggressive stance and spit my words at him, "Then you give me the price motherfucker or you call them. I am tired of these games you play with me. Did you not tell me that Leo said he gave Felicity to you to give back to me? Did you not just say a moment ago you would give her to me when I earned her. Tell me how to earn her now. I want my fucking lamb."

He shook his head. "I give you the lamb Maximillian because you demonstrated good behavior. That was all I was meaning. I didn't expect you to think I was asking for something." He tossed Felicity onto the rubber bed like she burned his hands with a frightened expression on his face.

I watched my lamb land on that uncomfortable mattress.

I shot a look of caution at that insane man. "What are you doing? I didn't agree to anything. I see the trick. I go to touching her then you get to touching me. You are a sicko."

The doctor gasped. "You think I want to molest you so you can have your toy? Oh, my God. You thought, oh no, I apologize Maximillian. I never meant for you to get the wrong idea. I am leaving right this minute. There is no trick. I swear to you this was an accidental misunderstanding." He moved closer to the door.

I hissed out. "Was it? Then get the fuck out of here and leave me alone. All of you keep your fucking hands off the boy. I am a Dominant now. You cannot do whatever you want. I am free to say no. You remember that you sonofabitch."

I watched with murder in my eyes as the middle-aged man knocked on the door three times. It opened a crack, and he slipped out of it. Whoever was out there slammed it shut and I heard the locks fasten. I stood there glaring at it for several moments. I suppose I was waiting for the swat team or group of brutes to come knock me onto the floor for restraining.

When after many minutes no one came, I cast my eyes on Felicity laying on her side on the bed. I cautiously slinked over to her then snatched her out of the open fast as I could. I tore off into the corner of the room and curled up with my back to the doorway.

I held her in my hands examining her little frame for injury. I found she was completely intact without so much as a bruise. I let out my breath with a sigh of relief and held her tightly to the boy's chest overcome with the emotions of joy and despair. I had missed her so much and now at last we were together again.

I hate to admit it, but I wept for quite some time like a little baby. I made promises to her that I would never let anyone hurt her again. I apologized for the poor parenting that led to our being separated and her pain. I asked her several times to forgive me for my stupid thinking Kilian could be trusted.

I was most grateful to find she held no ill will to this stupid Master of yours, Meine Leibe. I sat with her marveling at her ability to overlook the weak, disgusting and uselessness man I really am. I felt most unworthy of her affection, but as I held her in my arms, I realized she never was bothered that I was not perfect or even normal.

Felicity loves me without bounds, judgement nor end. It was her love that helped to slowly quiet the demons in my blood, chased away the shadows of crushing memories, and curbed the endless loneliness in that brutal world I could not escape from.

It is the animals, like the sheep, the hound, the kittens, which love us for no reason at all. They are the ones to lead our kind from our darkness. They never judge, and in truth they live their lives like we do. The animals have no guilt nor shame in doing what they must to live another day. Not even one would ever look down on you because you were forced to your knees for the special services.

You will find they aren't bothered if you are naked nor if you had to kill another in self-defense. They never would call you bad names nor think they can hurt you just because others have. The animals don't lock you up for rhyming, dancing, nor talking differently than they do. All of them accept you as you really are, a human being like any other one. To them you are not different at all. The lamb will treat you and your Master and others like us more like their brothers and sisters than our own fucking species ever will.

Master Maxx gently stood up holding me tightly to his chest. I gasped in fear as he walked over to his clothing that I had folded carefully still laying by the steal door of the basement. He leaned down and dug around in his inner jacket. Then with yelp of joy he produced a small, white lamb toy only the size of his hand.

I gasped in awe believing this was Felicity from his story. I ached immediately to hold her. I thought he could hear my thoughts when he held her in front of me just within my reach.

He whispered into my ear, "Here my wife. I give this Felicity to you. She will comfort you like she did Mad Maxx. She knows the secret location of the green fields and blue mountains of peace. All you must do is follow the lamb. They know the way. I once gave you the Golden hound to scare away the boogie man, but Felicity will show you the way home."

I took her into my eager hands while noticing her soft fur as I barely breathed out, "I thank you for the mercy, but I can't take Felicity from you. Debbie will get her like she did Der Goldene hound and then she will be taken away from me like he was."

Master Maxx chuckled then reached into his coat again. This time he produced a second lamb almost identical to the first. This one was off white and well-worn *from many long years of snuggles, tears, and hiding in pockets.*

He showed her to me. "This, Meine Liebe, is my Felicity. That one in your hands, she is yours. I give her to you because every lost soul needs a lamb to guide them to peace and keep them safe from the darkness inside their minds." He kept his Felicity in his hand and walked back to the mattress still carrying a very happy little Meine Liebe.

I snuggled my lamb toy to my chest as he sat his Felicity next to us. He laughed as he asked his "ladies" if all three of us were ready for the rest of the story. I nodded for me and helped my Felicity do the same.

He looked at his own Felicity with a smile then said, "Then I believe we are ready to go. Felicity always loved a good tale. You remember to hide your own lamb in the wall whenever your Master Maxx is not here. Debbie touches that baby of yours and I will gut that woman no matter the consequences. That would not be good for either of us. I am not worried you will disobey that order, my wife. I think you are ready for this responsibility of looking after a lamb of your own, yes?"

I nodded with happiness. "Yes Master. I love her. Thank you for the mercy."

He chuckled. "Well wait till she has to be house broken before you go thanking me for any mercy."

My eyes went wide as I pulled the lamb out to look again. I thought maybe she really was alive and not a stuffed animal. He saw me freaking out and laughed so hard he was brought to tears.

"Ah, you are such a treasure, Meine Liebe. I was teasing you. You thought that lamb would make the pellets all over this nasty cell? No wonder I love you so. Now settle down all you. We have things to discuss." I nodded with a laugh that I did indeed fall for his joke.

I snuggled into his chest holding my toy while he began his story again.

The days day passed slowly in that white rubber room. With Felicity with me once again, I was better able to bear it. Each day the staff would come to leave food, pills, or demand I take their many shots. I was still afraid of them, and not quite convinced this was not some plot by the House to fool me. It was hard to believe this was a real hospital that was in the world outside that hell hole.

Doctor Wagner came to that cell every day to speak with me. He and I fought constantly about my saying that the Kaiser House existed. That man told me that I was full of delusions and that nothing I told him really happened. He wanted me to say that it was Agnetta and her thug boyfriends that did all the damage to my flesh and the raping too.

Another two weeks passed. No matter what Dr. Wagner said, nor how many times he came to see me, I would not relent in my swearing that I was not psychotic with hallucinations. I could tell he was getting fed up with my lack of compliance with his wish that I merely agree with his lies.

On the fifteenth visit he come into the room without that woman Thema. He stood there watching me hiding Felicity in the white hospital outfit they'd made me wear. I would always put her in my shirt whenever anyone came to visit. I feared eventually they may try to take her away to gain my submission to their authority. That day, I could tell the man meant business.

He stood at the door with irritation in his expression. "Maximillian, it is now September. You have been here since June and still you show heavy symptoms of your illness. The staff says you run from them screaming if they come near you, and won't speak, or let them touch you without a fight. I cannot get through to you either. Every day I show you the evidence that your father Jonas has given to me that your delusions are in error. Yet, here we are, arguing repeatedly about this place that never existed and thank God never will. Tell me how I can help you understand you are mentally ill and this is all a terrible fantasy?"

I scoffed but didn't get up from the corner as I replied, "Why are you are speaking to the fucking Vampire? I told you a million times, he is a manipulator and a liar. He is not my father. You should try speaking to Leo. He will tell you I am not psychotic."

Doctor Wagner brightened up, "Wait, you are on good terms with your Uncle Leo?"

I nodded then said, "Yes, he is someone I can trust, though he is not my uncle."

The doctor narrowed his eyes. "He isn't? If not your uncle, then who is he to you?"

I looked at the floor feeling my ears burn with shame at having to admit the truth aloud. "He is, uhm, Leo is my lover."

Doctor Wagner nearly choked, then sputtered out. "You mean you claim your uncle Leo is molesting you like you've claimed your father Jonas has?"

I shook my head and smiled bitterly. "No, Leo is nothing like Jonas. I love Leo with all my heart. I am with him by choice, not by force." I felt better finally getting that off my chest because it is the truth.

I thought that Doctor Wagner was going to faint when he heard that. "You are only fifteen. You cannot choose to be a sexual partner with anyone. Plus, Leo is old enough to be your grandfather."

I snorted. "So are you. So is Jonas. What the hell is your point? Is there a law against it? If so, I don't think those cocksuckers in the House ever heard of it. Do you think it mattered to Peter when he raped me into my collar when I was the boy of only eleven? Leo never forces himself on me. I offer my services to him in return for his kindness. I did so with honor and honesty. Unlike those other fucking brutes. They took what they wanted and if I didn't like it, I got a beating for it or merely held down and forced anyway."

The Doctor wiped his brow with vigor and appeared agitated as he said, "Uhm, okay this delusion of yours has gotten too far out of control. Soon enough you will be accusing me of molesting you or maybe Doctor Altergott or perhaps even Thema."

I groaned. "Why the fuck are you saying that? Are you three planning to do such evil? I dare you to try it. If you think I will go down easy, you better think again. I will fight all you to the death over such dishonor. I am sick of this bullshit. Every day you come in here and call me a liar. I will never say anything but the facts no matter how hard you try to brainwash me to think otherwise. Please, ask Leo. He will vouch that I am a man of my word and one of honesty."

Doctor Wagner nodded. "I will be speaking to your uncle; of that you can be assured. I will also say Maximillian, you will not be leaving for home until you let this delusion go. You can stay alone in this room for all your days if necessary. There is no such a thing as Kaiser House, and Jonas is your loving father." He turned around and knocked on the door demanding to be let out.

I looked up with a startle as I replied, "What? Did you say I won't be let go until I deny the truth? You demand I recant my statements? But if I do, you will let me go?"

He turned around as the door opened and said, "Yes, you heard me. Stop this delusion and I will let you return to your father and your home. Good day to you, Maximillian."

The doctor walked out as I yelled at him, "I am never going back to Jonas or that fucking House, you cocksucker. Fuck you!"

The next day I was laying in my bed speaking with Felicity about the green fields when the door came open. I sat up with some terror because it seemed not enough time had passed for the orderly to bring my lunch. I had a rough night and they had shot me up with some sedative as usual. I was groggy but alert enough to recognize this irregularity could spell trouble.

I had to rub my eyes several times to believe what they told me. There in the doorway stood Leo with a huge smile on his face. I thought for sure my mind had snapped. He come forward with a dramatic squeal and embraced me with vigor.

He pulled back to investigate my face with tears welling up in his eyes as he said, "Little rabbit, I have missed you so much. Oh my, you have grown a yard. Look at you. Tell me, have they been treating you well?"

I shook my head still unsure if I wasn't hallucinating as I replied, "They are nice enough. No raping or beating that I can recall. How did you get here? Am I dreaming?"

He ran his hand down my cheek with affection as he said, "No my love. I am here. Your doctor was hoping I could speak some sense into you. They allowed me to visit you after many weeks of begging." He smiled and hugged me tightly again.

I groaned. "Speak sense into me? I don't understand. I am not psychotic, Leo. Please tell that damned doctor Wagner there is a Kaiser House and that I am being truthful. They think I am lying to them."

Leo frowned suddenly then shot a nervous look at the door as he whispered into my ear, "My little rabbit, you listen to your Leo. Never say those words again. Not to anyone. Don't you remember that you've given your oath? The House will have you murdered to keep their secrets. Surely you are aware of that."

I shook my head wildly. "No, Leo! The police must be told. They are killing children. Don't you care? I thought you were different. I am a Dominant now and I am going to stop those monsters that hurt the silvers. I beg you to help me. You must tell the doctors I am telling the truth, Leo."

He grabbed the back of my head and held me to his face looking me right in my eyes with sternness as he replied, "I will only say this one time, and if I am caught telling you then they will kill me too. So, listen closely Christian Axel. I have been sent here to get you to shut your mouth about the House as your last chance. If you refuse to relent and recant that story you told these people understand that the House has ways to shut you up for good. You need to accept the fact that the only way to change the lives of the silvers in the House is through careful policy and laws from within. The people that run that place have enough wealth to buy the doctors silence and keep you a prisoner in this cell till you are old and grey. Wise up my little rabbit. Whatever these fools tell you, agree with them. You do that, then you can come home, and all will be forgiven this one time. Your mental illness has bought you a second chance. Do not squander it. I love you Christian Axel. I want you alive, safe, and home."

I stared at him in disbelief as I said, "Are you insane Leo? I don't want to go back to you or the House! I want to live in the real world with a job and a wife. I want a normal life. I would rather rot in this rubber room than go back to that horror. If you came here to get me to give up and crawl back to the Vampire and your bed you are a fool. I am done with that shit."

Leo let me out of his grip and whimpered as he looked down at the bed then said, "I fear that you have no other choice in the matter, my little rabbit. You either stay prisoner here, or you will come home. If you will not listen to reason, then please promise me that you will stop talking about the House to these people."

I glared at him. "And what do I get if I stay quiet? You're asking me to allow the murder and raping of little children with my silence. I have nightmares, and I am plagued with guilt, Leo. What return do I get if I let them all hang and look out only for Christian Axel?"

Leo sighed, "Okay, at least you are willing to bargain. That is a start. I am willing to work with Rolf, Friedrick, and Byron to begin the House law changes that will make the worst criminal acts punishable if you will stop spilling the secrets of the House."

I snorted. "No, not enough. I want more."

Leo nodded. "Of course, you do and if I were in your shoes, I would say the same. I will offer to allow you to join our team. You were a victim of the House's cruel lack of protection for silver collars. No one would know better than you on what laws should be pushed through first."

I crossed my arms. "Keep going, Leo. Still not enough."

He chucked bitterly. "Well only the best for the best, yes? Okay, then I will bring you all the schoolbooks you need to catch up on your studies. You have nothing else to do from the looks of things. May as well use this time wisely."

I nodded. "Getting warmer, Leo. I am still not hearing what I want to hear."

Leo looked at me with shock as he replied, "Christian, I cannot assure you freedom after they release you. Do you really think Gretta, Cora, Jonas, and Peter will allow you to just walk away? You threatened to burn down the House in front of everyone. Then you killed Olaf and Vilber in plain sight. You also have told everyone within shouting distance that the House exists, and you have given names and crimes."

I shrugged. "So? They killed Ryker, Abelard, every fucking kid they ever bought. They've ruined me. The way I see it, I owe those sonofabitches nothing but my boot up their asses."

He nodded. "You may be right, but they won't view it that way, Christian. Be reasonable. The more you talk the tighter they will pull the chain around your neck. If you are waiting to hear I will help you escape, then so be it. You play ball with them, and I will do all I said. And I will aid your escape the second the time is right."

I smiled with joy as I replied, "I do believe we have an accord, my love. I want you to start changing those laws right this minute thought. I will shut up if you can, at least, save the silvers from being chronically misused and murdered for the smallest infractions. We'll work on the other horrors they endure as we can. I will study for doctor school, then when they release me, I will run like the wind. I will never come back. I want your promise that when I am gone you will keep on changing the rules till all the silvers in that place are free or you burn that fucker down, or maybe I will anyway." I held out my hand to him to shake.

He frowned as he shook it saying, "I will make this contract with you Christian Axel, but be aware you will not be able to run away so easily."

I giggled. "Ah, Leo. You let me worry about that. Now, I want out of here. Can you tell the doctors I am not schizophrenic please? These idiots think I am psychotic."

He sighed. "I can tell them all I like, little rabbit. They won't believe me till you stop throwing fits and speaking of vampires, fleas, and stereos. I see they did give you the toy I sent, just like I promised. Obviously, I am a man of my word. If you can stop acting like an ass, I will lobby to get you out. Deal?"

I nodded. "Yes, yes, I'll stop this very day. Did you bring my books with you?"

Leo smiled with wickedness. "Of course, I did, little rabbit. I know you far too well. I told that idiot Jonas I could reason with you. When I leave the staff will bring them in so you can study. I want to enjoy your company until then. Can you behave nicely for me? I've missed you terribly."

I laughed as I replied, "Of course I can! It is good to see you, Leo. I suppose I have missed you too. How is Der Makellos?"

Leo spent almost an hour with me catching me up on the growth of our hound, the news that Bladrick had finally succumbed to his cancer (Leo told me he died screaming after many hours of struggle with the reaper), and that the new House door guards were no longer the black collars that had the best connections. They had replaced Olaf and Vilber with black collars that had gone to security training school.

Thanks to my killing those two brutes, the next generation of guards could officially carry guns. Leo explained that escaping that House was more dangerous than ever with Guards in the yard and fellows at the doors carrying deadly weapons. I was not happy to hear that news.

Sooner than I would have liked, Thema came to the room to say that Leo had to leave. Visiting time was to be kept short because the medical staff didn't want me stressed, as if being isolated was not upsetting. Leo looked at me with a longing in his expression. I thought he would kiss me goodbye but to my shock he left with only a tight hug.

I sat there in full confusion at that lack of intimacy between us. It was not that I was not unhappy about it, mind you. It was very odd to me that in all my time in the hospital, no one had attempted to enforce special services of any kind. Not even the one that had already been with me in every way possible.

Not long after he left, an aide brought me my schoolbooks of every subject. I went to work on them immediately. I was grateful to finally had something to do. From that day until the day I was released, I studied them the second I awoke till the moment I went to sleep.

Eight to twelve hours a day for many months with no real interruptions led to my catching up and finishing my education. It had been severely neglected that last year before I'd broken my collar, and most of the one before for the same reason.

Since I was in a legitimate hospital, with a bullshit diagnosis, the school authorities allowed me to take all my tests from my room. I was in a hurry to prove myself an educated man. I passed them all with high marks and received the German equivalent of the high school education diploma, just before I was released. All of us Maxx boys and Christian were proud of the grand job we had done, together as the team.

The weeks spent alone in that white rubber room slowly turned into months. I did as I swore to Leo. I never claimed another harsh word about Kaiser House, and even managed to nod in agreement when Dr. Wagner demanded me to blame my mother for the damage done to me prior to my arrival there. I refused to agree aloud, but I no longer fought him over the details.

I think the reason they refused to let me go, despite my compliance of saying that the Kaiser House was a delusion, was my continued refusal to admit I have schizophrenia. That I simply couldn't do, no matter how much Leo begged me to. I knew if I was to be labeled with that mental disorder my dreams of being a doctor would be over. I was aware they don't let schizophrenics work in the hospitals.

I mean there is no law against it, but such a diagnosis would prevent anyone from hiring me. I also knew it could keep me out of medical schools, as well. As my sixteenth birthday came and went in June of 1974, I had been a mental patient for a full year without any talk of release. I was beginning to believe I would never get out of that fucking rubber room.

I had been quiet and compliant all that time. Leo had been keeping all his promises. Each week he would speak to me in whispers asking my opinion of the laws he was writing with the intention to force Gretta to approve them. He had already pushed through many changes to House law that would make a difference, in time, to those cursed at wearing the silver collar.

It was far from my dream of the full protection of children brought there against their will. I wanted to end the practice of human trafficking forever. Leo continued to assure me, that in time, there would never be a child treated the way I had been.

The cleaning up of the worst behaviors within the walls of the House helped me feel a bit better but only a little. I still secretly thought the only real way to end the horror and bring those criminals to heel was to burn that fucking House down. That is something I still believe to this day.

As I finished high school and began my studying for college that fall, the idea that I would have to find out where the Kaiser House was located became the only thing on my mind. Honestly, I was torn between running away and returning only long enough to make sure the place was destroyed.

Another seven months passed with no change in my circumstances. I had given up all hope of ever getting out. I was resigned to a life within that white cell alone with only Felicity and the other shards to keep me company. It all seemed hopeless. I had grown so accustomed to the scheduling of the hospital, I wondered if I was not being rendered useless, even if I ever were released.

I had grown by leaps and bounds during my fifteenth and sixteenth year. Long gone were the trappings of a young boy, replaced with a beard, and the hairy chest of a man. I had to have new hospital outfits almost every month my entire time there. I hate to admit I technically became an adult in a mental institution, but that was the way it happened.

With nothing else to do but study or talk with Felicity, I worked out in my cell for hours each day. I used the rigorous programs, as best I could without equipment, that Freidrick and Rolf had taught the boy. My muscles were lean and sturdy. It was not likely that anyone could have pulled the man I had become into any fucking closets or behind the stairs so easily as so many had done when I was a little boy.

I was what do they say here in the USA? Ah yes, the mean, lean, fighting machine, like now, yes? Master Maxx laughed when my eyes went wide.

I nodded in awe of his humongous size and incredible chiseled muscles.

He seemed like a giant to me, and in truth he did to everyone around him because he was.

That is why it was so hard for me to believe he had ever been a little boy that others could push around and abuse as they had. I wondered if any of them would have been so cruel to him if they had known he would become so fucking big one day.

By the time December 1974 gave way to January 1975, I was almost six foot two feet tall and weighed a whopping 172lbs. Leo was shocked at the changes and the unexpected height. What was more disturbing to him was that I was not finished growing yet.

When I would stand up to greet him, he always hugged me tightly with squeals. He'd been visiting me weekly and sometimes daily by then. Yet, he would always pretend to run away in terror screaming that a huge brute ate his little Christian Axel. I never stopped laughing at it, no matter how many times he engaged in his silly behavior. I think that is because he was correct. I had become one big and scary looking fatherfucker. *Mad Maxx laughed and so did I at that somewhat derogatory statement.*

Then only two weeks before I would start to hear rumors that the doctors were finally considering releasing me back into the world, I was awakened in the night by a loud crash. I rubbed my eyes while craning my neck about the room wondering what the hell was in there to fall and make a noise like that. I stirred Felicity and asked her if she saw anything out of the ordinary.

She shook her head, appearing as confused as me. I stretched and got out of the rubber bed to see if maybe my books had collapsed to the floor. I nearly screamed in full terror when I saw movement in the shadowed corner of the room. There were no windows in that cell but there was a small yellow light near the wall to cast a glare resembling the sun. The hospital staff left it on even at night, the assholes.

I grabbed Felicity and ran to the spot where the weak light was strongest. The rest of that cell was darker than my heart because the hospital had gone to 'lights out' hours before. I trembled as I sat down pulling my long legs to my chest never takin my eyes off that thing moving around in there with us.

A voice rang out from that corner, "Kneel before your Master, boys." I nearly pissed myself in fright upon hearing the voice of our Master Shard Der Goldene Hound.

I quickly knelt with grace and dropped my head with reverence. He hobbled out of the darkened space and approached the boy. I stole a look at him and gasped with surprise. He looked no worse than before he had been tossed away by the vortex. I had assumed he would be torn apart, or at least be in worse shape than he had been, after that trip into the nothing that he had endured.

He smiled at us lesser Shards as he came close enough to view us in full as he said, "The boy wears no collar. I've found all of you in the world outside the House. I must assume my shards were successful in completing the mission to escape the metal. I am proud of all of you."

I groaned as I trembled in worry at what I had to report to him. "Yes, Master Hound, we broke the collar, but the boy is a prisoner of a new cell. We've been kidnaped by outsiders. They call themselves doctors and have labeled us schizophrenic."

Der Hound frowned, as he replied, "How long has this been going on? Did the mission fail and these new hijackers merely remove the collar?"

I shook my head. "No, Master Hound. We took it off with the Sacred Bolt cutters, legally. But the boy was kidnapped shortly after and brought here against his will. These outsiders refuse to accept our status as a Dominant. They also ignore our reports of the foul deeds we endured to become Master Mad Maxximillian. We have obtained the boy's credentials for college and are poised for a life as an honorable doctor. Our minority is almost complete as well. All that is left to do is escape this cell and we are the freeman you've desired."

Der Hound snorted. "This is a cell. Where are we? Did anyone tell us why they've taken a Dominant captive?"

I nodded. "Yes, Master Hound. As I said, these men and women think us schizophrenic. We've been informed this is a mental hospital but not in the House. We are in a city called Heslach, Germany."

Our Master Shard growled angrily, "The boy is in a mental hospital? What did you do Mad Max?"

I looked up in fright as I replied, "What? I don't understand the question Master hound. Men came and abducted us as we were leaving the House."

He interrupted me with a loud screech, "Stop evading my question Mad Max! You know damned well why they've brought the boy here. I ask again, what did you do that caused the authorities to lock us up. These are not House people and had no knowledge the boy existed. Obviously, the outsiders have some fucking reason to see the boy as a threat to them. What was it?" He came forward with flames of fury in his eyes and grabbed the boy's chin with strength to force us to look at him.

I gulped down my terror as I replied, "We merely kept the oath to kill Olaf and Vilber. I swear this is all. Jonas has hijacked the guardianship of the boy and is telling these people lies. He says he's our father because he married Agnette. Our mother has run away and as usual left us to rot in the horror she's sold us to. It was also Jonas that told them we are schizophrenics. We've done nothing wrong. Please I beg mercy, Master."

He let our chin go with a bitterness in his expression as he said, "Fools, all of you! We had the fucking world in our grip, and you decided to take out an old grudge. Jonas taking guardianship didn't even matter until you gave him a valid reason to wield his power over us. He merely used the truth to trap the boy, idiots. You've let him do this to us."

I shook my head. "No! No! Jonas is lying, Master. We are not schizophrenic. We are men of our word. We had to kill those brutes because we made an oath to do it. Mercy please." Der Hound limped over and sat on our bed while we whimpered in despair over letting him down like we had.

He sighed loudly then said, "Calm down, Mad Max. You Max brothers listen to your Master closely. You too, Christian. The boy is schizophrenic. We shattered a long time ago. How could you so quickly forget all those terrible months we spent in the horrid dungeon cell before Peter uncollared us. Look at my face. Try to remember. I was not always like this. I cannot get back inside the flesh. Only the lesser shards can run the wheel thanks to this calamity we've suffered. The doctors will not release the boy until you admit we are mentally ill they claim us to be. Tomorrow, you'll ask to see the boy's doctor and tell that man or woman you're ready to face the truth. Then watch, they will let us out of this cell. Mad Max and Maximillian, it's about time you listen to your shard brothers Max, Christian and Mad Maxx. They've already accepted what you two will not. There is no coming back from a break from reality. Never mind, you need not believe what I say to you. However, you will obey my orders. I mean it. You tell those doctors you have schizophrenia without fail. I want the boy out of this hell hole. We can never start our life outside the House from a God damned rubber cell."

I bowed my head low with bile rising in my throat as I replied bitterly, "Your will is our own, Master."

He nodded. "Good, I am back now boys. Things are going to change. The time has come for college, work, and getting married. I want to be ready to enjoy our freedom by thirty-one when our future wife turns sixteen."

I gasped and said, "Wait! What do you mean? Are you saying we won't be free until we turn twenty-nine? No, Master! We will have it the second they let us out of this hospital. Oh my God! Do you think they're going to keep us here that long? Why would you say our wife will only be sixteen when we are that old. I intend to find a woman to marry and have our children the second we are released. You talk like we are going to choose a girl that is not even two years old at this moment. What the hell? Are you demanding I wed a baby? No way! I won't do it." I shot a look of terror around the room with tears welling in my eyes.

Der Hound stood up and calmly replied, "You will always be a dreamer, Mad Max. While it keeps the boy wishing for more, it can also blind him. You will see clearly soon enough. There is no chance to obtain that desired outcome you are seeking till we are near thirty-one, like it or not. Tell me Mad Max, did you or any of your shards really think Peter and the Vampire will let you out of their contracts with us? If you cannot figure out why our future wife is only two this year on your own, then I leave you to learn it the hard way. These delusions must stop one way or another. I am around if you need me. I cannot leave but I cannot stay. Be well and remember to watch the back of your brother shards." He returned to the shadows and disappeared without another word.

I think it goes without saying I spent the rest of that night weeping. I didn't like being dishonest or telling lies. I am not schizophrenic, but Der Hound is the Master of us all. I had no choice but to mind his directive.

So, first thing, the next morning, I asked for a meeting with Doctor Wagner. He came right away, since I had never once asked to visit with the man the whole nineteen months, I'd been his patient. I watched him walk in with his partner psychiatrist. That man was called Doctor Altergott. I sat quietly on the rubber bed with my head bowed low, staring mindlessly at my hospital slippers. I could neither look into the doctors' eyes nor stop the tears as they entered the room.

Doctor Wagner snorted as he stood there with the younger man, I barely knew but was aware was the head of my case all that time as he said, "Well? The breakfast orderly said you wish to speak to me. I am here, Maximillian. What did you want?"

I groaned as I shot a quick look at his dark haired thirty-something partner with a hawkish nose and cruel looking eyes, then replied, "I didn't expect you would bring Doctor Altergott. I kind of wished to see you alone Doctor Wagner."

Doctor Altergott looked up from the paperwork he had been examining, likely my records and said, "Ah, so you are bothered that I am here, are you? I will tell you anything you say to Doctor Wagner will be reported to me eventually. After all, I am the head of this wing, and you are my patient, Maximillian."

I nodded feeling even more defeated that I would have to confess to a lie with a larger audience than expected. "Yes, I know who you are Doctor Altergott. Well, no need to waste your valuable time I suppose. I called you here to confess that I am, uhm, schizophrenic."

Doctor Wagner and his partner gasped as he said, "What did you just say, Maximillian?"

I groaned as I responded, "You're torturing me, doctor. I said I am a fucking schizophrenic! I admit that I'm mentally ill. There, I said it. Now let me out of this Goddamned rubber room, please!"

Doctor Altergott smiled at me as he replied, "Well, Doctor Wagner, I am impressed. You finally got through to this disturbed young man. I was beginning to think he would spend the next winter holiday season with us as well. Good job. Oh, and Congratulations, Maximillian. You are on your way to rehabilitation."

I looked up with startle over his words, "Rehabilitation? What is that? How long will that take?"

He chuckled and said, "I've heard you received high marks in your school exams, but you've never heard of rehabilitation. Well, my boy that is when a disabled person receives extra training to learn how to manage their daily functions and symptoms."

I shook my head. "I am not disabled though. I'm just a little schizophrenic. I never said I am unable to function or anything serious like that."

Doctor Wagner frowned as he said, "Don't stress over this, Maximillian. It is standard procedure. Just calm down and listen. The rehabilitation will not slow down your release. Besides, you will require many months, maybe years, of this assistance. Luckily, we have a rehabilitation specialist willing to work with you for as long as it takes to get you functioning well in the world outside this cell."

I dropped my gaze and replied, "Ah, okay I see. So, you're saying this rehabilitation person will be living with me I guess."

Doctor Altergott chuckled. "No, Maximillian. However, they will spend many hours a day with you in your own home, but they go home after your sessions with them."

I sighed and responded, "Okay, I give up. You can assign this rehabilitation worker and let me out of here. I will behave myself; I swear it."

Then I looked up with a smile of wickedness in my eyes. "Can you assign a female for the job?" both doctors chuckled over my saying that.

Doctor Altergott cleared his throat and said, "Well, I can see you are a very healthy young man, indeed. However, the rehabilitation worker assigned for you is my own brother. He is the best in the business. I do you a great honor entrusting your future to the one man on earth I trust above all of them."

I nodded. "I thank you for the mercy of it then. Did all your family go into the psychiatric profession? But he only became the rehabilitation worker, and you are the doctor though. I must assume that is because you are the oldest?"

Doctor Altergott smiled with pride as he replied, "Yes, I am the oldest, but my father encouraged all three of his children, including our sister, to pursue a life in the psychiatric world. Anna became a psychiatric nurse and Kilian a rehabilitation counselor."

I nearly choked as I replied, "Kilian, you say, and Anna. Those are lovely names, common no doubt. Even in my short life I've known two people with those names and they both favor you a little with that prominent nose you have there. Uhm, yeah, I think I am tired. I'm pretty sure I need nap." I began to weep, realizing at last that I was in one hell of a trap.

"No doubt, Meine Liebe, you've already figured out like me that Kilian is not a common name nor is that nose of Doctor Altergott. Kilian had one just like it. What you may not recall is that woman that aided Malfred and Karl in that second gang rape incident and was known around the House as one of Jonas's creatures was named Anna. Her brother is that bastard Kilian." Master Maxx sniffed and paused a moment making me a bit anxious before he returned to his story.

I said nothing as the two doctors stood there praising each other for a "job well done." I couldn't stop the tears at this horrible revelation. Kilian had managed to get his hooks into my future functioning. Which could only mean he had managed to do what his sister had failed to do. He'd caught Jonas's trust. He did even more as I was to sadly discover, but we get ahead of ourselves, yes?

The men finally left me alone to wallow in misery. I heard from the lunch staffer that there were already signs that soon I would be released. They had banned me from all visitors. I wondered why they were punishing me by keeping Leo away as they prepared for my eventual release.

One of the aides informed me they would do all they could to keep me quiet, subdued, and calm until the paperwork went through. She said I was not being punished but protected. I didn't see it that way, but I was in no position to argue. I wanted out so badly I didn't even breathe a word of argument. Even when they told me they had assigned my case to Kilian and recognized Jonas's right to guardianship. I felt like a fly trapped in a jar, slowly running out of air.

I worked day and night with the Max shards, Christian, and Felicity to come up with a plan to run. I intended to hide in the country the second those doctors let me out until they stopped looking for me. I knew that would forfeit any chance for me to become a doctor, but I wanted freedom from those evil men more than anything else on the planet. I would merely have to be happy as a factory worker, grocery store clerk or janitor. I was resolved to suffer a lifetime of poverty, if necessary, but I consoled myself by realizing no matter what job I would be free to choose my destiny.

Then on the first day of February 1974, Doctor Wagner told me the next day I was to be released to return home. I smiled with joy that I was finally getting out, but I said nothing about his bullshit home statement. I frowned when he handed me a box. I took it but merely stared at the card on it, which read "To my Maximillian. From Jonas with love."

I wanted to throw it to the floor and scream, but I held my fury. The doctor noticed my lack of enthusiasm at this gift from my so-called father.

He stepped toward me. "Are you not going to open it, Maximillian?"

I shook my head. "Uhm, later maybe. I am sure it is nothing important. You know father." I flashed a fake smile at him.

Doctor Wagner scoffed. "Ah, well you need to open it soon. I happen to know that it is an outfit your father sent you to wear for your trip home. You have no street clothing to wear outside of this hospital tomorrow. I suppose you planned to walk out naked. Well, that would get you sent back in short order, yes? Go ahead, open it." He laughed.

I growled at him as I replied, "I have not seen my father in almost two years. How the hell would he even know what size I wear? I have grown a bit since I first arrived."

He cleared his throat and said, "Well, he uhm, he sent the wrong sizes I confess. He is obviously unaware of your growth spurt. I had your uncle Leo return the first outfit and get the right size when he came by yesterday hoping to visit with you."

I opened my eyes wide as I yelled out, "I desire to visit with Leo, please. I promise his visit will not upset me. Doctor, I beg of you. Let me see him."

Doctor Wagner looked at the floor as he replied, "Okay, tell you what. You open that box and put on the outfit to be sure it fits. If you do that, I will allow him to visit for a few minutes when he comes in today, like he does every day. Deal?"

I glared at him as I growled, "Ah, I thought you didn't understand service for service doctor. Seems I am the fool to teach you such things or maybe for believing you were ignorant of them."

He snorted while flashing me an angered look as he said, "I don't know whatever you mean. Do we have a deal, yes or no? Maximillian, you're wasting my time."

I smiled with evil as I replied, "There it is the thing I have waited a long time to hear. The truth of my sorry lot. You know doctor, that expression of 'wasting time' I know all too well. Someone else I know has said it often enough to me. I suppose I'd better do as I am told, or it will not go well for Maximillian. Sure, we have a deal Master, oops I meant Doctor."

Doctor Wagner stormed to the door and knocked three times with a furious expression as he responded, "Enough! Put the outfit on. Your uncle will be here soon. I will see you tomorrow when you are released. I expect no difficulty out of you as promised." He took off out of the room leaving me there with the Vampire's chosen outfit.

I looked at Felicity. "He desires to make me look like the freak, thinking if I try to run, I won't get far because everyone will recognize me. Well, fuck him! He is wrong. I will steal laundry from a clothesline or out of trash cans. It will not even slow us. You see, my love, I told you that Jonas owns this hospital and Doctor Wagner too. Kilian owns that fucking Doctor Altergott as well. It is the reason they chose this place to hold us. It was their way of beating us down until we bowed to their wills. Won't that motherfucking bat be surprised when tomorrow night his bed is cold without Christian Axel to keep it warm for him, ha." I opened the box.

I groaned out as I pulled the crimson lined long jacket, red waist coat, black blouse, trousers, and boots from the box. I noticed the pervert didn't include a pair of underwear. Inside was a letter from the Vampire in which he demanded I come to visit him in the apartment the second I got back to the House. I tore it up and threw it into the corner.

He was careful to offer no real details that could prove my story of the House being a den of sin true. Not that such a thing mattered anymore. I now understood these doctors and maybe the whole staff already knew what I'd been telling them was really happening. Obviously, they were all in on it.

Leo came to see me maybe half an hour later. He found me sitting there in that wretched outfit feeling blue but looking black and red. He smiled as he came inside and hugged me tightly. I looked to the floor barely able to keep from breaking into tears while I told him of Kilian's betrayal, and the truths I had found out about the hospital. Leo listened with an expression of pity on his face.

When I finished, he leaned in and whispered into my ear. "I tried to tell you, my little rabbit. You cannot escape Jonas nor the House. Please listen to me. Tomorrow when they come for you, just do as they say. Like it or not you are coming to Kaiser House. Once you get back inside, I want you to go straight to your fourth-floor apartment. You remember, the one Rolf has provided for you. He told me to tell you he is proud to call you brother and will visit with Jakob very soon. I beg you to stay in your apartment until I come to get you. You will escape from the House, my little rabbit, but when the time is right. If you give them any trouble, they may shoot you just to pay you back for all the stress you've caused them."

I glared at him. "Fuck you, Leo. I am not going with them. Tell Jonas and Kilian or any others to leave me alone. I choose to be free of the House. I am a Dominant. That means I have the right to leave!"

Leo kissed my forehead, which surprised me as he replied, "My little rabbit, you have always done everything the hard way. It only gets you injured. For this one time, please trust me. Do as they say and come home to me. I will help you escape eventually, but you must do it my way this time. I love you Christian Axel and always will. No matter what happens in this life I will never rest till you have all that will make you happy. That I vow."

I nodded with tears welling up as I responded, "I hear you Leo, but I can't do this. If I do, then you must realize that Jonas and Peter will want me to return to satisfying their twisted lusts. I hope you can understand why I just can't obey you this time, Leo." I fell into his chest weeping loudly.

He patted my back and hushed me as he calmly, "Christian Axel, I have seen you be strong for so long. You can be strong a little longer. Do it for your Leo. Do it for your future wife. Do it for your children. No matter what they try to do to you, it is only flesh deep. They can never reach your heart. That I own exclusively until the day I give it to the woman that will bring you all your dreams. You stop crying. You are a man now, so be a man. Stand on your feet and make all of them kneel to your desires for a change." He let me go while he watched me wipe my eyes.

I nodded. "As you say Leo. I will think about what you told me. You do have my trust and heart. You have been a man of your word."

He chuckled. "I'm an old dog but I've learned new tricks, my little rabbit. I'll see you tomorrow. Der Makellos is so excited he piddled in his hound bed. I didn't have the heart to spank him for it. I admit, at my age, I piddle when excited too. Our Christian Axel is coming home. We have reason to be losing our decorum, yes?"

I giggled with him over that funny statement. He visited a bit longer but was then called to leave. He kissed my forehead again and told me to remember his wise advice. I nodded that I would, but I was planning to ignore him. I was running away and that was that.

I spent many long nights and mornings in that cell, but that one February 2nd in 1975 was the worst. It seemed time stood still as I waited for that door to open letting me out into the world to resume the life I had never yet lived.

When at last the huge orderlies came to lead me to the front door, I nearly forgot myself and took off running like the kid I still was. They wore stoic expressions as they took me by the upper arms. I was dressed in the freakshow outfit Jonas had sent me as Doctor Wagner ordered the men to haul me down the winding hallways. I didn't look at anything but what was ahead. I was ready to flee the second I figured out where the exit was located.

Well, I had grown quite large and was very strong. That said, I still was not capable of breaking the hold of the two big brutes about my size. I saw the shiny glass doorway and made a move to get out of their grips. They held me tighter and told me to be still or they would call for the sedatives. I decided to wait to try again after they opened that blasted entry.

To my shock and horror, a black car pulled up in front of the door. Four big Russian brutes stepped out and walked up to greet us. I gasped for air in a panic realizing the House sent them to collect me. I spun my head around wildly looking for any escape route before the orderlies could hand me over to the House Guard.

The big hospital staffers roughly pushed me toward two of the Russians. I began to struggle and kick with all my might. Despite their having much more difficulty than they ever had in the past, I couldn't beat the huge males. They worked together seamlessly. No matter what I tried, they easily managed to get me handcuffed and hauled to the back seat of their awaiting car.

I was pushed inside headfirst while another produced a syringe. I cursed and kicked with all I had but that needle found its mark. They slammed the door on me the second they got the sedatives into my hip. My last memories are of laying in the back seat watching the clouds crossing the beautiful sun while the car motor started up and took me away to wherever the fuck the Goddamned Kaiser House is located.

I turned around with a gasp. "You mean you still don't know where the House is Master?"

He frowned and spat out his words. "No, they've never told me. I am always dragged back to the House sedated to this very day. Those stupid motherfuckers."

I nodded. "But Debbie knows and Russell. Ask them, yes. Beat it out of them Master."

He growled while glaring at the ceiling of the basement listening for their footstep sounds. "If I thought they knew where it is, you're fucking right I would. Yet, they don't know either. No outsider is allowed to travel there without a blindfold. That is the House law. One day I will find out where they take me. When I do, I will sneak back to that fucking place and burn her down, or maybe we go together, yes?" Master Maxx smiled and ruffled my hair.

I looked at my Felicity then smiled back. "Your desire is my pleasure, Master." We both laughed for a moment then he went back to the story.

When I awoke the car was still. I laid there unsure what was going on. Then suddenly the memory rushed back into my mind. I found my hands were no longer handcuffed and no one was at the wheel. The car was empty except me. I reached into my pocket and grabbed out Felicity. She was there. I sighed in relief while holding her to my chest.

I took a deep breath and told Felicity to hang on. I sat up ready to jump from the vehicle. I didn't hesitate to grab the handle and rip open the door ready to flee when I was suddenly surrounded by the four big Russian brutes from the hospital entryway. I backed up in fear with nowhere to run but back into the car.

The largest, and hairiest man, pointed to the right, "You go to the House. You have five minutes. You try to go anywhere but through that front door, Ivan will shoot you dead, Priceless. You go now." He yelled out in his thick Russian accent.

I nodded then took off walking as fast as my legs would carry me to the front door. I confess I was frightened. I saw Ivan aiming his rifle and following me with it from the furthest side of that parking lot. Those boys weren't kidding. If I had so much as stumbled, I would find myself deader than Olaf and Vilber. I decided to worry about getting out later, but for that moment the House was the safest place to be.

I jogged up the porch steps then looked back to see if the brutes and Ivan were still watching me. They were of course. Without another moment's hesitation, I knocked on the door and it opened with speed. I nearly choked as the dust and dankness filled my nostrils. I took one last look with regret at the blue sky and fluffy clouds as I took a step back into the darkness that haunted my soul.

The second I was through the entry; the door guards closed and locked it behind me. I turned to glare at them. Two large brutes dressed like normal police officers stood there smiling at me. I quickly cast a nervous look to their hips. It was obvious that Leo had told me the truth. They both were armed.

The redhead one with a mustache said, "Welcome home, Maximillian, sir. I am Toby and this is Neil. We are here if you should ever encounter difficulty. It is an honor to finally meet you in person. We are humbly at your service." He chimed out with awe in his expression, his eyes settling on Felicity in my left hand.

I nodded then said, "I desire you open that door and let me out. I wish to leave and never come back, Toby."

He looked at the ground while hitching up his weapon heavy breeches. "I apologize, but I cannot do that. If there is anything else you desire then Toby is your man. I thank you for the pleasure of serving you most honorable Master."

I nearly fainted when he called me that. "Huh? You call me Master? I own no submissive, nor do I wish to."

The other Guard with dark hair called Neil smiled then said with a chuckle, "Forgive me for explaining facts your honorable person already knows but we are black collars, Master. We serve all the Dominants of this House. Do you require aid with any baggage from your trip? The fourth floor is quite the trip, right?"

I shook my head feeling mildly disconnected realizing that while being addressed as a Dominant, I could not fucking leave like one. I took off walking for the staircase without replying to Neil. Immediately every silver and black collar knelt as I passed them.

I stopped briefly, mildly freaked at their overly reverent behaviors. Silvers are required to kneel for all the House Leaders or their personal Dominant. Black collars are only expected to take to their knees for the Head Voter or Head Elder.

After a frustrated gasp I rushed toward the staircase. I did my very best to ignore the fact that every submissive I encountered fell to their knees all around me as if I was the fucking king of Kaiser House.

To my surprise, many of the collared people gasped and some murmured apologies for getting in my way but all appeared in complete awe. I was upset by my most unhappy situation of being forced to return to this hell hole, but this weird welcome was sending me right to the edge of madness. I couldn't handle that stress. I practically ran to the apartment that Rolf told me was mine the second I broke my collar.

I was hauling ass down that hallway when two things sunk into my thick head. The first was I had not seen a single Dominant the entire way to the fourth floor. Secondly, I didn't have any keys to the apartment. Once I arrived, I stood quietly at the entryway unsure what to do. I walked to the banister and looked down at the rushing residents and familiar scenery that plagued my nightmares for as long as I could recall.

Then I stepped back from the railing with a sigh, positive that I needed some peace and quiet to think. I recalled someone told me there were armed guards at that back door too waiting for me to try to escape. I thought I would check that out for myself after a moment to recollect my thoughts and shake off the left-over fogginess of the heavy sedative I'd been shot up with only a few hours before (I assumed it was a few hours, but I really can't be sure).

I walked back to the door and gripped the handle. I wished I had a screwdriver to break my way inside. To my shock, the knob turned, and it opened easily. I smiled over the only bit of good luck I had all day. I stepped inside and turned on the lights.

The second the room brightened people jumped out from almost everywhere screaming at the top of their lungs "Surprise! Welcome home, Maximillian."

I immediately dropped to my knees in a cower. I groaned with terror as the world began to spin. I saw a man that looked like Byron catch my head just before it collided with the floor, then darkness overcame me.

There had simply been too much noise, and too much stress. I was indeed surprised to be back, but to be welcomed home. Well, I unfortunately was already aware many in the House were very thrilled to have me returned to them in fact. There were three residents in particular that had been waiting almost two years to remind me of why I'd tried so hard to escape in the first place.

Chapter 3: Welcome Home

I don't know how long I was out after I fainted but during that time someone moved me to the couch. I slowly regained consciousness after that terrible fright. I heard much mumbling and whispers all around me. I opened my eyes to the hovering vision of Byron staring right into my face.

I sat up with a startle. "Ah, what the fuck! Get your hands off me, motherfucker!" I screamed in pure terror at the Voter.

He had been leaning over me using a wet rag to bring me back from the darkness.

"Maxx, it is me, your lover Byron. Calm down. You must have hit you head when you fell and don't recognize me." He shot a look of confusion at the people gathered all around us.

I shook my head while backing away from this rapist as I said, "I know who you are, Byron. You are not my lover, cocksucker. Not now and not ever! What are you and all these sonofabitches doing in my apartment. Everyone, get out!" I cast a look of anger at the crowd recognizing the large array of Dominants that hailed from the first to the fifth floor.

Rolf came out of that mass of people with a look of mild humor in his expression. "Holy hell. Look at the size of the boy. I almost thought a giant mistakenly came to the wrong apartment. If it were not for that scar, I wouldn't believe this is the same little guy I used to call my buddy. Christ what the hell have you been eating." He stood there in front of me with his eyes wide looking me over from head to toe while letting out his breath appearing impressed.

I furrowed my brow as I growled out in irritation, "I am glad you can see I am not one that can be easily bullied any longer. I said to get the fuck out, all you! Anyone that wishes to ignore me should be warned. I intend to show them out the hard way." I pointed at the apartment door.

The huge brute Friedrick came out of the group frowning as he said, "But Maxx, we went to a lot of trouble to put this welcome home surprise party together for you. Be reasonable. These people are happy to see you. Can't you cut them some slack?" He crossed his arms.

I got off the couch and stood at full height which caused gasps among the mob as I yelled out, "I am a lot of things Friedrick but reasonable is not one of them. I didn't ask for anything from any of you. As for everyone being thrilled to see me, oh I bet they are. I on the other hand would rather be hung from my toes above a pit of poisonous snakes than see any of you ever again. I would trust the serpents to be more merciful when they tore me apart." I shot a hateful glance at Byron as he backed up.

Rolf shook his head with a groan. "My goodness, Mad Maxx. Aren't you the just the hateful one? Well, fellows, and ladies, I think you all better do what this big man says to do. It would appear Maxx is grouchy from his travels. Come on, we'll leave him to rest a little. I am sure he will apologize for his impulsively being ungrateful to his friends for their hard work after a nap."

I stood there keeping my eyes on each of the Dominants as they began to scatter. Many grumbled and a few shot me looks of anger. Each glare was met with an expression of disgust from me. I watched with immense fury as I saw Audrey, Fritz, Valitin, Roland, Hedy, Magnas, Bruno, Matz, Fiona, Louis and Nelda leaving.

I shook my head with complete disbelief that those criminals in particular thought I would be excited to see them. The hubris of these so-called Dominants were a complete mystery to me. The way I saw it, every one of them should be barricading their apartment doors, praying I had forgotten the cruel shit they had done to me when I was just a little boy. I had to assume they thought me still the helpless, beaten, submissive without a choice. Well, they were dead wrong.

Within only a few minutes I was left alone with only Friedrick, Byron and Rolf lingering behind. I refused to relax my stance of aggression as the three of them stood there in the living area shooting sheepish glances at each other. They appeared unsure what to say or do while I glared at them like an angry bear.

Byron looked at the floor when the last of the lesser House Dominants had exited my House as he said, "Maxx, look we are sorry to have embarrassed you with such a nasty startle like that. We meant well. The intention was to demonstrate to you how many new friends you have and to welcome you to your rightful place among the Dominants. I swear it."

I sneered at him, "Oh? You thought I would be appreciative of coming back to this fucking hell hole to find all the molesters, abusers, and scum awaiting me in my only God damned sanctuary on this motherfucking planet. I merely thought you delusional Byron but now I see you are a fucking moron."

Rolf let out his breath while Byron dropped his head appearing hurt by my words. "Now you just wait a second there Maxx. This party and invites was my idea, not Byron's. He wanted to greet you alone. You have no right to be ugly to him or to any of us. We've come to welcome you to our ranks with open arms and no ill will. How dare you act like an ungrateful ass?"

I laughed with bitterness. "Ah yes, fuck me, what was I thinking Rolf? I am shocked you are surprised though since I'm known for my ass. Well, I wish to apologize for my lack of polite protocol. How rude of me? I totally forgot myself. Allow me to kneel to my old Masters and offer to suck their cocks and thank them for the mercy of it," I yelled out while Friedrick looked to the ceiling and Byron dropped his head even lower.

Rolf covered his eyes as he said, "Oh, fuck Maxx. I suppose I wasn't thinking. I guess if the boot were on the other foot, I wouldn't be in a hurry to visit with people that had hurt me. Shit, you are right. I am a moron."

I nodded. "Yes, you are. Now that we have established that fact, you may go." I pointed at the door again.

Friedrick shot me a look of shame as he said in a pleading tone, "Please Maxx don't be like this. We know when last we met it was not on good terms but I for one would like to prove we can be your friends, despite all that has happened between us. Couldn't you give us the chance to know you on our own level and let the past go?"

I scoffed as I replied angrily, "I don't need friends. What I need is to be left in peace, but just so we are clear. I didn't like you before I broke my collar but was unable to do a fucking thing about it. None of you considered how I felt about you before forcing me to fulfill your baser urges. I am Dominant now, so I am free to do as I please. What I want is to never see any of you again."

Rolf crossed his arms as he said in a tone of frustration, "You've forgotten I pay the rent for this so-called sanctuary of yours, Mad Maxx. If I were you, I would remember that. I have been most generous to you to make up for my short falls when you wore the forbidden silver. I would also like to point out my brothers and I have been working with Leo to get laws changed around here. You say you need no friends? With Gretta, Peter, Jonas, Cora, and that fucker Kilian are all gunning for you. Friends, I do believe, is the one thing you require in abundance. If you hope to survive much longer that is."

I looked to the floor as I nodded and replied, "Exactly. If I did wish to survive is the question. You'd do well to remember that too Rolf. I say once more, with my temper in check, to get out. Next time, I'll use my fists to remove you. If you wish to stop paying for this apartment, that you claimed I had earned, then do so. You are a free man, unlike this fucking idiot that stands before you. Your wish I must accept when it comes to that. However, I do have the right to not set my eyes on you while you decide if you are a man of his word or just another Goddamned liar." I looked up and glared at him angrily.

Byron, Friedrick and Rolf let out their breath, but all three began to head for the door.

Byron turned and cleared his throat just as they started out into the hallway with me hot on their heels ready to lock them all out. "Here Maxx, you dropped this when you fainted. I am sorry for everything. We all are. Maybe after you settle in, you'll change your mind. If you do, I cannot speak for these other two brutes, but Bryon's home is always open to you. For what it is worth, I thank you for always serving me well and for the wonderful memories." He handed Felicity to me.

I snatched her from his grip while I growled out, "Oh and I thank you for the nightmares, Byron. As for changing my mind, well, I wouldn't hold your breath, cocksucker. I don't associate with people that demand someone pay with their dignity to receive assistance that should have been granted pro bono. Bye."

Rolf stood there a second holding the door so I could not close it on him. "What happened to you out there in that mental hospital Maxx to make you so fucking heartless? Where is the sweet boy I once adored?"

I chuckled with bitterness. "Before this moment you've never bothered to know a thing about me Rolf. The House killed the boy you knew and all of you helped House do it to him. Reap what you sow, I know I must. So, why should any of you get a free pass?" I pushed him out of the entry with vigor and slammed the door locking it tightly to guard against them trying to re-enter.

Alone at last, I walked back to the living room. I found the China Geraldine with diamond eyes sitting where I had left her on the fireplace mantle. I went from room to room investigating with some surprise the changes since I'd last been there.

Apparently, all or one of those three brutes had packed it with fine furniture and modern appliances. I even found dishes in the kitchenette cabinets and towels in the bathrooms.

I sighed as I examined the master bedroom. In the closet I found that the Vampire had also aided in furnishing my apartment. It was packed with long jackets, waist coats, boots, breeches, and blouses of his interest. I found a new makeup case, also packed with new items, which had a note from Jonas attached. I took that piece of paper and sat down on the bed to read it with irritation rising within.

It said, "Welcome home my husband. You likely are very tired from your long trip. Take the night to rest up. I expect your visit at our apartment by nine in the morning to discuss our living arrangements. Under the bathroom sink you will find the typical hygiene items required to make yourself ready to greet me properly. Use them as you have been trained to do. You will look your best when we meet, or I will be forced to demonstrate my displeasure. I have missed you greatly and look forward to our reunion tomorrow with thrill. Do not be late. It will not go well for you if I must come seeking your excuse for it. Till the morning, love your Jonas."

I growled with fury as I crumpled up the note and threw it across the room. "Do you believe this shit Felicity? That bat thinks he can still order me around. As I have been trained to do? Look my best? Who the fuck does he think he is?" I shot a look of anger at Felicity sitting next to me.

She merely shrugged. Felicity knew I was already aware of what his note would say. It was obvious Jonas still thought himself my Master. Well, he could kiss his own ass. I wasn't going to do a fucking thing he ordered, not anymore. I knew by House law he was considered my husband, but I was a Dominant now. Not even your blood bonded spouse can force the special services when you are not their legal submissive. The Vampire was an arrogant cocksucker to think I was not aware of that.

My first issue of business was finding a way to replace the only clothing I had to wear. I was going to be damned if I would dress the way that monster insisted. The real problem was I had no money, nor a job to get any. If I didn't want to be stuck running around naked, I had to address that matter immediately. Without an income, I was not only at the mercy of Rolf paying my rent, and the Vampire's choice of what I wore, but I also had no way to get food.

You see Dominants must pay for their meals whether from the kitchen or the Great Hall. Nothing is free for them. The submissives needs and care are paid for by their Dominant, but they are forced to pay back with the only thing they have, their flesh. I was not a submissive anymore and no man or woman could own me.

While that all seems good on paper, I would be like any other free person out in the world even within the House. Without a way to pay I was in danger of homelessness and starvation. That threat was heightened by the fact that I wasn't allowed to leave the property to seek my fortune.

I decided right after I visited with Der Makellos and Leo, I would head down to the kitchen to seek out the Black Collar Mistress. I was hoping she had some sort of job opening. I was aware that if I couldn't get out of the House quickly, this would be my only shot at least of earning my supper. The black collars get a paycheck if you recall.

I sat there with Felicity wondering how expensive clothing or food may be, and how much a fair wage is for any job, when there was a loud knocking at the door. I was going to ignore it thinking it was one of the Voters. I assumed they'd returned to start arguing again, but the longer I refused to answer the harder the visitor pounded. After a few moments of enduring the noise, I stormed from the room with Felicity ready to knock whoever was out there right the fuck out for disturbing my peace and quiet.

I put Felicity in her hiding spot as I tore open the door, my fists up ready to strike. I threw a right hook right into a man's face without bothering to identify him.

I pulled back to hit the fellow again when the person yelled out, "Goddammit, Maximillian. You hit me one more time and I will kill you." That familiar voice caused me to back up with a tremble I could feel all the way to my soul.

"Peter? What the fuck are you doing here," I said with a bit of a stutter in my words.

My father stood there rubbing his jaw with an angry expression as he replied, "What the hell did they teach you in that hospital? Apparently not manners when receiving a guest. Shit, that hurt you little, I mean, (he looked me up and down with his eyes wide in horror) big motherfucker. Holy shit, you have grown Maximillian. What the fuck happened!" He backed up with what seemed like fear overcoming him.

I nodded as I looked at the floor to hide my grin as I responded, "Not what you expected, am I? Puberty is what's happened, Peter. You know the thing that eventually changes everyone. I am not a little boy anymore. Well?

Now you have seen the error in assuming I wasn't human just like everyone else. So, what the fuck are you bothering me for? As you can see, I am in no mood for visitors. State your business then move on. You're wasting my time." Ha, I had waited for years to throw that last sentence back in his face.

Peter cleared his throat appearing mildly anxious as he said, "Uh, yeah, okay. I have come by to arrange a formal meeting with you. You and I must jointly go to the Hall of Records with the Honorable Gretta present to witness the details of our contract."

I rolled my eyes. "Seriously, Peter? Do you not see me? I am not a cute little boy anymore. I am an ugly brute. Surely you don't still desire to control the rights to call on the special services from such an unsightly man. See here? I have a fucking beard if I don't shave every damned day. I am already almost taller than you are. Ha! I bet you didn't consider the cuddly pup would become the hairy hound when you pulled that trick of yours on me, did you."

He snorted then glared at me with fury as he replied, "You assume I care if you are small or large? All that matters is that I find desire for your subjugation to my will. You always were the hardheaded one, Maximillian. You've never listened worth a shit. How many times have I told you that it thrills me to break your heart? Seeing your impressive girth and size today only makes my interest higher. It is easy to bully a tiny child, but to force a giant man to his knees. Oh, well now that is power." He smiled with wickedness.

I scoffed and replied, "Well, maybe I'll kill you rather than see our contract fulfilled. Bet you didn't consider that, did you? I am more than capable of such a thing, even more so than I was before. We both know I am just as experienced in that kind of service as the sexual ones you're interested in now, don't we Peter. Just give me a reason why I shouldn't break you in half, then throw you from the banister behind you." I took a step toward him and to my thrill he stepped back with fear in his expression.

He stuttered out, "Back the fuck up, Maximillian! If you kill me, the Guard will send you to hell before my flesh goes cold."

I smiled with evil and took another step sending him back one himself. "So? You think I give a fuck? Maybe it would be worth it just to watch you bleed out."

He glared at me with sudden fury. "How dare you threaten me Maxx. Like it or not you agreed to this contract with me willingly. You have always been a man of your word. Am I to believe you've suddenly become a criminal that breaks his bond?"

I nodded while I replied, "You tricked an eleven-year-old boy into this contract by withholding information. That agreement between us is as much bullshit as anything else you ever told me Peter and you know it. If I were you, I would go and tear up that fucking thing and keep my door locked tightly. I will be coming for you soon enough. Better watch your back, cocksucker." I grinned even wider showing him all my busted-up teeth.

He nodded with intense anger. "Fine, I will go and tell Gretta you refuse to uphold your end of our bargain. After I do, then it is you who had better find a place to hide. The Guard will have you in the dungeon awaiting another trip to the rubber room the second I tell the Heads of this House of your betrayal. Even if they let it go, you will rot inside this apartment for the rest of your life, without work or any way to support yourself. If you don't starve to death, then you will end up killed most violently by those still looking to take out old vendettas. You won't be able to afford protection from them any more than food. You try escaping out the doors, the Guards will shoot you. If I were you I would go ahead and get that over with. Bullets are less painful than starvation or beaten to death."

I growled at him, "Fuck you, Peter."

He smiled bitterly as he replied. "Yes, that is the right response, Maximillian. That is, if you ever want the chance to escape this House. As it is, I see you are hell bent to forfeit all you earned by being a dumbass. Well, enjoy your freedom Mister Dominant Maximillian for as long as you last. I see you around. Oh wait, no I won't. I don't hang out with corpses." He began to walk away.

My eyes went wide over his cryptic words as I yelled after him, "Wait, what is this you say about escaping the House? Are you saying I will be released if I honor my contract with you? I don't understand!" I was feeling fear rising within faster than floodwaters in the desert after a sudden storm.

He stopped marching away but didn't turn around as he replied, "Medical school, Maximillian, is not in the House, is it? Our contract states that I must pay for that luxury in return for the rights to your special services until you produce a child for the House or your forty-second birthday. Did you forget the details? I am surprised if you did since you seem so angered over them now that the time has come to fulfill it."

I shouted angrily, "You tricked me, Peter! That deal is unfair, and you fucking know it! You had no business making bargains with a child that had no idea what he was agreeing to!"

He halted then turned around with a look of indignation on his face as he replied calmly, "Unfair you say? Well shows you still know nothing. I am forced to provide for your living expenses while attending college, medical school, and residency. You're going to cost me a minor fortune. It was a fair trade to demand you service me in return for the hole you will put in my pocket."

I shook my head and plead out, "Then allow me to pay your coin back when I acquire work as a doctor, Peter. I'll even pay you interest. Hey, you can set the amount. Go ahead and give me a number. I won't refuse it, I swear."

Peter chuckled with a look of disbelief in his expression as he replied, "You are indeed mad, Maximillian. I won't live long enough for you to repay all that you will owe, even without asking interest. Besides, I told you this years ago. I don't want the money back. You already agreed to pay the price I demanded long ago. So, you either hold up your end or kiss medical school and a life outside this House goodbye. I refuse to argue, nor am I open for renegotiation. I am leaving so you can think about it. If you come to your senses, then I will meet with you in the Hall of Records tomorrow at five in the afternoon to finalize the contract. If you don't show, be ready to be arrested. I warn you Maximillian. I am not going to drop this. If I don't get what is mine by contract, then I will see it removed from my sight forever. Good day to you, Maximillian." He snorted then took off with speed down the hallway.

I stood in the doorway watching him till he took off up the stairs out of my view. I turned and slammed the door shut with a yell of fury. I was so fucked. I hated my life. I hated that House. More than anything at that moment I hated me. I walked over to the couch and dropped onto it ready to weep like a kid when I spotted a romance novel on the coffee table.

I picked it up then opened its cover to the inscription, "For the lonely nights. Love Leo."

I smiled bitterly. "Felicity, we need to meet with Leo. He will know what to do. He promised to help us escape this nightmare, right? He is a man of his word. If he cannot help, then we can just jump from the banister. Deal?" I could feel her nodding in my pocket.

I stood up to leave, almost forgetting to grab my keys to the place that I still call my sanctuary in that House to this day. I took them into my hand, dropping them into the hidden pocket with Felicity. Without any further hesitation I tore off down that hallway rushing up to the sixth floor, and my real home with Leo and Der Makellos.

I was moving so fast, the silver and black collars on the staircase had some difficulty kneeling in time when they saw me coming. I was still startled by this strange honor they were paying to one of no worth, but I didn't have time to ask any of them about it.

Until one silver boy of twelve knelt in front of me. His bad judgement almost sent me back down the steps to end my days just as that old Doctor Briton or Drexel had. He yelped and cowered as I caught myself just before rolling to my death.

I was panting in anxiety as I cast a worried eye behind me and wiped the sweat off my brow. You have no idea how grateful I was that I managed to catch the railing just in the nick of time. I looked at the silver collar that was trembling prostrated terror at my feet.

He wailed out, "Please. I beg mercy Master. I apologize for my clumsiness. It won't happen again." He was weeping heavily in fear.

I let out my breath and felt my heart breaking for the poor boy as I replied, "You have nothing to apologize about. It was my rash behavior, not yours, that caused this collision. I am the one that begs your mercy." I held out my hand in offer to help him to his feet.

The brunette boy gasped but kept his eyes down as he responded, "What? I don't understand Master. I must beg your punishment. You were nearly killed because of my thoughtlessness."

I chuckled at that familiar sounding plea as I said, "I was nearly killed for being a thoughtless oaf. Punishment denied. What do they call you?" I took his upper arm and pulled him to stand when he didn't take my offer to aid him readily.

He looked around wildly at the silvers, blacks and a few Dominants watching us as he said with fear and tears in his eyes. "I am called Marc, Master. You are not angered at me?"

I shook my head with a friendly pat on his back while I said, "No, at least not at you, Marc. I will have to remember to be more careful when I am running like a fool up the steps. I could have injured you even more than me. Are you hurt in any way? I may owe your Mistress for damaging her most sublime silver collar."

He looked at the floor nervously as he replied, "Uhm, no. I'm not hurt, Master. Mistress Karsten will surely beat me for tripping the Priceless, as I have done."

That made me laugh as I said, "The Priceless? I think you are mistaken Marc. I was the Priceless but that was long before you came out of the dungeon for your submissive training. I am only a lowly fourth floor Dominant now. Perhaps you would do me a favor and tell these other submissives they need not kneel to this unworthy man any longer."

He shook his head then stole a look at me with an expression of awe in his eyes as he said, "Forgive me, Master, but I cannot stop them from kneeling to you. They honor you willingly, as do I."

I narrowed my eyes as I said in a suspicious tone, "Huh? Why do you do that?"

Marc smiled while wiping his tears as he replied, "Because Master, you are our hero. You broke the forbidden silver. Since your rise our lives have been better. For the silvers you're our legend, for the blacks a beacon of hope for a better day. We kneel before you because to us you are the real power of this House, and of our hearts. You are the King of all the collars."

I gasped as the world began to tilt slightly. "I think you have it wrong. All wrong. Thank you for the mercy, Marc. I must be going now." I began to stumble up the stairs unable to wrap my mind around his words.

He called out, "Forgive me Master, but will you report my stupidity to my Mistress Karsten?"

I shook my head but didn't look back. "No, Marc. Have a good day. I'll see you soon, I hope." I wandered up the rest of the way to the sixth floor feeling disconnected and afraid.

The blacks and silvers continued to show their reverence to their hero as I traveled. I was reacting this way because it was all a lie. I wasn't free of my forbidden silver any more than any of them. I had indeed been working with Leo and the Voters to improve the lot of the subjugated, but the rules were slow acting. Many new laws that had been voted in had long transition periods thanks to Gretta's interference. She continued to stall many of the worst excesses with the excuse that the Dominants would need up to five years to adjust to the changes.

For example, while it was now illegal to force special services from a silver collared child under fifteen, it was still happening in secret. Leashes with silver collars under eighteen were also forbidden by this time, and you could not kill nor sell a silver to the circuit for being soiled, no matter their age without approval from the Voter Council.

I was most unhappy that all around me the silvers and black collars still lived a colorless life of abject subjugation, fear, and hard labor. I was a Dominant without wealth, power, or the ear of the ones with the real ability to change things. I sighed as the emotion of despair washed over me. I realized that Marc and all of them like him could still expect to find their grave before adulthood thanks to the House residents working together to hide their cruel practices. Those children and other impoverished people that served the wealthy residents deserved better.

I walked to Leo's door quickly. I feared that Jonas, Claus, or even Malfred, may come out of their apartments and catch me. The last thing I desired was to be found wandering around within their grips and no witnesses. I knocked with only enough sound to alert Leo inside. That is if he were in his usual spot sitting on the couch reading a romance novel.

To my relief Leo came right away. He stood there smiling, with his eyes shining brightly. I dropped my gaze to the floor but smiled back with nervousness. Leo backed up without a word. A black muzzle pushed past his waist. I nearly let out a yelp when I realized this huge hound was my baby Der Makellos. I had not been the only one to find adulthood during that long nineteen months I'd been away.

Despite our lengthy separation my best buddy knew me immediately. He spun around in excitement as Leo grabbed my arm and pulled me inside with him. I leaned down to pet my old friend. Der Makellos didn't think that was cozy enough of a greeting for ones that shared such familiarity as we had.

He knocked me to my ass and pounced. I giggled and struggled as my hound bathed me in thousands of eager tongue kisses. Leo stood there laughing as Der Makellos wrapped me around his dew claws once more. I had certainly missed him, and the feeling was more than a little mutual.

When at last my hound had convinced himself I was completely subjugated to his will, he allowed me to rise from the floor. I was grateful for the mercy of his not holding my long absence against me. I told him gently I wrote to him every day even though I had not been permitted to visit. I said that while patting his head.

Leo chuckled as he said, "Ah, and Leo read him every single word of your letters, my little rabbit. Come sit down. You must be so tired. Please tell me what you think of your apartment decorations. Rolf, Friedrick, Byron and I worked day and night to get it ready for your comfort." He sat down on his couch, and I sat down next to him.

I shook my head while scoffing. "Leo, I do appreciate the beautiful new things in the apartment, but was that surprise party necessary? I don't want to be here in the House and sure don't desire being welcomed in such a shocking way."

Leo let out his breath in a loud gasp. "What? A surprise party. I am afraid you have puzzled me. I didn't know about a surprise party."

I rolled my eyes as I petted Der Makellos who was sitting at my feet. "I am to assume that this party idea was the Voters exclusively?"

He groaned. "You are not teasing me then or speaking in code? You must be kidding me. Rolf and his dumbass brothers Voters actually went through with their threats after I warned them such a thing would upset you. Shit, what the hell is wrong with those boys?"

I chuckled bitterly. "I think I made believers of them, Leo. I was not the happy host they expected. I am afraid I lost my temper along with my manners. It is not their fault that I am back in this hell hole. Yet, I took out my anger on them. I will apologize later. For now, I need to ask for your good counsel, Leo. I am in a lot of trouble. I think you are already aware. I as usual didn't listen to you when you tried to warn me."

Leo interrupted me. "Christian, drop the self-loathing. It is not only likely to cause you wrinkles before your time, but it is worthless to engage in. You are a Dominant now. That means you must do what you do without apologies. Remember, you are free to choose even if the choices suck. I no longer have the authority to make you mind my desires and neither does anyone else in this House. That said, what is it that you are unsure of and how can I help you figure out?" He frowned as he reached out and pushed my hair out of my face then crossed his arms.

I leaned back with a loud groan. "Leo, Peter came to see me. He said he is calling in that fucking contract. He didn't even blink upon discovering that I am not little Maximillian anymore. He says that if I don't come to finalize that agreement in front of Gretta tomorrow, he will demand my arrest. Then he plans to send me back to the rubber room till I relent."

Leo nodded. "Okay, and how can I assist you there? You were aware of that contract long before I even knew you, my little rabbit. You also are aware that Peter is not kidding. If you don't show up, he will come after you. That is a no brainer. You go, honor the contract, and live. Or you don't and find yourself in a cell for life."

I glared at him with a bit of irritation. "That is all you got to say about this, Leo?"

He snorted. "What the hell do you want me to say, Christian? I don't have the power to do shit about this contract between you two. That deal is with Peter. Only he can choose to release you from your vows to him. You know how I feel about your father's unnatural attraction to you, little rabbit, if I report it you're both dead men. Gretta will not be the fool to allow such an embarrassment to become public. Plus, she is implicated in that plot of Peter's too. While seeing that pervert get his at last would be wonderful, I won't say a word for your own good health."

I groaned casting my eyes to the ceiling as I whined out, "Then there is no escaping his foul touching is what you are telling me. I really thought, I guess I hoped, that something could be done. I don't know what the hell I was thinking coming here. You are as useless as everyone else. Maybe you are in on this plot to keep me in the beds of these horrible men. I am the fucking fool to think you ever cared about me, Leo. I am going to march to the front door this moment and allow Toby and Neil to shoot me dead." I stood up with rage filling my chest.

Leo sat forward his own fury building as he grabbed my wrist pulling with strength and yelled out, "You sit your ass down, Christian Axel! I have had enough of this fit throwing. I have done things for you over the last two years that nearly got me killed. I will stand for any others being nasty to me, but not from you. I mean it. You will calm down or so help me I will fucking call the Guard myself. I am ready to go to hell if you are. Just say the word, my darling, and we can be dining with the devil in no time,"

His sudden aggression set off old terrors and I found myself minding his orders without thinking. "I am sitting down as you wish Master, oh, I mean, Leo. Let me go, mercy please."

Leo nodded then glared at me with sternness. "Christian, you must do what suits you. You are the boss of your choices now. However, if I were you, I would be there tomorrow to meet with Peter and Gretta."

I started to interrupt, but Leo snapped at me with fury till I hushed as he continued in a furious tone, "You listen, I was not finished! I would go but not because of fear of being arrested but because that is your only honest ticket out of this House. If you comply then Peter will be forced to hold up his end too. You'll be sent away to medical school, then to a residency. That will take a long time to finish, yes? Well, maybe Peter will die, and others around here looking to hold you as their hostage may fall too, right? Come on and use your big brains, Christian. Such a thing as keeping Peter interested in your favors would get you protection from him. It also buys you time to get you ready for life out there in the real world." He smiled at me with a bit of sadness in his expression.

I shook my head. "Leo, didn't you know those doctors at the hospital made me say I am a schizophrenic? They don't let the mentally ill become doctors. I tell you this is a trap. Surely you can see it. Even if Peter comes through with his promises, that fucking Dr. Altergott and Kilian will block me from getting a medical license. They've written in my records that I'm a dangerous psychotic, Leo.

I am so fucked!" I began to weep but I covered my eyes with my hand, so Leo didn't see that unmanly display.

Leo sighed deeply. "Yes, I am aware that Kilian is up to no good. I am not a blind man. He has taken up with Jonas deeply. He moves that idiot Vampire like a puppet master."

I uncovered my face startled out of my despair. "What? Did you just say Kilian has taken up with Jonas? I don't understand Leo. Jonas doesn't listen to anyone!"

Leo clicked his tongue then sat back with a loud sigh. "When they took you away Christian, all the Elders beds got cold and lonely. Well, Claus and I are not beasts. The lack of affection was of no serious interest to us. Malfred, well, he has been slipping around with a FemDom on the fourth floor, but he was already doomed to such a life thanks to his early rise as Elder. Jonas, on the other hand, was not happy to wait till you returned. Kilian managed to be there when that idiot was grieving for you, his lost Priceless collar. A few months after that day you cut off your metal the two of them publicly became partners. Lovers to be blunt. Jonas apparently fell hard for that hawk nosed snake, go figure. You no longer see one without the other."

I gasped in full on terror. "Leo, this cannot be. Elders cannot be openly with one under their rank unless they are blood bonded. Jonas cannot marry Kilian. He and I are, and the law says only one husband per Dominant. Wait a minute. What is it that you are not telling me, Leo?" I closed my eyes trying to escape the pain of what I already knew he was going to say.

Leo sniffed then looked at me with pity. "My precious bunny, Jonas used Malfred as the precedent for Kilian's rise to Elder. The man was given Bladrick's slot and apartment without quarrel before my old buddy's corpse was cold in the grave. Jonas threatened Cora and Gretta to tell of their association in the death of Xavier and plot using his Priceless collar in their own rise to power. Peter, Rolf, Friedrick and Byron were helpless to stop the motion from going through. Gretta is the power of this House; her word is law."

I wept harder, this time not bothering to hide it from Leo as I replied, "Well, that is that I suppose. The man that can block my life on the outside is an Elder and the lover of the Vampire. Jonas claims to be my husband and guardian with ultimate power over me in this House. Peter's contract is no good to me anymore. So, he is barking up the wrong tree. Plus, I have no job or money to survive in this fucking place either, Leo. What the hell am I going to do now? Did you know the Vampire left me a note in my apartment? He demands I come provide him with his husbandly rights tomorrow at nine. I don't get it. If he has Kilian to attend his lust, why is he still bothering me? What kind of sex fiend is he? Jonas knows I'm not interested in him, and mostly straight. Kilian is homosexual. Why not just let him attend those creeps twisted desires."

Leo reached out to stroke my cheek. "Christian, I know this is all so difficult for you to deal with right now. It is overwhelming no doubt. You must trust your Leo to never lead you astray. I learned my lesson with that Malfred business long ago. You go tomorrow and make good on the deal with Peter. Then you can go to medical school the second you are accepted. I will do all I can from within to assure that Kilian and his family don't block your medical license when the time comes."

I nodded, still weeping. "Okay Leo, I'll do as you say, but what of the Vampire's demands? Can I merely ignore them? What rights does a husband have to force my compliance with his desires?"

Leo smiled with bitterness. "You are a Dominant now. He can demand to you attend his lusts all he likes. However, sex isn't something he can force on you anymore. You have the freedom to say no, my bunny. Peter is the one with the power to force you to mind when it comes to who you sleep with or deny. I already spoke with him about that, and he says he will not intercede on Jonas's behalf. He also said he will not block you from taking all the lovers you wish if they are male. He said thanks to your husband he must block all females except for the one that becomes your wife."

I wailed. "I can only have sex with males until I choose a wife. Are you fucking kidding me?"

Leo hushed me gently. "Easy, little rabbit. You need to think outside the box here. Yes, I realize that not getting to sow your wild oats will be a hard thing, but let's face it you didn't get to do that before all this anyway. What is a little more time? You have your studies to focus on. Becoming a doctor is time consuming. You wouldn't have time to run around with the girls anyway. When your residency is over, you can select your wife and make up for all the lost time, yes? Peter is not saying he will force you to have sex with males, only that he will turn a blind eye if you decide to have any boyfriends. It is only the girlfriend he is denying you right to obtain."

I glared at Leo. "Oh well, I suppose I misunderstood. I thought Peter was a man. All this time I thought he had a cock. Must have been a hallucination of all those blow jobs and penetration sex with him. Thank God I won't be forced to have sex with men anymore. Leo, are you listening to yourself? Fuck me!"

Leo shrugged, "Christian, I am saying other than that brute father of yours you don't have to put up with any other foul molestations. Sure, Jonas will attempt to force you to his bed, but he has no power to make you. Just remind the bastard when he starts to bully, you are supposed to be seeking your wife. You know that female Priceless he wants so damned bad." I gasped so loud he dropped his words.

I dropped my head into my hands. "Scheiße (SHIT), I forgot about the fucking promise to leash my wife to Jonas for the collar selection. He will use that dishonor to attempt a hijacking of my children. I cannot allow any woman to carry my children, Leo. The House will force them to the silver collar for sure! Fuck this! I am throwing myself off the banister. I cannot take anymore." I wailed as I tried to get up and run from the apartment.

Leo, with Der Makellos's help, managed to tackle me to the floor. I struggled against him and my hound but the two of them pinned me adequately. I fell into a weeping jag while Leo held my head doing his best to comfort the most miserable boy on earth. I was trapped solidly and there was nowhere to run, other than to the grave.

When I had calmed to a silent weeping Leo cleared his throat then said, "Well my bunny, you go tomorrow to assess what Jonas and Kilian are up to. Then seal the deal with Peter. After all that is done, report all you learn back to me. I feel confident together, in time, you and I can be the winners in this game. You must believe me when I say I want to hold your children in my lap one day as their Uncle Leo. I agree with you that you must never have children with any girl until you can get rid of Jonas, Kilian, and above all Peter. I don't know what Peter's interest is in you, but you can bet it has something to do with his grandchildren and perhaps your future wife. Promise me you'll keep an eye on that sneaky bastard. Until then, keep big Christian in his breeches and his cute button nose in his books, okay?"

I nodded feeling empty inside while I stammered out, "I can do that Leo, but Peter is going to want me to, I mean, I am not. Oh, you know what I am worried about, right?"

He looked at me with sadness as he replied, "You are a man Christian and have handled worse suffering than the kind he'll cause when he rebreaks you in during his penetration. The sexual shit he will pull on you won't be any worse than what you already have endured. After the first couple of times, it will be more of a psychological torment than real pain. The sooner you go off to college the better. You have performed special services hundreds of times. Please, my love, don't let Peter get to you. That is why he continues to harass you, you know. The sooner you learn to pretend you could care less about his foul demands, the sooner he will lose interest."

I sniffed loudly. "That is maybe the one thing you say I must agree with you about, Leo. He told me many times it is the heartbreak he sees in my eyes that makes him desire me. If only I could learn to hide that somehow. I wish there was a way to get the Vampire to lose interest in me as well, but so long as he thinks I will bring him the, wait a second. I am a Goddamned fool!" I yelled with a sudden epiphany while looking deep into his eyes.

Leo jerked in a startle from my sudden shout. "What? Christian Axel, why are you looking at me like that?"

I sat up and looked at the floor coyly as I said, "Leo, you can help me fix this."

He snorted. "Me? How Christian? I suppose you want me to kill Peter, Kilian, and Jonas? They will catch me and you. Then we can all dance together in hell."

I laughed then looked at him with seriousness. "No, you need not kill anyone Leo. Quite the opposite. I want you to be my lover, Leo." I stroked his cheek then looked down coyly again.

Leo near sputtered with shock. "What? No, I cannot do that!"

I looked back at him with surprise as I replied in a confused tone, "Huh? You're denying my offer? But why Leo? I thought you loved me. If so, then why can't you be my lover for real. I swear, I'm choosing you willingly this time, see no collar! Besides, if Jonas believes I am truly gay, then maybe he will give up his stupid fantasy of trying to get me to find him a female Priceless. The homosexual man isn't interested in marrying women! Just think about it for a moment. This won't break Peters rules and when he sees that I am with you by choice, he will also think I'm truly gay. He will then lose interest too. You see my problem has always been these perverts think I'm straight and get a thrill by torturing me along with their physical release. So, if being straight is the problem, then Christian Axel will not be. Problem solved!"

He grabbed my wrist and closed his eyes appearing unable to speak for a moment then said, "I have waited so long to hear you say this to me, my little rabbit, but I must deny this offer with much regret, believe me. I cannot have an open love affair with one under my status by House law unless he is blood bonded to me. I think your idea is magnificent. That said, you must choose another to be your lover, Christian Axel." He opened his eyes and a tear rolled down his cheek.

I reached out and stopped the water with a finger as I replied, "Okay, fair enough. You cannot be my lover in public. You can, however, still be my lover in secret. I ask you to take me for your own, right this minute. I beg you to make love to me in the bed we have shared many times when I had no choice. Now I do, and I choose you."

Leo shuddered. "You don't realize yourself Christian. You are merely being kind to me. I thank you from the bottom of my heart, but I cannot take advantage of you anymore. I accepted I would be alone till I die. Please have mercy on me and on yourself. Never bring this up again."

I smiled with deep affection in my expression as I said softly, "You have called me hardheaded and say that I don't listen. That may be true, Leo. However, I must have learned that from my foolish Leo. I also think maybe you need better glasses or maybe you are going blind. Can you not see that I love you and always have?"

Leo was beginning to pant with wantonness over my words as he responded, "But Christian, I am a man. You said you didn't want to be involved in penetration sex anymore. I will always be a top and never can change my heart. I respect that you are neither a bottom nor gay. Please stop teasing me with offers you don't mean. It is cruel."

I pulled him to me and engaged him in a deep, heated kiss full of lustful passion then pulled back watching him gasping in thrill as I said, "That was teasing, Leo, better learn the difference. I am not straight if you must know. I am bisexual or possibly pansexual. I do not enjoy being the bottom during sex that is true, but I do find my pleasure when you make love to me. I am begging you to be my lover. Break me back in before Peter or Jonas gets the chance. Allow me the mercy of your gentleness while you bring me back across to the place I cannot escape. Tonight, when I cry out in the darkness, let it be the name Leo that falls from my lips." Leo gasped out unable to hold back his urges any longer.

He grabbed the back of my head with strength forcing his lips to mine with eagerness. I pushed him back with fury. Leo growled as he pushed me to the floor with all his weight. I kicked him off laughing with thrill. That only set his fire for me to inferno status.

I yelped as he grabbed my upper arms pulling me to my feet. I stood there with a cat smile daring him to try pushing me around again. Leo narrowed his eyes then came at me plowing both of us into the wall behind me. Der Makellos thought we were wrestling. He jumped and yipped trying to get involved in this brutish wooing ritual.

Leo told Der Makellos to "sit and stay" as he grabbed handfuls of my hair from the side of my head and forced his deep kissing. I allowed this for a few moments then with great care, but with strength, I pushed him off. He fell to his ass on the floor.

He groaned as he flashed me a look of angry confusion and growled out, "What the hell are you doing, Christian? I thought you said you wanted me to take you. If so then why do you keep pushing me away?"

I laughed as I said in a teasing tone, "To remind you that I can, anytime I wish, Leo. You seem to have forgotten that I am aware I can say no. Next time I tell you I have made a choice, do not question me. Catch me if you dare or are you too old to handle the youth you've desire so much?" I took off running for his bedroom giggling like the kid I still was.

Leo of course came running with great contentment. He found me waiting for him on his bed. I had removed Felicity's house, my jacket, but nothing else. Leo came through the door and tackled me with heavy kissing and fevered touching. The man behaved as if he had been without a lover for his whole life.

I gasped out in thrill as he tore off my shirt and kissed me on my naked flesh. I pulled him onto me removing his own shirt as he came down. Our heated kisses and petting became a unified process of stroking with passion filled rubbing. He didn't have to say a word. I was well trained in the special services. I rolled him then dropped to his lap readying him for his task at re-breaking in my flesh for the horrors of being the bottom of male same gendered sex.

When he was fully ready, he pulled my face back to his kissing and biting with vigor as he rolled me to my back to take me in the missionary's position as truthful lovers do. I closed my eyes and braced for his entry. Leo as usual was gentle, patient, and careful in his penetration. I gasped and recalled why I hated this shit so much but was grateful to be enduring it with the right lover, for a change, for this kind of sex.

He waited till I was as comfortable as I was ever going to be, then began his strong but careful intercourse. He leaned down and engaged me in deep kissing as he made love to me with eagerness. I felt him reach down to my own manhood to enjoy all my flesh had to offer him. Leo panted with thrill into my mouth as he found my erection more than a little happy to be handled by his skilled stroking.

We found our apex's pretty damned close to the same time. He yelled out in ecstasy as I moaned in my own grateful release. For that moment, I couldn't imagine ever hating this man's lustful interest in me. I had proven to him, and myself, once and for all that I was at the very least a bisexual, if the partner was the right man.

The one thing I am is neither purely straight nor purely gay. It is the truth that other than Leo; I have never been completely thrilled to be with any other man, but I believe if I met another like him, I would not be opposed to enjoying his interests in me. That is if just once I could be the fucking top, sheesh.

Anyway, Leo rolled off me and held me tightly in his embrace sweating and gasping for air while I chuckled and said, "You are either out of shape or getting old Leo. That was great. I think I better stay the night though."

Leo cut his eyes at me appearing mildly humored and mildly irritated over that statement as he replied, "I've told you I am an old man, Christian. I've never lied about such an obvious truth. That said I am not so fucking old that you need to stay the night. I assume you are saying that you wish to make sure that I don't stroke or have a heart attack over this mild exertion."

I laughed loudly as I hugged him rubbing my face into his neck with affection. "Ah, well then, I suppose I can leave you now that you found your thrill. I merely thought that I would need to have seconds or even a third helping of your affection tonight. I really need to be vigorous as possible if I wish to properly prepare for Peter's bullshit tomorrow. But since you are tired, I understand. I thank you for at least getting me through the early stage of this painful process." I started to rise and get ready to go back to my apartment.

Leo dramatically moaned out loud sounding like a wounded calf, "Oh, wait Christian! Christian, are you here, honey? I am feeling lightheaded. Maybe you better stay the night after all. My heart is feeling most irregular. Perhaps, I am having a stroke or heart attack." He looked at me doing his best to appear pathetic as he grabbed at his chest.

I nodded. "Oh my, yes you do look ill my love. I think I'd better stay then. It is just as I thought. You need me here to take care of you, Leo." I kissed his forehead with a teasing smile on my face.

He replied laughingly, "You are one sexy bastard, Christian Axel. I never been so fucking turned on in my life. Look at all that beautiful hair on your chest, and that gorgeous beard you wear! Oh God, I swear I almost blew a gasket when I got your clothes off and saw those muscles you have grown. Then to be able to kiss you during our love making without having to struggle to reach you for a change. My, my, you have grown into a humongous hunk of man!"

I laughed then coyly looked away as I responded, "That is good to hear Leo. If my plan is to work. I am going to need to catch the eye of an eligible bachelor soon. I can be with you in secret, but I need a trophy boyfriend for the public. Do you have any single friends?" I grinned with wickedness.

Leo frowned as he poured out, "Oh, I am jealous already, Shit! Tell you what. I'm going to resign my position as Elder in the morning and move down to the fourth floor."

I nodded then looked at him with seriousness as I said, "You are more than welcome to live with me, my love. However, I only want a cover but not the real thing, Leo. I'm not interested in sleeping with another man. So, you are safe and have no reason to be the jealous. No other but you shall ever truly possess my heart until that lucky day I am free to choose a wife. That I swear to you, Leo." I kissed him deeply.

When I pulled out of our loving tongue embracing, he smiled and replied, "When you are finished dealing with Peter and Jonas tomorrow, come back to see me. I will contact Jakob and the homosexual sect of the House. There are many of us scattered on every floor. I may not be able to be your public lover, nor can Jakob, but we can out you to the other boys. With our approval they will take you under their wings. Then with their help your cover will not only appear convincing but no doubt those lucky fellows will half beat each other to death just to gain the honor of sporting you on their arm. I must admit this plan of yours may actually work, Christian."

I smiled. "It will Leo. Now, I have one more big problem. Well, two actually."

He frowned. "Huh? What else is there to cause you to fret?"

I looked down. "I need money Leo. I cannot afford to eat without a job."

Leo groaned. "Oh shit, I forgot about that. Okay, no problem. I can give you that."

I shook my head. "No, Leo. I cannot take anything more from you. You have been generous too me already. I will allow you to tell me what I can do for an honest wage and help me with the other issue."

He nodded with a look of interest. "Okay fair enough. So, what is the other issue?"

I laughed as I jumped up and straddled him with speed while saying in a breathy voice, "I have been alone a long time. Can you help me out?" I winked with a diabolical grin.

Leo wailed out loudly, "Oh, my God, I am going to have a stroke for sure. Help! Someone help me! I am being ravaged by a gorgeous young man. Please bring the heart paddles, oh, and a camera. I need evidence of my amazing good luck because no one will believe this otherwise." I shut up his silliness with another series of lustful kisses and much heavy petting.

That night Leo did me the favor of soundly rebreaking me in for penetration sex. When the sun rose the next morning, he was so worn out by our wanton greed, and many trysts, he couldn't even get out of bed. I laughed and teased him about his age until he threw a shoe at me to shut me the hell up. I took a shower then redressed as he nursed a cup of coffee while still under his sheets with fatigue.

When I came out, I was clean shaven everywhere. I knew that Peter would raise hell at my appearance as the man (not boy) I had become. Leo frowned the moment he saw my suddenly more youthful appearance.

He pouted as he groaned out, "But I liked the beard! Please tell me you left the rest of your incredible fur untouched. I don't understand those idiots demanding you remove all your body hair. If they are interested in fucking a man, then let him be the man, not smooth like a woman.".

I smiled bitterly. "Leo, you said you would give me money if I needed it. I want to purchase something of some worth. How much does it cost to leash with a silver trainee on average?"

Leo frowned at that. "Uhm, not too much, why?"

I nodded. "And the lamb that Rolf bought me, how much would it cost to buy say six to eight of them?"

Leo sat up with a look of concern. "Christian, what is this about? The silver trainee leash is kind of hard to get now with the rule against sleeping with them. It will likely cost you a favor rather than cash. As for the lamb toys, you would need about fifty dollars for that many if you could get them."

I smiled. "Alright then, can I borrow fifty dollars? If so, would you take the money to Rolf and have him get me as many Felicities as possible with it. Hopefully he can get at least six."

He nodded. "Sure honey. Where are you going? I was going to take you to breakfast, my bunny. I know you must be hungry. You need to eat something." He started to get out of bed as he watched me getting ready to leave.

I walked over and took his hands into mine. "Stay there, Leo. I am headed down to the first floor to see Mistress Karsten before I am expected at Jonas's place. I will allow you to take me to dinner, Leo. Besides, I already had breakfast." I smiled with wickedness then kissed him goodbye.

Leo yelled out as I left the room, "That is only twenty-five calories you've had for breakfast. Do not miss our date for dinner or I will kick your ass, my bunny."

I chuckled over the fact that Leo remembered the number of calories I'd told him jism contains while I stopped briefly to pet Der Makellos. Then without further hesitation I hauled ass down the stairs. I was headed to the first floor with important business on my mind.

Upon my arrival at ground level, I rapidly approached the door that I recalled belonged to a young Mistress named Karsten. With gentleness I knocked and the submissive called Marc answered almost immediately. His eyes went wide the second he recognized me. Marc didn't move a muscle, appearing too terrified to do anything other than stare.

I smiled with pleasantness as I asked, "Is your Mistress here Marc? If so, please ask her if I may gain an audience with her for a moment. I wish to discuss an arrangement she may find useful."

He nodded and replied, "Oh, uhm, I apologize for my rudeness, Master. I will go get her for you." I watched the trembling boy go to fetch his FemDom.

Within a few minutes a heavy-set, mildly unattractive woman in her late twenties with stringy brown hair came to the door.

She had a confused expression on her face as she said, "Why Mad Maxx, to what do I owe this most appreciated visit? My collar Marc told me, you're desiring to conduct business of some kind with me."

I nodded. "Uhm, yeah, he's reported my reason for calling on you correctly. I wanted to know what price you're asking for a leash with Marc. I am only requesting one afternoon with the boy, but I demand that no questions be asked about my interest in him."

I heard Marc gasping from just beyond my sight as the FemDom stepped out into the hallway and closed the door behind her. "Oh, well this is more of a shock then I first thought Maxx. You desire a leash with my most talented Marc, do you? Well, such an arrangement could be made. I had heard the rumor you prefer the boys." She giggled but then cast her eyes down appearing embarrassed.

I grinned widely as I replied without flinching over her most rude and incorrect belief, "Ah, well you know some rumors are more truthful than people think. That said, I wish to make this arrangement quickly. I have been, uhm, without company for a while. Tell me your price and if possible, I would like to leash with him no later than tomorrow afternoon." I cleared my throat feeling sick that I was having to lie about my intentions with the boy Marc, but that is how the game in the House is played.

She nodded and responded, "Well, normally I would ask for money, but I happen to know that despite your level as the High Born Priceless, you are broke as a church mouse."

I growled, "I've come here in good faith with the offer of an honest deal, Mistress. Yet, you insist on insulting me. I find that most inappropriate. Perhaps I was mistaken to desire a leash with any silver collar trained by you. Surely, he must be poor in providing service, and no doubt insolent. He must be because his Mistress doesn't know her place either." I began to storm off, feigning anger.

Karsten gasped and grabbed my upper arm appearing desperate as she yelped out, "Oh my, no, no! Please, Master Maxx I must apologize. What the hell was I thinking to dare to question one of your obvious honor and worth! Of course, I am willing to grant you a leash, but perhaps you'd be willing to do a favor for me rather than pay in cash for it."

I turned back around. "Well? You waste my time Mistress. Name your favor request or I'll move on to find a silver worth keeping me entertained elsewhere."

Karsten came close, then whispered into my ear, "Please, this information is to be kept confidential. Well, you see I have this gambling habit, Maxx. I've lost a lot of money recently to one of the Dominants that runs the betting tables here on the first floor. I don't have the cash to pay my debt, and he is threatening to harm me. You can have Marc, no questions asked, anytime you wish, for as long as you wish. That is, if you could, uhm, get this man to relent his demands for payback."

I sighed, rolled my eyes, and replied, "Anytime I want for as long as I wish you say. Wait a minute. Just how much do you owe this Dominant, Karsten?"

She sniffed as she teared up then leaned closer and breathed out anxiously, "Over twenty thousand dollars."

I nearly choked as I replied, "Huh, what the hell? I don't have that kind of money! For that matter, twenty thousand I could buy twenty trainees' leashes. You are insane, Mistress. I bid you a good day!"

I started to leave again but she released my upper arm quickly, then to my shock fell to her knees at my feet. All around us silver and black collar people hurried past, trying to look the other way. They were pretending to mind their own business, but it goes without saying Karstin was making a spectacle of herself.

She sounded wretched as she sobbed out, "Please Maxx. Don't leave. I'm so frightened and unsure what to do. Hell, I will give you Marc's collar if you can help me out of this terrible mess, I'm in!"

I shook my head and glanced around us nervously as I angrily replied, "I cannot own a collar until I am twenty-two and you know that. I already told you that I don't have that kind of money either. I told you rumors are truer than many wish to admit to. Well, the one about me being a poor man is one is more fact than gossip. So, why the hell are you dropping this bullshit on my head? I tell you I cannot help you."

Karsten nodded wildly as she blubbered out, "Oh, but you can, Mad Maxx. You are maybe the only one in the House capable of making this bastard release me from the debt. The Dominant I owe is openly gay. If you were to go to him and offer him a tryst with the Priceless of legend in my name he would relent. I know he would because I've heard him speak of his desires to taste your metal for years. Look, I can sweeten this deal. If you do this favor for me, then you can leash Marc anytime you like. Also, I'll hold his collar for you until you are twenty-two and the boy can become your property officially. I will sign a contract in blood with you if you're worried, I'm not trustworthy to keep my promises."

I nearly fainted as I replied through numbing lips, "Oh hell no! Are you really asking me to sleep with your loan shark to pay off a debt you owe to him? Christ you are indeed out of your mind. Wait, did you say if I do this horrible thing, you'll sign Marc over to me?"

I'd suddenly had a change of heart regarding her offer. An idea to save the poor little boy's life from the terrors of being a pleasure submissive had come to me. But I knew if I went through with my plan, it could cost me much more than just my dignity.

She nodded. "Yes, you heard me correctly, I will give Marc to you. We can go and file a valid contract valid the second you get Matz off me."

I groaned loudly as I yelled out in disgust, "Oh hell no, not Matz! You are kidding me, right? That creep has already tried to rape me once! I think you'd better choose another favor, Karsten."

She wailed loudly as the tears rolled down her cheeks, "No! Please Mad Maxx! Marc is worth the trouble. He is pure and pliant! You could train him to please you with ease."

I took a deep breath recalling that young man, Matz. I recalled he'd been the ringleader in the group of first floor ruffians that attempted to pull me into the closet from hell, with the intent to gang rape me. That attack had directly led to the hideous contract I'd made with Friedrick and Bryon to gain their protection.

I glanced at the sobbing FemDom, while thinking of the innocent little boy only inches away. I knew Marc was slated for death if no one helped him survive the curse of silver.

It felt like I was floating as I nodded while I said, "Okay Karsten, you have a deal. I'll go to speak with Matz right now. After I've successfully cleared your debt, then I'll come back for the contract you've promised. But you will not give his silver to me. Instead, you will paint him black."

She gasped as she replied, "I cannot paint him black until he is collared Maxx. You know the law."

I nodded. "That is true Karsten, but that contract you write will assure the boy is painted black the second he is judged submissive at age fifteen. You will sign it in blood and put in writing he is never to be put to the yard, chains, or beaten without my approval. I will visit often to check that my boy is handled with care, affection, and well-treated. You will agree to my demands, otherwise, I will leave, I mean it. You've placed a high price on a trainee that's not proven himself, yet." I blew out my breath in anger as I said that.

Karsten nodded wildly as she replied eagerly, "Fine, yes! Yes! I am happy to do this for you honorable Master Maxx. If you get that man off me then I swear to you Marc will be treated in the manner you command for the rest of his life."

I glared at her with disgust as I said, "I think you need to end your gambling habit. You are not any good at it, Mistress. I see you soon. You best beware. Marc better be without signs of harassment, or I'll take it out on you with my cane. I will not show you mercy twice in this lifetime. I know you have heard other rumors about me. Those are true too, honey. Ask Fritz, or perhaps Olaf and Vilber? Good day to you." I stormed off headed to Matz apartment unsure just what the hell I had gotten myself into.

As I approached his apartment, I was taking deep breaths reminding myself that Marc's life was worth whatever I had to pay to save it. I stood at his door bracing myself as I began to knock.

The pissant answered after rudely yelling through it, "I'm coming dammit! Hold your horses, asshole!"

When he opened the door, he stood there staring at me appearing dumbfounded. His mouth was hanging open so wide I was sure he would trip over it if he'd attempted to take a step.

I glared at him with as much menace as possible in my expression as I growled out, "Well, Matz? Are you inviting me in, or do I stand out here to air out our business for everyone to hear?"

He barely whispered out, "That depends, Mad Maxx. Are you here to kill me?"

I chuckled and replied, "Oh, that is a topic for another day, Matz. Sadly, I've not got the time today. Maybe tomorrow I can fit you into my busy schedule. Are you as much an idiot as you are a pervert? I wouldn't knock on your fucking door if I'd come to murder you. If that was my desire, I have other ways to do it that would not leave me as a suspect. That aside, I have come on behalf of Karsten. I wish to discuss a way to pay off her heavy debt to you."

His face fell as he said with bitterness in his tone, "You've come on Karsten's behalf, you say. That Mistress owes me a fortune Maxx and I don't believe that has anything to do with you. I happen to know you have no money. So, if you think you can talk me out of breaking that bitch's legs over her failure to pay me, you are mistaken."

I smiled with evil as I replied, "Oh, I was planning to use my mouth to get her out of that debt with you Matz, but

142

in a way I think you will be thrilled to hear. You really should ask me in. I would like to discuss a way to end this debt for Karsten if you would entertain such a discussion? I am quite skilled in conversation services. I can promise I will make you feel better than you ever knew you could. My Masters used to say that my tongue was more silver than my Priceless collar. You want to find out if that rumor is true, yes, or no?"

Matz smiled with sudden eagerness as he finally caught on to my inuendo and said, "Uhm, yes, yes! Where are my manners. Come on in Maxx." He backed up while wiping the sweat from his brow.

I checked the clock. It was seven-thirty. I had only had an hour and a half to save Marc's life before I had to meet Jonas. I hoped that I could talk Matz into dropping that debt by bargaining with the only thing of value I had to trade, my dignity.

If Matz would accept my deal, then for the first time in my life I could truly call myself a whore. But what is a human life worth? The answer is: it is Priceless.

Chapter 4: Hustling to Earn an Honest Income

I followed Matz inside his apartment. I noticed immediately the smell of garbage, dirty clothing and witnessed, to say the least, that his place was poorly furnished. The man was using a cardboard box for a coffee table. Filth was everywhere from wall to wall.

I covered my nose and felt I may retch. "Christ Matz. Do you ever clean this nightmare you call home? Fuck me! I am going to barf." I swallowed hard trying not to vomit.

He sat down on the only furniture in the room, a battered armchair as he said with a bitter smile, "I am not handy with the mop Maxx. I am also poor. I cannot afford the House's black collar cleaning service. Hell, I can barely afford this fucking apartment as it is. Sometimes I must go without dinner just to make the rent."

I stood there in shock as I replied, "Huh? What the hell man? I thought all the Dominants in this place were rich as thieves, Matz. What happened to you? Did you piss away your fortune on the tables like that stupid Karsten is trying to?" I pulled my blouse over my nose to attempt to block out the stale stench while wondering if I should run away before this situation got any worse.

He chuckled. "Well, you were brought here as a kidnapped child so you would not know much about the way this House works. It is most rude to ask such questions of another Dominant, but you have not learned Dominant manners yet. So, I'll tell you and expect your confidence as

144

a gentleman. Valitin, Roland, Magnas, and I are what they call the legacy members. That means our families all were wealthy and important residents of Das Kaiser House back a long time ago. Well, then the wars came. Our family's fortunes were confiscated, wiped out or lost in those dark days. We still have our powerful names but not a fucking penny to back them. Since our mothers and fathers could not pay the freight, they were forced to leave the House for good. The other boys and I grew up in the outside world, hearing the fabulous stories of our parents' time here when they were rich. It was all I ever wanted, to reclaim my rightful spot as the High-Born Dominant of this House. The other boys shared this dream too. We all saved our money till we turned sixteen. Between us we had enough to rent two apartments on the first floor. Thanks to our old valuable names, we were granted entry with no questions asked, but without work or a way to earn money, all of us faced eviction almost within the first months. That is when I figured out that gambling here is all corrupted and the Dominants know this. Valitin and I set up "honest" games and Roland and Magnas took the position of enforcers. They do what they must to collect the cash owed to us when losers don't pay up. Over the last four years, our arrangement has managed to allow us to each have our own place, but not much else. Still, it is better than nothing. Except when assholes like Karsten try to shaft their debts. I need the money she owes me badly. I planned to use it to hire a black collar maid. So, I am listening to what Karsten thinks you can say to talk me out of collecting from her. But beware, unless her payment plan is solid, I am not interested. I sense that she sent you here to calm me down.

I bet she wants me to offer her more time to collect the cash with a returned service from the Priceless of sweet talking or maybe a little bit more?" His eyes traveled down my body as an interested smile broke out on his face.

I glared at him with irritation while I began to realize Karsten was a fool. This fellow needed cash and I was not sleeping with him to buy her a few months of time to pay. I had to talk him into releasing her from the debt if I wanted to save Marc.

A shook off the sense of shame that had tried to take root within me as I flatly replied, "I thank you for your honesty and giving me information that would prove me an ill-mannered ass if I had not been schooled. However, I believe I've made a grave error by coming here, Matz. I desire something Karsten currently owns and for a moment lost my good sense. I've been suckered into trying to aid a loser, I fear. Forgive me for my brash and misdirected interruption of your schedule. I will not waste any more of your time."

I turned to leave but Matz yelled out, "Wait, Maxx, please. You are not interrupting anything. I was without a thing to do this morning. I beg of you to not to give up so fast. If you still desire that item Karsten has, I am willing to listen to the details of the offered bargain. How can you be so sure I won't be interested in what you've come to trade?"

His response caused me to stop abruptly and yell out angrily, "I can clearly see this hell hole you call a home,

Matz. What I've come to offer to pay off her debt with cannot pay for a black collar maid. I thought you were like the rest of these rich board asshole around this House that had everything he needed but a reason to thrill. Obviously, I was mistaken. Again, I apologize for bothering you. Have a good day." I strode to the door while trying not to gag from the smell.

Matz jumped up from his chair and shouted sounding upset as he shouted back, "I will give you three thousand a night, Maxx. That would pay off Karsten's debt in seven days. I even give you the hundred dollars left over in cash right this minute if you're willing to agree to my terms."

I stopped dead in my tracks again and turned around in a full-on stun as I barely choked out, "What? I don't understand what you are saying, Matz. You'll give me three thousand a night for what exactly?"

He looked down at his shoes putting his hands in his pocket with a stupid grin as he replied, "Ah, I find it rude to discuss the specific details of my desires, other than to say whatever I want, and as much as I want."

I shook my head and responded, "I am still not getting you, Matz. I've come to work out a trade to pay off Karsten's debt. Then she gives me what I desire from her. But I thought you said you don't have any money. Yet am I to understand you are now offering three thousand dollars a night to, uhm, sleep with me?"

Matz howled in mirth as he replied, "Oh, my God! You really are ignorant of how the House works, aren't you? I don't want to sleep with you, Maxx. I want to fuck you and I am willing to erase Karsten's debt by receiving your Priceless sexual services for seven nights. That will give her a credit of three thousand for each payment you make in her name. In return, I'll get to do whatever I like to you, as often as I like for the duration of our agreement. When the contract between us is completed, I will owe you a debt of one hundred dollars. I will pay you and that money is yours to do with as you please."

I felt my breath become shallow as I said, "You think my skills at the special services are worth three thousand a night? Holy hell man that is insane!"

Matz looked me up and down while nodding as he replied, "Hell yes, you're worth that, and maybe even more. If I were you and offered to trade such a coveted service, I would certainly charge more. That said, three thousand per night is all I can justify paying you given my compromised situation. I am out the money that bitch owes me if you take my deal. To be honest, I really need the cash more than I need the sex, but I would be a stupid fool to turn down this offer. You have no idea how long I have desired to have you for myself. I wouldn't entertain this trade with anyone else on Earth, even if they promised me a lifetime of great sex. But you, my man, are the Priceless! You are gorgeous, rumored to be a sexual artist of the highest quality, and a fucking legend. I am willing to forfeit the maid for this once in a lifetime chance to make such a beautiful memory."

I rolled my eyes as I responded in an irritated tone, "You are indeed a fool, Matz. Your apartment is a disaster area. I would break the idiot's legs for the cash if I were you. However, that said, seven nights of enforced special services is a lot to ask of me. That is far more than I was willing to trade."

Matz sat back down laughing as he said, "Really Maxx? What did you think I would say when you came to see me? Maybe you thought you would threaten me to back off? Or perhaps blow me one time and I'd suddenly forget the smell of this hell hole?"

I sighed and replied, "I told you I don't know what the fuck I was thinking. I merely did what I always do, impulsively rush into shit. You tried to rape me I seem to recall. Perhaps you are right, and I came to bully you over it. Well, whatever I was planning, I see you have your mind made up. I will be on my way. I am not letting you have your way with me for seven nights. That is for damned sure."

Matz took one hundred dollars from his pocket and laid it on the cardboard box coffee table as he replied in a serious tone, "Are you sure Maxx? I happen to know you have no money or job either. When was the last time you had a meal? How do you plan to survive without any cash in this House? I have heard a rumor that you cannot even leave the yard without an escort. A hundred dollars would feed you for a week and those seven days will get you the thing Karsten owns that you covet. You say you came here impulsively. I say to you, don't repeat that error by leaving

149

the same way. Think about it a minute. I am willing to provide a written contract, give you a hundred bucks up front, plus, you can go collect the thing you want from Karsten this very morning. I will even swear to space out the seven nights. What the hell Maxx? How many times did you perform your skills by force for free when you were a submissive? I've offered to pay you good money for such a glorious performance. What the hell else are you going to do for food? Beg? Good luck with that brother." He leaned back in his chair smiling at me.

I frowned as I replied, "I will get a job. In fact, I am going to see the Black Collar Mistress this morning. I can do honest labor. I don't need to be your whore to earn my money, Matz."

Matz's nodded with a look of sarcasm overcoming his expression as he said, "Okay, fine you do that Maxx. Reality is not going to be kind to you, I see that plain as day. I will say that this offer is good only for another few minutes. Then I am done with this conversation. You walk out that door we will not bargain again. Take the money Maxx and get the thing you wanted with the rest. Your call, brother."

I closed my eyes thinking of Marc laying there on the steps, trembling and scared. I knew I was to meet with the foul Vampire and his snake Kilian in only an hour. The meeting with Peter was later in the day, but I knew all three of them had disgusting designs for my flesh. I opened them up to look at Matz and that money, realizing that he was asking nothing more and nothing less, but offering something I believed I needed in return, the life of that little boy.

It felt like I was moving across the floor by levitation as I approached the hundred dollars. I reached out and took it shooting the smiling Matz a look of menace.

He nodded, still grinning as he said calmly, "Intelligent and beautiful. What a great combination. Okay, you wait here while I find some paper. Karsten will require I provide you with prove she is off the hook. I will fill it out now and sign it. That money is yours Maxx. I look forward to doing business with you more than you can know." He jumped up and rushed to another room.

I looked at the money feeling sick to my stomach, and it wasn't from that smell this time as I said aloud, "Felicity, what the hell are we doing? Is this the right thing to do? Maybe we should just kill this man and be done with it?"

Felicity shrugged in my pocket which made me sigh. Things were so fucking complicated now that I was Dominant. I wanted to help the silvers find a better life, but I couldn't do anything without money.

I calmed my anxiety over this horrible situation by reminding myself it was only this once I would have to endure such humiliation. I would forget about the indignity of it the second I saw the smile on Marc face when he learned he was safe. I hoped I would anyway. That little boy was worth it I told myself.

Matz was right, not like I hadn't dealt with unwanted touching for years. What the hell. I could save Marc in a week when it took me three years to do it for myself. I smiled as I dropped that money in with Felicity. I was proud that at least I could pay Leo back the fifty I had borrowed only thirty minutes earlier. It was good to erase debt even if it was by such shady means.

Matz came back quickly. He and I bickered about the details of our arrangement, until at last he had that contract filled out in a way we both could accept. He pricked his finger, then my own, and we signed it in our blood.

I took it up with a frown folding it to put with Felicity and the money. "When do you desire to begin this payoff arrangement? I will need at least a warning of twenty-four hours. Such things require preparation and do me a favor and at least clean your bathroom if you will desire bath service." I groaned out.

Matz grinned with thrill. "Ah, so professional. I am a lucky bastard. All my trysts before were clumsy, dirty and less than the romantic encounters I had hoped for. I love it that you know that such things require hygiene rituals and proper preparations. I am super excited to experience the charms of one professionally trained in all the sexual arts."

I rolled my eyes with a scoff. "Be that as it may, you didn't answer my question, Matz. I need to know, and you are wasting time I don't have with this stalling and unnecessary attempt to make a whore into a prince. I need to be on my way."

He snorted with a chuckle. "You are no common whore, Maxx. Not with your experience. I would call you a sexual artist. That sounds better and is more the truth. I wonder will tomorrow night be too soon to start?"

I shook my head. "No, it would not. I prefer to get this over with as soon as possible myself. I will bring nose plugs to deal with the smell. I see you tomorrow night at what time?"

Matz looked around his apartment frowning. "Uhm, let's do nine to nine, okay?"

I shrugged. "Fair enough. Have a good day." I rushed to that door and into the hall gasping for fresh air, okay, fresher than that nasty ass apartment anyway, yuck.

Karsten came to the door after my first knock. Her face wore a look of fear as she invited me inside. I took a deep breath, in case her place smelled too, and followed her. Marc was kneeling by the front window trembling. Her place was neat as a pin, and well organized. Thankfully, it smelled nice too.

She sat down while rubbing her big arms. "Well? What did Matz say, Maxx? Am I to run for my life?" I could see she was about to break down into tears again.

I stood there never taking my eyes off the frightened Marc. "No, Karsten. Matz has released you from your debt. I have accepted it in your stead. The details of our arrangement are none of your business, but I have the proof here that you are off the hook. Now I request that you contract what you promised me for this favor. I must be somewhere very soon, so please let's make this quick." I handed her the letter Matz wrote that stated she was forgiven, and I had assumed her place as the indebted.

Karsten gasped and a huge smile broke out across her face as she read it. "Oh, you are an angel, Maxx. I cannot thank you enough."

I turned to glare at her with irritation. "Uhm, I didn't do this shit for your thanks Karsten. Get that fucking contract ready as I've requested. I want what I am owed. I told you I am in a hurry."

She shot a look of pity at Marc then nodded as she stood up to rush from the room. "Oh, my where are my manners. Of course, you wish to have your plaything soon as possible. I'll go get your contract ready right now, you wait here. Marc, get your Master a cup of coffee or attend to anything else he wants." She took out of the room.

I winced when she said that but never took my eyes off the boy. He stood up shaking like a leaf, keeping his eyes down caste as he approached me. I watched as he knelt at my feet. He was so fucking small. I wondered, had I looked like this once myself?

He stuttered out with tears welling, "Do you want me to get you a cup of coffee, Master?"

I shook my head. "Not right now, Marc. Tell me why are you crying? I do not bite. If we are to get along you will need to be relaxed when with me."

Marc gasped. "I uhm, cannot help it, Master. You will have to punish me because I am frightened. I don't know anything about sex, especially with a man."

I nearly choked as I realized what he must have been thinking of me. "Huh? What? You don't know about sex, holy hell I hope not. I am a fucking idiot. Oh, you poor boy! You thought I bought your collar for, oh my God! Well, I must apologize to you little one. Taking advantage of your innocence is not my intentions with you not now, not ever."

He looked stunned. "I don't understand, Master. My Mistress told me I had to learn to have sex with you. She said that is why you came to leash with me and wanted to own my collar too."

I chuckled with bitter humor. "Well, Marc, I admit I led her to believe that, but I can assure you that is not true. I bought your silver to paint you black. I want only to see you grow up, smile, and stand up like a man. You remind me of someone I knew once long ago that didn't get the chance to do any of that."

Marc gasped as a look of disbelief came over his face. "Am I dreaming, Master? You say you intend to see that I am freed from the silver collar? How can I ever repay you for your kindness?" His tears fell fast but this time a smile was breaking under them.

I smiled as I pulled him to his feet. "You can live happy and free of unwanted molestations for all your days, Marc. All I want is for you to be a kid, without being forced to be anyone's whore. I ask in return that you grow up to be an old man without regrets. I beg you will do this for me but not because you call me your Master. Please do it for the one I couldn't save, okay?"

Marc smiled with glee as he exclaimed, "You are the legend everyone says you are Master. I can't believe it! I am owned by Mad Maxx, the Priceless King of the Collars himself! Oh, Gregor and Brutus are going to be so jealous of my good fortune!" He giggled like the kid he was.

I laughed out loud and replied, "Ah well, I think you are celebrating too soon, Marc. No doubt, when your buddies find out about this situation, they will believe what you did before I corrected you. In fact, everyone is going to assume your warming my bed as my personal plaything."

Marc shrugged. "Let them, Master. I don't care. I know you are different than the other Dominants and that is all that matters to me. I believe you'll keep your word and not force me to have sex with you. So, they can call me a catamite, a horse's ass or whatever they like. When I am painted, black everyone will have to eat their words." He clapped his hands with thrill as he said that.

I marveled over this amazing boy. He wasn't the least bit worried that the other silver collars would say I was using him in the way I had been at his age. Marc also trusted me completely even before getting a shred of proof that I was an honest person. He didn't seem worried I could be merely manipulating him. I swear to the God, he was everything I'd ever wanted in a little brother. I was immediately overcome with deep affection for him and next to Felicity, he'd become the most important person in the world to me.

It was the truth that a more beautiful soul couldn't be found anywhere else on the Earth. Marc was pure, innocent, trusting, loving, loyal and everything else I was not. I swore to myself privately I would do anything necessary to protect him from being ruined by the evils of the House. He became my first adopted silver collar child that morning, and there would be many others.

Marc stood next to me appearing thunderstruck while I signed Karsten's contract in blood. I handed the paper to him so that he could see for himself that he'd been formally released from the oppressive lifestyle of a silver collared pleasure submissive.

I finally retrieved the contract from Marc and dropped it into my hidden pocket. I intended to deposit Karsten's agreement and the shameful one I'd collected from Matz earlier into a secure spot in my apartment the second I finished dealing with my next pressing matter.

Karsten sat down on her loveseat grinning at Marc as she said to me, "So, you understand Marc is welcome to stay with me until you can make new arrangements for his care, Maxx. There is no hurry, of course. Paying for his upkeep a little longer is the least I can do in return for the help you've granted me in this most delicate matter."

I replied with a gasp, "What are you talking about, Karsten? I thought you understood that I cannot own a silver nor keep this boy in my apartment until I've finished my Dominance training. You know the law just as well as I do. Where the hell am I supposed to put him in the meantime?"

The world began to spin as it sank into my head that since Karsten no longer owned Marc, she was not responsible for his care. To my terror it became obvious she wasn't going to continue it out of the goodness of her heart either.

Karsten's expression of joy melted to one of concern as she responded, "Oh dear. I thought you had a friend or lover that you would leave him with when you are not enjoying his favors. Oh, my goodness this is going to be a problem, Maxx."

I nodded and said, "Hell, yes it will be. Couldn't you keep him here with you for the next three years, Karsten? Afterall, he is used to serving you, so why no allow him to continue as he is?"

She interrupted me with a snort, "That's impossible. You've contracted with me to see his collar painted black. The law makes it clear he must now live as all the black collars do. The pleasure submissive lifestyle is much different than that of the House submissive. Once trained as a silver collar they don't survive well if switched to House duties. Luckily, you've bought Marc at the right age to save him from that terrible situation. He's not even a year into pleasure submissive training. Now, I am not opposed to allowing the boy to stay with me, but he requires clothing and must be fed. Plus, despite being on the first floor, this apartment isn't cheap Maxx. If you can find a way to pay for his freight. Then he can stay with me while he completes his training in the black collar program. I admit I adore this boy and I think what you are doing for him is wonderful, but I am not rich, Maxx. I don't have the extra cash to see to the needs of another mouth that is not my own. Especially when Marc can't repay my sacrifices for him in any way but his smiles and non-sexual company." She glared at me while crossing her arms to demonstrate she was not going to budge on this subject no matter how much I begged her.

I glanced at the observably panicking Marc as I replied, "Uhm, okay, so you want me to pay for Marc's upkeep. That's fair and not a problem. I am already seeking employment and intend to meet with a connection that can assure I'm a man of means this morning. How much are you asking to permit him to stay with you until I can make other arrangement?"

She rubbed her nose then looked over at Marc while she responded, "Well, it costs about a thousand dollars a month to cover his expenses properly. If you give me that amount at the end of each month, then I'm happy to let him stay here with me as long as you wish."

Marc's face lit up with fear as he cried out to me, "A thousand dollars every month, Master. Oh, but that is too much. I thank you for the mercy, but I don't think I am worth that."

I groaned as I patted his back and replied calmly, "Ah Marc, you are wrong there. You are worth more than I can earn in a lifetime. That said, okay Karsten. I agree to your price for this arrangement. I swear to meet the payments on time, but for now, I must go to attend to other pressing business. I will return tomorrow morning and ask that you have Marc ready to visit with me. I intend to spend a little time getting to know the collar I've granted the honor of my honest labors without unnecessary delay."

I smiled with bitterness at Marc. He gazed at me with unabashed awe and joy. He didn't appear to realize that while he understood my interest in him were pure, his ex-Mistress didn't have a clue. She shook her head with an expression of concern while watching the little boy fawning over what she assumed was an unfortunate arrangement for him.

Karsten turned her attention back to me and with an anxious sounding laugh she said, "You are something else, Maxx. As good looking as you are, you could sleep with any of the House Dominants for free or hell even charge them a minor fortune just to escort you on their arm. Yet, here you are making deals that cost you more than I paid for Marc's silver, just so you can lay claim to his innocence. What is wrong with you? Is it that you can only find sexual thrill with a young virgin?"

I felt fury rush to my cheeks as I bellowed out angrily, "If you ever insult me like that again or mistreat Marc over your perceptions that he is nothing more than my plaything, I'll kill you, Karsten. What I do or don't do with him is no longer your business, now is it? I've agreed to pay for Marc's care and will do so with honor. So, you will keep your opinions, questions, and information about our dealings to yourself. Do you hear me? I warn you Mistress. You'd better take excellent care of Marc, or I will demonstrate that I'm indeed a man that keeps his promises, all of them. I must go now, but Marc, my dearest boy, I cannot afford to pay extra bills. You stay healthy and be careful. Doctor's can be expensive, yes?" He nodded while covering his mouth trying to hide the smile, he wore over my berating his ex-Mistress as I had.

Karsten nodded as she replied sheepishly, "Don't worry, Maxx. I swear I'll take good care of him. Please accept my thanks for all your help and apologies for speaking out of turn. It won't happen again. Marc will be ready to attend you in the morning." She dropped her gaze to the floor as she finished saying that.

I nodded with a grimace and glanced at the clock on her wall. It was nearly nine. Without another word, I rushed to the door in a near mad run. I realized it was rude to leave without a formal goodbye, but there wasn't another moment I could spare. I was in danger of being late for the meeting with Jonas.

I'd been so busy trying to save Marc's life from subjugation and eventual death I had almost forgotten about my own pitiful lot. I hauled ass up the stairs wondering how many hours I would have to work to earn one thousand dollars. It was a daunting task, but I was sure with my strong back and serious resolve nothing would stand in my way of keeping Marc safe at Karsten's place.

The truth is, Meine Liebe, I was biting off more than I could chew. I was in a hurry to make the lives better for those poor children in silver all around me. There were hundreds of them and only one Mad Maxx to care for them all. This idiot Master of yours didn't have the pot to piss in nor a window to throw it out of. I was myself still submissive to Peter and as I knocked on the Vampire's door that day. I was about to add another invisible collar to the one my father already was trying to fasten around my neck.

Kilian answered Jonas's apartment door with an evil grin on his ugly face. I noticed immediately he was wearing a crimson, velvet vampire coat and had grown his hair long. He had also dyed it black just like Jonas does. He'd grown his fingernails to resemble long claws as well. If I were at a distance and couldn't easily see his long-pointed nose. I easily could have mistaken him for the Vampire Jonas, instead of the snake Kilian.

I glared at him for a moment before rolling my eyes as I said, "So I see he's bitten you, motherfucker. Well, that is unfortunate there are now two bats in the belfry of this House. I have said a million times this place needs an exterminator to rid its ancient halls of all the nasty vermin that have infested it."

Kilian's smile melted to a frown as he growled back in an irritated tone, "You would do well to watch that insolent mouth of yours, boy. I do believe you and I have become partners in the attendance of your good welfare. If you insist on being difficult, my brother would be most unhappy to hear of it." He waved his creepy hand, ushing me to enter the apartment.

I chuckled as I said, "Ah, yes, I had forgotten. You managed to gain a sixth-floor apartment by sucking the right dick. Plus, you were assigned some bullshit status as my rehabilitation counselor by being related to another one. Well, fuck me Kilian! Since you seem to enjoy dick so much, I'll happily let you suck mine." I stared at him menacingly while stepped inside, grabbing my crotch immaturely.

I was so busy engaging in aggressive behaviors with Kilian I didn't see Jonas sitting only a few feet away on his velvet couch. He'd been witness to the less than warm welcome I was giving his roommate/lover.

Jonas angrily shouted out with suddenness, "Enough of the insults, Maximillian! You will shut your mouth and kneel immediately. Wait a minute. Oh, holy hell! What the fuck? You're fucking huge." He stood up as his look of irritation melted into one of incredulity.

I glared at him refusing to break eye contact as I replied in a laughing tone, "Did you just tell me to kneel? Oh, I think not, little Vampire. As you can clearly see, I am now much bigger than you or your ugly butt buddy Kilian. Guess you should have come to visit me at the hospital. While you were off biting snakes, I grew into a giant. Ah, but I digress. So, go ahead and try to make me fall to my knees, if you think you still can, lover. I dare you."

The five foot ten Jonas sat back down appearing anxious as he turned his attention to Kilian and said "Your brother Reece never said a word to me about his size Kilian. I suppose he didn't tell you about it either. You'd think he or Doctor Wagner would have warned one of us about this serious complication. For God's sake how are we supposed to keep this insane boy under control now that he is a brute?"

Kilian shook his head while looking me over then smiled as he said, "Yeah, I agree. Thanks to his unexpected bulk his management will be more difficult than it has been in the past but look on the bright side. As a child he was an uncommon beauty. Now he has become a breathtaking vision of masculine perfection. Often puberty erases the favor nature gifts a pretty boy, but this young man has been overly blessed by maturity. Plus, unlike before, there is plenty of him for both of us to enjoy. Your fear that we would overwhelm him during our lovemaking was unwarranted. He looks sturdy enough to handle anything we wish of him, don't you think?" He crossed his arms while keeping his place by the door.

I turned my head to caste him a go to hell look as I responded in an irritated tone, "Why is he here, Jonas? This business you wish to discuss with me has nothing to do with snakes in the grass called Kilian. I am your husband, not his. Nor is he yours. I demand you send him away or I refuse to continue this meeting."

164

Jonas shook his head as he replied, "No. I will not send him away, Maximillian. This is Kilian's home now, plus he is your rehabilitation counselor. If something happens to me, he will take over for me as your guardian. So, obviously, anything we discuss is as important to him as it is to me."

I nodded and with a disgusted expression said flatly, "I've come to see you as you requested. Of course, I assumed you wanted to see me so you could pull shit on me like you always do, Jonas. Well, you can try to play games all you like, but if you think I'm going to put up with it, you can forget it. If House law would allow it, I would divorce you. I'm aware I can't escape our blood bonded marriage, but I can refuse to sleep with you. Just so we are clear; I'm saying you and I are through, and I am leaving for good! I'm warning you. Do not bother me again. I mean it." I turned and rushed for the door intending to leave.

Kilian jumped in front of the door with a threatening smile on his face as he said, "You go out that door Maximillian and I will I call my brother Doctor Reece Altergott to report you're noncompliant with your treatment plan. Go ahead and test me. I'll have you back in that rubber room before you make it to the fourth floor. You'll discover that you've no choice but to obey the commands of your husband and me, your counselor. If I were you, I would go take a seat and listen with the reverence owed the both of us."

I smiled back demonically as I growled in reply, "Oh, is that so? Well Kilian, the House law says that I'm free to refuse to even speak to that bat that calls himself my legal husband. As for you. Ah, if you know what's good for you, you'd ask for a reassignment. Better do that quickly, before I decide to put you to good use feeding the worms. From the moment you injured Felicity and hit me in the head with a baton, I have been meaning to demonstrate for you why they've leveled me Priceless."

Kilian glared at me like a reptile as he said, "You dare lay a finger on me and you will join me in the grave, Maxx. If you want to survive outside a white room without windows, then I suggest you sit the fuck down. Jonas is more than just your husband, you fool. He is also your guardian. If it were not for him, you would still be rotting away at the Heslach Institute. You were only freed for his pleasure. So, sure the House law says you can refuse to associate with him and deny him his husbandly rights. But if you don't keep him happy, he can return the favor by making sure you suffer a fate worse than death. Either way you decide to go is fine by me. I will enjoy your torment no matter the choice you make."

I stopped dead in my tracks. Leo had warned me that Jonas's guardianship gave him immense power over my future and my freedom (or lack of it to be exact). It was possible Kilian's threat that the Vampire could have me returned to the rubber room was true. I glared at Kilian for a moment while considering my options before angrily turning around and returning to the armchair across from Jonas. Kilian came over and took a seat next to Jonas's flashing smiles of triumph my way.

I plopped down onto it emitting a frustrated sounding sigh as I said in a bored sounding tone, "Well? Here I am, Jonas. So, what the fuck do you want?" I glared unwavering into his eyes.

Jonas continued to look me over and replied sounding still a bit awed over my appearance, "I uhm, can't get over how big you've become, Maximillian. I suppose I will need you to inform me of the size you wear in clothing these days and bring the outfits I put in your apartment back to me. I'll have the black collar shoppers replace them with ones that fit you."

I scoffed, "Sure thing, dad. Anything else? I find it hard to believe you've interrupted my life only to fuss over the hideous wardrobe you've insisted I wear."

He snorted in reply, "No, I merely was making that observation."

I nodded the said angrily, "Of course not. So, I'm listening. Hurry up and make your demands, so I'll tell you to go to hell. Then I will leave and get on with my life and you can go back to hunting for snakes while leaving me the fuck alone."

Jonas flashed a look of concern at Kilian then leaned back in his sofa as he turned his attention back to me and said, "For starters you are going to go back to your job as my donor, Maxx. I have been patiently waiting almost two years for a transfusion from you. I am growing older by the second and now that you're healthy again. There is no further excuse for you shirking your duties to me."

I chuckled heartily as I replied, "Well, that was easy. Nope! Not going to happen, dad. You're getting older because that is what happens to everyone, Jonas. Then again, maybe Kilian is stealing your youth, but what do I know?"

The Vampire growled angrily, "You will return to my bed and do your duty to me, Maximillian. That is not a request. It is an order! If you deny me, I'll see that you're sent back to Heslach without delay. Don't test me, boy. You know I mean it."

I sat forward aggressively and spit back, "You know I am getting a little tired of all this threatening about that rubber room. Go ahead Jonas. Send me back. Do you really think I give a shit?"

Kilian purred out suddenly, "Oh yes, we think you do, Maxx. You can bluff all you like. Being isolated, without anything to do will cause that madness of yours to return in no time. This time, you'll never return from that place of inner torment, my brother can make sure of it. Jonas, my love, forget about arguing with this idiot. Let me call Reece. I think Maximillian needs to be reminded of your power over him."

Jonas smiled with evil and took Kilian's hand into his as he said softly, "No, wait a moment, my dear. Let the boy calm down and think about his lack of options for a moment. He has always been hotheaded. He thinks he is convincing but we both know he is bluffing."

I glared at Jonas and said hotly, "You both are freaks and I swear that I am not bluffing. Go ahead Kilian call that asshole brother of yours. I'll go without a fight nor need for any cowards to hit me in the head while I am not looking. It's the truth that I would rather die than put up with nasty vampire habits or snakes touching me."

Jonas refused to break from our stare down as he replied calmly, "Oh my, aren't you brave these days. Not at all like the whimpering little boy that cried every time he had to satisfy his husband that you used to be. I suppose you want me to believe your will has grown as strong as your muscles have. That said, if I send you back to the rubber room you won't find a wife, Maximillian."

I laughed loudly as I said, "Do you really think remaining a bachelor bothers me, Jonas? I don't need a Goddamned wife. Sleeping with Gretta was horrible. I almost failed to lose my virginity to her it was so unpleasant. It was a real surprise but turns out I am gay after all. I only thought I was straight when I didn't have any choice in the matter. Well, thankfully, my honest sexual preference was determined before I made the horrible mistake you have made. You know, marrying the wrong person. Just think, I almost ruined my life by blood bonding to one of those disgusting creatures." My response made both Jonas and Kilian gasp loudly.

The Vampire appeared startled as he stammered in reply, "No, you are lying! I happen to know you are straight. I happen to know for a fact that you've never found pleasure during our intercourse, and I've seen you lusting for girls on many occasions."

I smiled with wickedness as I replied in a humored tone, "You are only half right, Jonas. I never found passion in your bed. As it is, I did find lust with Leo many times. Gretta however, yuck. That woman made me want to puke. I couldn't stand her. I've lost all interest in females ever since having to sleep with her."

The Vampire shook his head wildly as he practically wailed in return, "You are full of shit, Maximillian! How the fuck would you know anything about what turns you one anyway? You've never been with anyone willingly. You've always been a submissive and nothing but a sexual plaything for your Masters. Now that you are a Dominant with the freedom of choice, you will choose to be with women. I am sure of it."

I smiled even wider as I said cooly, "Ah, but I know what turns me on, Jonas. In fact, after all those months locked away, I could barely wait to attend to my pent-up sexual tensions. I started looking for someone to scratch my itch the second I arrived at the House. It only took moments for me to find a perfect boyfriend to do that for me. You may know him. His name is Matz, and I am head over heels in love with that sexy man. He's everything I ever wanted and believe me I've found immense joy in his arms, several times last night. He's such an awesome lover that I am thinking of moving him in with me. You know, so I can have him handy anytime I get the urge to rut." I closed my eyes and feigned a shutter as if enthralled by the thought of my imaginary relationship with the shady low-born Matz.

Jonas stood up with fury reigning in his dark eyes while he shouted, "Bullshit! You've always hated having sex with men! I know you are lying. Besides, even if you were gay as old Claus, I know you'd never choose to be the bitch of that no account Matz. He is nothing but a criminal and a low first floor Dominant to boot!"

I stood up to demonstrate that I towered over him now as I yelled back, "I don't care if you don't believe me, dad! For your information, Matz is gorgeous and unlike you, young! I am in love with him and for a change there is nothing you can do about it. Why the fuck do you bother me anyway? Kilian happily keeps your bed warm. Why not be satisfied with that disgusting thing you call a lover and leave me free to find my own thrills?"

The Vampire in full on shit fit mode as he bellowed out, "I forbid you have lovers outside this apartment! I am your blood bonded husband, and you are my ward and personal blood doner. You are not a gay, because I say you are not. Get to my bed, attend to my desires and then you will return to seeking a female to marry. You are going to return to your duties to me like it or not! That is a directive."

I shook my head still laughing as I howled in reply, "I don't wear your collar anymore, Jonas. Peter owns my special services, and he said I can have all the boyfriends I want. He did say I am forbidden sleeping with women but that is okay by me. As I said, I am not interested in girls anyway. I suppose all you perverts fucked me so much I finally learned to love it, just like you always forced me to say I did. Consider this my official 'coming out,' to you, Jonas. Thanks to my homosexual nature, I'm never going to provide you with the female Priceless you want, so deal with it. Well, this family reunion has been great, but Matz is waiting to ring my bell, so guess I'll be seeing you around, dad or hopefully I won't." I got up to leave while laughing so hard it was bringing tears to my eyes.

I halted my attempt to exit when I heard Kilian say, "Calm down, Jonas. I'll call my brother and be right back in a moment. This time I'll have them work Maximillian over until he is too fearful to deny anyone anything they ask. While they break his will, I can arrange visits so you can get your transfusions. The staff can strap him down and you'll have full access to do as you please. Besides, the doctors wanted to keep him longer. They have some experimental drugs they are trying to get government approval on. Reece told me the hospital is willing to pay you a handsome sum if you'd let them use Maximillian in their trials with no questions asked." He got up and headed for the phone.

Jonas growled out at me with a huge grin breaking across his face, "Oh, I will see you soon, son. Enjoy that rubber room. I know I will. Did you hear Kilian? He said they can offer me what I want without my having to beat you to get it. Shit, they're even offering to torture you for me. And they will if I don't pay them to keep their hands off. I suppose you didn't realize the weekly fees I paid all these months are the only thing that prevented them from turning you into a human guinea pig. Ah, but this is the thanks I get for being so kind. Oh well. At least, Peter will be most pleased to hear you refused to obey me. He and I had a bet you know. He said you would act an ass and end up returned to the hospital before a week had passed. Oh well, I suppose you made him a rich man twice over. First because he wins the bet plus now, he doesn't have to spend all his ill-gotten gains sending you to a fancy medical college." I stopped dead at the door trembling as Kilian picked up the phone and began to dial.

I turned around with a start, nearly hyperventilating as I said, "You wouldn't dare, Jonas. You told me a long time ago that you love me and want me to return your love. Forcing me into your bed isn't the way to earn my heart."

The Vampire chuckled as he listened to Kilian's call to Doctor Altergott before he said flatly, "I also told you I don't like things waved in front of me that I cannot have. You either submit willingly or I will have them tie you up so I can take what I want without your consent. The choice is up to you, Maximillian."

I rushed over to the chair and sat down quickly sweating like a Baptist preacher hiding whiskey in his back pocket as I stammered to the Vampire, "Tell Kilian to hang up right now, Jonas. I am not going anywhere, and I am willing to bargain. Please, don't send me back to the hospital."

The Vampire nodded with a look of victory on his face as he called out with humor, "Kilian love, tell your brother to keep handy but don't send out the ambulance, just yet." Kilian nodded as he stretched the phone cord into another room to talk to my doctor where we couldn't hear him.

I wiped my wet brow as I said in a tone dripping of desperation, "He is telling them to send the white coats for me, Jonas. Stop him, please! I'll stop acting insolent, and I'm listening to your demands with seriousness I swear it!" I cast a frightened look in the direction the snake Kilian had retreated.

Jonas laughed as he responded, "Calm down Maximillian. It's tragic to see that you are as paranoid as you were before they treated you at that expensive hospital. That damn disease of yours is a stubborn bitch to get control of, isn't it? Anyway, Kilian can't have them pick you up unless I say so. With that in mind, I want you to understand something right now. There will be no bargaining over these things I'm demanding of you, Maxx. You are going to return to attending my lust and your duties as my blood donor. You will also choose a wife as per our agreement from the days before you broke my collar, or I will send you back to the hospital for good. It is simple as that." He leaned back onto his couch while crossing his arms.

I dropped my gaze to the floor feeling more than a little sick as I said in a near whisper, "I beg to differ, Jonas. There is always some room for bargaining in any deal. If I agree to satisfy your lusts as your donor every two weeks, and seek a wife, despite being gay, then I want something in return. I want to live on my own, away from this apartment, and I want you to give me an allowance if you are going to force me to tolerate the foul touching of your lover Kilian. It is unfair to expect such indignity when he is not my guardian, husband, lover nor even a human."

The Vampire growled. "Denied. You'll move back into this apartment right away, and I will not agree to a fucking taste of your skills every fortnight. That is bullshit."

I startled as I replied in an incredulous tone, "But you have Kilian to attend your daily urges, Jonas. What the hell do you need me for? Surely, he can do for you anything you in the bedroom that you think I can."

Jonas shot a look of humor at me as he replied, "Really Maxx? You were a pleasure submissive all those years for how many men but still you understand nothing about male sexuality? I find that hard to believe. Besides, Kilian is a top, like I am, you fool. I do believe you are already intimately aware of that."

I groaned and covered my eyes with my hands as I whimpered, "No, this cannot be happening. You are kidding, right? How can you two be lovers but neither enjoy the intercourse with the other completely or even at all? Look, you are older and more powerful than him. Make Kilian submit as the bottom. Hell, you never cared what I wanted, so why do you care what he does?"

Kilian returned and sat next to Jonas the said with a big smile on his face, "Reese said to tell you hello Jonas. What did I miss?" The two of them kissed as I tried not to gag over watching that gross display.

I growled in reply, "The mark is what you missed, you idiot. I am not moving back into this House, Jonas. I may as well go to that hospital if you insist on such. As for everything else you demand, I seem to be at a disadvantage. I will give you no further quarrel but must beg to be allowed to leave the second you are done enforcing me to attend your foul lusts. Since you won't give me a fair allowance for the hard labors I provide you, I'll need to find work, or I will starve to death." That statement made both men laugh hard for several moments.

After a moment Jonas recomposed himself then said, "Oh, you intend to find a job. Here in the House? Really? Where exactly, Maximillian? Do you honestly think they will pay you when all around they have skilled labor that already is hired cheaply?"

I shook my head and fought back tears of frustration as I replied, "I've no choice but to find work in the House since you bastards won't allow me to leave. What the hell am I supposed to do for rent and food Jonas?"

Kilian snorted then said, "That's why we demand you move back into our apartment, you idiot. Jonas and I will take care of your bills and you will take care of our needs in return."

I glared at him as I growled out, "I would rather live under the stairs and starve to death. And what is this our and we shit Kilian is spewing, Jonas? I don't take orders from a snake, nor was I informed his name was on your apartment lease."

The Vampire smiled as he took Kilian's hand and practically cooed out to him, "Oh, don't mind his poor manners, my beloved."

He then turned his attention to me and said flatly, "You will take care of both of our desires without argument or extra payment for it, Maxx. You'll also move back in with us and obey his command just as you will my own. If you behave yourself, we will make sure you are spoiled and well-treated. If you refuse our most generous offer that is fine. After we finish using you as a sex toy each day, you can leave to starve slowly in your makeshift bed under the stairs for all I care. Or perhaps you can move in with your new boyfriend. I'm sure that poverty stricken Matz will make sure you eat often, but will the meat he puts in your mouth keep a growing boy from being hungry?" The two of them laughed like hyenas over Jonas's cruel statement.

I stood up abruptly and yelled in fury, "This is bullshit, Jonas! I am not blood bonded to that, cocksucker. Bad enough I am forced to tolerate your gross interest, but him I'm not doing it!"

Jonas growled out, "You'll agree to do whatever I tell you to do in my bedroom, or I will have him finish his call to his brother, Maximillian."

I stood there damning myself. For the millionth time I wished I had not stupidly come to this apartment that night so long ago begging for the Vampire's help to block Peter from keeping me trapped in his collar. If only I had realized I was only trading one terrible situation for a much more horrific fate.

With an observable shutter I breathed out, "Fine, but I refuse to live in this apartment with you fiends. Just wait and see. I will find work. I can take care of myself without any help from you or anyone else."

Jonas smiled diabolically as he practically purred in response, "Good luck with that, my boy. But again, you have forgotten an important fact. Your behavior and diagnosis were carefully examined by a court and legal team. It was determined you are severely disturbed, and a probable threat to yourself and others. In other words, those learned men judged you to be mentally incompetent. They also decided that you can't be trusted to attend to your daily functions independently. Since I am married to your mother and assumed to be your father, naturally I was asked to assume responsibility for your best welfare. Of course, I eagerly agreed to do take on such a heavy burden for the son I love so much. Now, if you are still confused about everything I've just said. Please allow me to break down what all that means for you in a way you can easily understand, Maximillian. Even if you manage to get a job, your employer will be obliged to hand all your paychecks over to me. Kilian has been tasked to do his best to help you manage the symptoms of your disease, but how best to spend your money is up to me. Enough of this stalling. I command you to get going to my bedroom and strip, boy. I have been waiting a long time to get all my dark lusts fed. You can look for that fantasy job after Kilian and I are finished with you. I've no doubt that after a few weeks of suffering hunger and homelessness, you'll be ready to move back in. When you do, be ready to show gratitude that I'm the patient and forgiving husband to you that I am."

I felt the breath leaving my lungs as I whimpered out, "No! There is not a court order that says I must turn all my income over to you. You are lying to me." I trailed off and tears began to roll down my cheeks because deep down I knew he wasn't.

Jonas had worked hard to make sure I was trapped in a corner. No matter what I did I was fucked. I mean that literally. Before I could say another word, the Vampire stood up and grabbed me by the arm. I was too stunned and despaired to put up much of a fight as he forced me to my feet and dragged me after him down his hallway to the bedroom. I'd been taken captive by the two villains, and I knew struggling would only make this painful situation worse.

For the next three hours, I was held hostage in their bed. After the Vampire bonded me to his headboard he cut into my left shoulder and drank the blood that rose from the wound. Once his blood lust was sated, he and Kilian took turns using me as their personal sex doll. They brutally tagged teamed me without granting me any rights to refuse their advances. It was exactly the way I'd endured hundreds of times in my sad days as the Priceless pleasure submissive.

Many things went through my mind as they forced their foul touch and penetrations on me. The thought that I returned to several times was how grateful I was to my beloved Leo. Though this sexual assault was humiliating and more than a bit painful. It wasn't nearly as bad as it would have been had he not prepared me for a return to be playing the bottom in male-on-male intercourse.

I confess, I had to hide a smile when I saw the confusion and worry in Jonas's expression just as he began his brutal thrusting. He knew after spending nineteen months chaste in a rubber room cell, his initial penetration should cause me to bleed mildly. The absence of this sign of freshness caused Jonas to realize that I was telling the truth about sleeping with Matz. In fact, I he discovered me 'seasoned' enough to have engaged with the man more than just one time since I'd returned to the House.

My plan to fool the Vampire into believing I was a strict homosexual was starting to take root. Like it or not I had to look on the bright side. Had I not been forced into a tryst with them that morning, Jonas could have disregarded my claim as a complete lie. This way he was the unhappy witness to physical evidence that he couldn't easily discount.

A sudden awareness of my significant problems with finances endangered Marc's freedom as much as it did mine. This knowledge worked as an added insult to the injury of my fast-tanking self-esteem. I was now facing the unfathomable idea that not only did Kilian and Jonas have the power to rape me as often as they wanted, but eventually their economic stranglehold would result in my complete failure to survive on my own.

My consciousness ached with the realization I needed to find and apologize to Rolf quickly. I had arrogantly assumed it didn't matter if he was willing to cover the rent. Well, I was wrong because it sure as fuck did! While having my living space covered by his kindness helped. It still wouldn't put food in my stomach nor pay for the little boy that depended on me to keep him safe.

I decided my only option was to apply for a black collar job anyway. I hope the Mistress could be bribed to keep my employment and paychecks secret. I knew, if it came down to it, Leo would make sure I was fed. Though, I dared not ask him to pay the fees Karsten needed to continue her care of Marc. Leo is a wonderful and generous person, but he would view my actions as a useless waste of efforts. He truly believes the only way to save the silver collared people is by changing the House laws. I agree with him, but children like Marc don't have the time to wait for his vision to take effect. Plus, I was already planning to purchase another submissive trainee.

Marc had a biological sister who also wore a silver collar. He didn't know I'd found his face familiar when I pulled him to his feet on the stairs after he'd accidentally tripped me. I noticed Marc was the spitting image of that little silver collared girl I'd punished during my thudding exam.

You may recall, Meine Liebe, I had to give her five lashes because she had been caught stealing food. I'd asked around about her after that situation and found out she'd committed the crime because she'd been desperate to save her biological brother, an unclaimed silver collar called Marc, from starvation. His rations had been withheld by the cruel Dungeon Mistresses as punishment for his natural clumsiness.

Well, obviously Marc's older sister had successfully kept him alive until he'd managed to catch Karsten's eye, but she'd suffered a bit of trauma for her valiant efforts. I knew from experience that if he had suffered such a harsh punishment in the dungeons before even being sent to auction, he was poor submissive material.

You see Meine Liebe, some of the simple silvers don't even make it through their first year of training once auctioned. They are clumsy, slow, rebellious, or just not talented enough to please their Dominant adequately. Poor little Marc was not a handsome boy, and he was without a doubt hopelessly clumsy. This unfortunately marked him as a likely candidate to be sold off to the circuit before the end of his first season in Karsten's household. That is why I was in a hurry to get his collar painted black. I knew a dead silver walking the second I met one.

Sadly, that day I met her I noticed Marc's sister was not blessed any better than he was. Yet the females, even the clumsy or unattractive ones, usually survive till the collar selection in their fifteenth year, at the very least. Since most in the House are heterosexual her coveted virginity would buy her a little more time in the House but only three more years than her less valuable brother Marc. I knew she was around twelve or thirteen years old that day I'd punished her. It goes without saying that nineteen months had passed, which meant she was fast approaching the end of the line for an untalented pleasure submissive.

If I didn't work fast to save her, she was soon going to suffer a fate worse than death. She'd be forced to give up her virginity to her Master then passed around to his friends to be raped to death. Worse still, I assumed he'd be like so many other Dominants around the House by that time. Most had found ways to work around the new laws that forbad selling used silver collars to the circuit once their Master had tired of them. If she was collected by the circuit coyotes, dying from the horrific conditions, and repeated rapes she'd endure on her way to the work camps would be a mercy compared to what was waiting if she didn't.

I knew she was still alive because I'd briefly seen her in the hallway the day I returned to the House. That helped me feel more secure that I had a little time left to work on the way to get her collar. It was likely that her Master was not going to be as willing to work out a trade as Karsten had been. I also didn't even know which first floor bastard held her training metal.

It was trying to solve my many problems and thoughts of Leo's loving embrace that got me through the nightmare tag team rape that morning. I admit I cried through the entire thing, but I managed to keep them from seeing my tears. Nothing I tried could keep my eyes dry, not even reminding myself that soon I would be sent away to medical school. I couldn't help it. I just felt so fucking helpless.

When at last the two of them were satisfied that I'd been completely sullied by their brutal lusts, I was finally given permission to take a shower. It seemed like I couldn't get that water hot enough nor scrub hard enough to clear away the foul evidence of their misuse of me. I gave up trying to feel clean again, and decided it was best to hurry up the process so I could leave as quickly as possible. Before either of them decided to demand a second performance, yikes!

Jonas was still in bed with Kilian whispering with contentment when I emerged fully dressed and smelling to high heaven of heavy cheap cologne. I attempted to rush by them before they could say another word to me, but as usual Jonas wasn't going to let me get away so easily.

Jonas cleared his throat loudly then said with a big smile on his face, "You are ordered to return to provide us with special services tomorrow. In fact, you are commanded to do this every day until you are ready to move home for good."

I refused to look at him as I replied flatly, "What time?"

He laughed over my lack of attempting to argue with him for a moment then said, "Tomorrow be here around noon. After we are done with you, I'll give you the time you are to return the next day. Oh, and in case no one has told you yet. You are not permitted to leave the interior of the House without an escort. If you wish to go outside to enjoy the gardens, you must come for Kilian or me to take you. I warn you, if step a toe off the House grounds when we take you out for a stroll, Ivan will shoot you dead. Oh, and Maxx, good luck job hunting. You're going to need it. Welcome home, boy. It has been a real pleasure to visit with you."

I shook my head as I angrily replied, "I would rather starve in the dark than ask either of you for anything. I will never be moving back in with you Jonas, so forget it. Don't bother to get out of bed perverts, I remember the way out. I hope you fall down the stairs Jonas and as for you Kilian. I will push you down them personally the minute I get the chance." I tore from the room with the sounds of their laughter echoing off Jonas's hallway walls.

I hauled ass down the stairs at a near run. All the while I was lamenting the day my father fucked my mother without a prophylactic. My wild attempts to put distance between myself and the Elder's floor was abruptly interrupted when I saw Matz coming toward me.

He stopped in front of me then laughed loudly as he said, "Damn, Maxx you're a hard man to find. Where are you heading in such a hurry? I was just coming up to see you."

I glared at him then replied in an irritated tone, "What the fuck do you want now, Matz? I told you I be there tomorrow at nine. Did you think I would dare to break our contract or are you trying to collect on the debt I owe you sooner rather than later?"

Matz frowned as he responded, "Neither. I know better, Maxx. I'm honorable in all my business dealings, you'll see. I wanted to ask if you are still seeking employment. If so, I've got a line on a job offer you may be interested in."

My sour expression brightened immediately as I replied eagerly, "Really? Ah, I'd be interested in accepting any job offer! When does it start? How much does it pay? What are the tasks expected? Oh, never mind that last question because I can do almost anything if they're willing to train me. I'm willing to work hard to please." I smiled with thrill over my sudden good fortune.

Matz dropped his head and watched a Dominant walking past us, appearing nervous. I found his behavior odd, but I was too excited to care enough to ask about it. I continued to bombard his ears with a string of inquiries regarding the proposed solution to all my problems. Well, most of my troubles anyway. The moment the traveling Dominant was out of earshot he grabbed my blouse and pulled me close to him.

I yelped and started to struggle in his grip when he leaned toward me and whispered loudly, "Shut up, Maxx! Look, this information is to be kept just between us. The pay for this job offer is the usual three thousand for the night. You can start after you pay your first installment to me. That is if you are interested. This fellow is willing to pay for no less than three nights with the Priceless of legend." He released me and pretended to be checking his nails for dirt.

I stood there unsure if I understood his words correctly, then I replied angrily, "How dare you claim you've come to offer me a job! What you are proposing isn't honest employment. It's not only illegal but it's dishonorable! What the hell do you take me for, Matz?"

He shot a humored glance at me then with a sigh said, "I took you for a man that needs an income so he can eat and pay bills. Like all the rest of us broke blokes, you must rely on the skills you possess if you hope to earn a living. The way I see it, you are blessed that an opportunity for a lot of money for very little effort has fallen into your lap. If you put your faith in your buddy Matz, I can assure you that you'll have all the work you need to keep you financially stable. I of course would take the usual ten percent finder's fee, and make sure you stay safe. That is fair I think, but I am willing to bargain over the details. I would most definitely be interested in taking out a small portion of my cut through trade. You know, be my lover from time to time." He smiled widely at me.

My face burned with both fury and shock as I growled back at him, "So you are saying not only do you want to be my pimp, but also to call me lover occasionally. When exactly would you desire to honor me with your deepest affection? While you whore me out to your friends or while I take the day off to recover from all the cocks I've been sucking. Oh, my God, I think I'm going to be sick! Stay the hell away from me Matz! This House is nothing but a den of perverts, I swear it!" I turned around and stormed down the stairs, nearly running over everyone that got in my way.

I was livid beyond imagination by the time I reached the House kitchen. I managed to track down the Black Collar Mistress with some effort, despite my deepening fury. The moment I set eyes upon the elderly woman I successfully had shaken off the ill emotions the Vampire and Kilian had caused me. Matz's offer, however, was still bothering me a great deal. I was having difficulty believing he'd even dared to bring up such a horrific solution.

Truth was what Matz suggested upset me because I understood I had led him to think of me that way. I assumed the deal I'd made with him to save Marc had tarnished me in his eyes. So, he naturally thought my dignity could be purchased for the right price.

I decided I would have to be far more careful about what I'd be willing to offer in return for favors. No doubt I'd probably have to agree to many foul arrangements in my bid to save as many silver collared children as possible. One mistake with someone with more power or influence than Matz could haunt me for life. It could even prove deadly if the rumor that I had earned any income through hustling became common knowledge among the House residents.

Anxiety over my perceived reputation as a professional catamite plagued me while I stood there patiently awaiting audience with the plump Head Mistress. She was busy correcting a couple of her black collared trainees.

I was deep in self-loathing and self-punishing thoughts when the Black Collar Head Mistress Vebber approached me and said in a stern tone, "To what do I owe this pleasure, Mad Maxx? I am a busy woman Sir, but if you tell me who service has left you unsatisfied. I swear I will see the submissive punished and the behavior will be corrected immediately."

I smiled with as much pleasantness as I could muster as I politely replied, "Oh, dearest Mistress, I didn't wish to visit with you to grumble or complain about one of the trainees. If you would be interested, I am seeking a position among your ranks. I swear that I am handy and work hard. Any job opening you could offer me is fine if it is the paying kind. I can also provide references that I am skilled in many areas, easily trained, and reliable." I kept my gaze down but smiled coyly while holding my breath in anticipation.

The Mistress stood there silently for a moment then suddenly broke out in wild laughter as she said, "Oh, my God, Mad Maxx! That's a very clever joke. Hell, you had me going there for a moment. I swear I've always adored your fine sense of humor. This one was so good that I'm not even angry that I rushed over here ready to listen to your complaints. I tell you I'll laugh for years every time I think of it. Thank you for this most unexpected gift." She started to walk away.

I cleared my throat and halted her retreat as I replied, "Wait, please Mistress, I beg of you. I am not kidding nor playing a prank. I really am seeking employment with you. I need a job badly."

The Mistress's chuckling came to an end, and her face was overcome with an expression of concern as she said, "Are you serious, Mad Maxx? This had better be a joke, because surely, you're aware it is forbidden to hire you even if I did have a job opening. That said, I wouldn't give you work even if it were not against House law to do it. To dare to put a Dominant to the plow in their own House, is undignified. I'll be damned before anyone can accuse me of being responsible for putting my betters in such a humiliating position."

I fell to my knees at her feet and plead out in a panicked tone, "Mistress please help me! I need employment. Honest work is not humiliating nor undignified, but starvation most certainly is. Surely, you've heard the rumors that I have no money, can't leave the House. This isn't empty gossip, but a sad truth! I beg you to help me. Listen, I will work any job, no matter how lowly you think it is, without complaint. I will happily clean trash cans, or you can put me deep in the dungeons moping the stoney floors. Just give me the task and I swear it will be done to perfection."

She seemed freaked out over my kneeling to her. Before I could plead my case further, she reached down and dragged me back to standing.

I watched her cast anxious glances around the nearly empty room as she whispered in a harsh tone, "Mad Maxx, stop this insanity immediately. Holy shit, seeing a King act like a desperate child is scaring this old lady half to death. I've already said I cannot hire you and I will not. You already have one of the most important jobs in this House. I suggest sticking to that one and leave your loyal servants to handle the mundane tasks."

I began to weep silently as I whimpered out, "Mistress, I am doomed if you don't give me a paying job. Nothing is free for a Dominant and I cannot leave the House. What am I going to do?"

The Mistress shook her head and smiled with bitterness as she replied, "Mad Maxx, you are a good looking fourth floor Dominant and our Priceless King to boot. I find it hard to believe no one in this House is willing to keep a beautiful young man in all the champagne and bubble baths he could desire. I suggest you send word that you're available for wooing. I bet a lovely high classed Mistress will snatch you up so fast it will make your pretty head spin. If I were a young woman and it wasn't against the law to mix with Dominants, I confess, I would beat my own sister to death to have you decorating my bed. Now get out of here and stop tormenting an old woman with visions of young perfection she shall never know. Take my advice, get a wealthy girlfriend. She will look after your every need, wait and see." She winked then looked me over with a yearning expression on her face, sighed, and walked away leaving me standing there suffering in abject misery.

If only I could've taken her advice, you can be sure I'd have not despaired over my status as a House prisoner. What I wouldn't have given to be the latest plaything of some beautiful young lady or an old, ugly one for that matter. Believe me, I wasn't picky when it came to the wiles of the woman. That said, you already know why that wasn't ever going to happen. By five that afternoon, so did I.

I killed the time I had left before the horrific meeting to start Peter's contract clock wandering around the House. I approached and told every black collar submissive I encountered I would do their job for a minor share of their weekly paycheck. Most of them freaked and ran away before I could do more than make the offer. A few laughed thinking, I was pulling an elaborate prank, until they realized I was being serious. They were not too friendly in giving me a resounding hell no after that. A couple of the older ones even accused me of trying to entrap them into an illegal discussion just so I would have reason to see them punished.

The anxiety within me built to near panic attack levels as I watched the time get ever closer to five o'clock. With only five minutes left, I finally gave up my fruitless hunt for a job and headed for the Hall of Records.

Gretta and Peter had arrived long before I did. I found them sitting at a large round table in the center of the huge room. An unconscious groan escaped me when I saw the original contract Peter had tricked me into agreeing had been placed on the table between them. It had grown yellow with age, and the edges were peeling but to my regret my signature upon it was clear as the day the ignorant boy I'd been had put it there.

Gretta glared as I quietly took a seat across from Peter. I kept my head down, to hide my wincing while she read the agreement out loud. Once the Head of the Voters had finished repeating aloud the stupid things I'd hastily agreed to, she asked if I agreed nothing had been added or subtracted from the original contract. My shame at having been so badly fooled had robbed me of the ability to speak. So, I replied to her question by nodding slightly.

Gretta snorted as if irritated by my lack of verbalization. Then without addressing my observably subdued behavior she asked Peter if he agreed that the contract had come to full maturity. In other words, she wanted to know if he felt I'd held up my end of the bargain and he was now prepared to complete his side of the arrangement.

Peter eagerly and loudly replied, "Yes, I happily agree the condition have been met that cause this contract between Maximillian and I to become active." Gretta nodded at him then stamped the aging paper with the House mark that indicated it was legally binding.

Gretta stood up and walked over to file the document while haughtily saying, "Peter, I was expecting trouble the way you were acting but I see that Maximillian is docile and as submissive to your will as he's always been. I wish to add I am not disappointed by it. Merely surprised is all." She flashed a snotty smile at me.

I shrugged off her attempts to goad me into losing my tempter as I turned my attention to Peter and asked. "So, what does it say in the contract about your responsibilities to me before I start medical school? Like specifically, are you obligated to pick up my living expenses outside of the ones I'll require while attending college?"

Peter appeared startled by my question but replied, "Uhm, no, Maximillian. I don't have to pay a dime until you are accepted into an accredited program. That was the agreement."

I nodded with a frown and got up to leave as I responded, "Ah. Okay, that's good to know."

Peter watched me walking away for a moment then yelled after me, "Wait a second! Where do you think you're going, Maxx? I want to call in my rights to your special services. If you recall, that is how you agreed to pay back all the money I'll have to spend to make sure you become a doctor."

I turned around and smiled at him bitterly as I replied, "I am sure you do want your payments Peter, but as you can clearly see I am not in medical school nor in residency. I do not pay up front for services that I have yet to receive. If you are not obligated to cover my expenses while I rot away in the House that you helped to trap me in, then I don't owe you anything in return. Equal service for equal service, Peter. That is what you taught me while I wore your collar, right? I'm an honorable man, even when dealing with one that dishonorably tricked a little boy into an unfair agreement. You can be assured that when I get your services, you will get yours. I just heard you admit that there is nothing in that contract that says I owe you a fucking thing until the day I get into school. I do understand you managed to gain control of my ability to take lovers other than you or my husband. You've made it clear I'm forbidden to engage in relationships with females, but because I am married to a man, you can't stipulate I remain completely monogamous. I can sleep with as many men as I want. That is fine by me. I'm not interested in women anyway. You can thank Gretta for helping me discover my disgust for the fairer sex. Now, I need to be going. My boyfriend is waiting to wine, dine and then ravage me most soundly. Oh, he is such an animal that one, but I tolerate his overeagerness because he is so damned good to me. However, I do not have to put up with your foul lusting, not yet anyway. Smile Peter! Maybe you'll get lucky, and I will collapse from overuse before you must shell out a single penny on me. If not, well you'll still get to play third, oh I mean, fourth, or is it fifth fiddle in my ever-increasing boy band. See you around, partner."

Peter growled out in fury, "You're a bastard. It's obvious you are attempting to rip me off by twisting the words of our contract. You know damned well I intended to have unlimited access to your special services the moment that contract went into effect. I'm calling in my rights immediately, Maximillian. If you know what is good for you, you'll get on your knees when I say to without feeble attempts to shirk your duties to me."

I laughed, then resumed walking away slowly as I shouted in reply, "I learned how to ignore what I think I see and go with what I know is real from the best teacher in this House, Peter. Do recall it is you that taught me what appears to be a girl is really a boy in a dress? You also demonstrated that a cheap fake can be Priceless. Oh, I do I thank you for the many useful lessons I learned both inside and outside your bed chambers. However, you should have been more careful with the way you worded that contract old man. I suppose you thought since you easily fooled me as a little boy, that it would always be a simple task to mislead me. Well guess what? I have grown up Peter to become a wise man. I think it best you do the same. Good day to you both." I turned and bowed my head slightly then left the records room, slamming the door behind me.

I walked down the hallway and to my relief ran into Rolf. He I managed to get his attention. The expression on his face told me he wasn't too happy to see me.

As I approached slowly, he growled out, "What do you want Maxx? Whatever it is you want to bitch about this time, better make it quick. I am already late to meet with a sexy little Mistress and I dare say I'm not willing to risk her leaving before I get there. Especially not for the likes of someone who's made it clear we are not friends." He glared at me and rudely checked his watch to demonstrate he meant what he said.

I hung my head and stared at his shoes as I sheepishly replied, "Rolf, I would like to apologize for my outburst yesterday. I admit I was being a rude asshole. I would like to say my bad behavior was caused by the left-over effects of the sedating drugs given to me at the hospital. But to be honest, I was angry that I had been forced to return to this House. I took it out on you and your brother Voters. That was an immature and stupid thing to do. None of my problems are your fault. I want to repay your kindness but as you know, I have nothing to my name other than what you generously have given to me. If you can find it in your heart to forgive me, I can promise it will never happen again. You have been a good friend to me. I appreciate you more than I can say."

To my relief his angered look softened immediately as he replied, "Oh, hell Maxx. You don't have any reason to apologize to me. It's unfair for me to be angry over your Dominant right to throw us out of your apartment. We were both guilty of being rude assholes. I never considered that you might be fatigued from your long trip back nor your feelings about those people that I'd invited. I meant well, as usual, but wasn't thinking clearly, also as usual. Tell you what, let's just agree we both fucked this one up and start over with a clean slate, okay?" He held out his hand.

I smiled while I took it and said happily as I shook it with vigor, "You've got a deal. It is a pleasure to meet you, uhm Rolf, isn't it? I am Mad Maxx at your service." I chuckled over my joke.

Rolf groaned as he replied sounding a bit humored, "No, you are not at anyone's service. Not since you broke that bat collar, anyway. Oh hey, I ran into Leo this morning. I bought you those lambs you asked about. I managed to get eight of them. I'd asked Leo what this weird request of yours was all about, but he said he didn't know. So, I am asking you. Why so many Maxx? I mean you are a little too old to be playing with toys now. Look at you. You've grown into a strapping young man. The way I see it, you should be trying to pet a woman's wool not a sheep." He chuckled over his vulgar comment.

I frowned then said in an irritated tone, "Don't I wish! Peter, Jonas, and that fucking Kilian won't allow it. I am in as bad a situation as I was as I ever was when I was submissive. I cannot leave the Goddamned House to escape their nasty lusting either."

Rolf frowned as he replied, "Seriously? That is bullshit. Look, I would love to chat with you longer, but I have a hot little redhead waiting on me. If you are available, we could catch up over breakfast tomorrow."

I nodded and replied, "I would love to, but I have a date in the morning. I could meet you in the Great Hall at nine the day after tomorrow, if that works for you."

The Voter laughed till he snorted then said, "Wait a minute Maxx! Did you say you have a date? I thought I heard you say Peter, Jonas and Kilian forbid you from chasing women."

I smiled with wickedness as I replied, "They did, but because they are all men, they couldn't ban me from hunting boyfriends. I've decided to get so many of those that those three bastards will have trouble fitting into my busy schedule. I wish to thank you for the apartment and beautiful furnishings you have generously provided, Rolf. I hate to ask it, but could you keep paying the rent until I can get employment and handle it myself?"

He appeared surprised by my response as he choked out, "Uhm, uh, yeah. I never expected you to take over the payments anyway. I've told you that apartment was payback for my taking advantage of you that day in the closet. Wait, a second. Did you just say you are seeking the company of boyfriends? Maxx, what the hell are you up to?"

I turned around to head down the hallway and yelled back to him, "Four, Rolf, that is what I am up to. I have that many men that can honestly call me their plaything. Ask me again when next we see each other. I bet I can do better than that. Hell, I was the sex toy to that many when I was only the novice at thirteen years old, ha! See you the morning after next, brother." I left a startled Rolf standing there in the hallway scratching his head with a confused expression on his face.

Without further interruptions I traveled down the winding corridors of the first floor until I reached my ultimate destination. I walked to the apartment door that belonged to Matz and knocked softly.

He answered it with a frown that immediately became a smile as he chimed out sounding surprised, "Mad Maxx! I wasn't expecting to see you so soon. Come in. Come in." I followed the low born Dominant inside.

To my surprise the place was clean and more importantly smelled fresh. Though it was still mostly empty.

I took a cautious deep breath to make sure I wasn't hallucinating the clean scent as I said, "Wow, you hired a black collar maid? But I thought you said you were suffering poverty. Where did you get the money, Matz?"

He chuckled as he replied, "No, I didn't hire anyone. I cleaned the place up myself. I wanted it to be pleasing because, oh never mind, you would think me stupid."

I shot him a look of surprise as I responded, "I know you are stupid, Matz! There is no thinking to it. So, now that we have established that, I ask again. Why did you do this? Not that I am complaining or anything."

Matz laughed then blushed as he said, "Ah, so you've come all this way just to bust my balls, have you, Maxx? I think not. So, why are you here? Oh, wait, I know. Someone loaned you the twenty thousand and you've come to pay off your debt to me, right?" He sat down appearing saddened at the idea that was a possible reason I had sought him out for an audience.

Suddenly I realized the thing I'd missed as I gasped and replied, "Matz? Did you clean up this apartment because you thought if you did, I would agree to become your lover?"

Matz covered his face with his hands as he blushed deep red and responded, "Okay, you got me, Maxx. You're right. I am stupid because I really believed you might want to be with me willing without that God damned contract if I could demonstrate better manners. Roland told me I am not only a moron, but I am also too caught up in fake romances to realize the reality of this situation between us. Shit like I've read in those fantasy books doesn't happen to 'nobodies' like me, he said. Roland tried to warn me, but did I listen? No, handsome men don't share their beds with unattractive, poverty stricken, low born Dominants. Not in this House, anyway."

Matz uncovered his face appearing shocked just as I broke out in loud laughter over his words and replied, "Seriously, Matz? You really think I'm that shallow to let looks, income or even status determine whom I sleep with? Well, you can tell Roland he is the moron not you because I came here to accept your most generous offer. Though since you've never tasted my skills you may be disappointed once you discover I'm not the legend in the bedroom you've been misled to believe me to be. However, that said, I need a boyfriend and I already am contracted to you. Plus, I already told Jonas you and me are in a serious relationship. You wouldn't want him to punish me as a liar, would you?" I shot him a coy smile.

Matz gasped and turned pale as he barely whispered out, "Is this really happening? The Priceless Mad Maxx told his husband the Elder Jonas that I am his lover? Maxx, are you really standing here accepting my offer saying I will be disappointed with your special services to me? No fucking way! I got to be hallucinating this. Perhaps I ate bad eggs at breakfast or I fell and hit my head while cleaning up this pig pen apartment. Nothing this amazing ever happens to Matz!"

I frowned as I replied, "Well, if you believe you are hallucinating now, then you are about to discover yourself in a full-blown delusion. While I don't care about your status in the House, it is against the law for me to date below my level. This first-floor apartment will not do, Matz. I've thought it over and decided the only way we can legally be seen together is for you to move in with me. I will have to charge you a fee to help me cover the costs but after our contract is finished, you are welcome to stay. If you pay on time and continue to play my fake boyfriend, then you can stay in the spare room as long as you wish. Please understand, the minute my debt to you is cleared, I will only require you be seen on my arm in public but in private you will keep your distance. I'm only looking for a cover lover, but I'm not interested in the real thing."

Matz sputtered out sounding incredulous, "What am I hearing this correctly? Are you inviting me to live in that fourth-floor palace of yours and saying that I can sleep with you? In your bed!"

I nodded and carefully kept the irritation from my tone as I replied, "You can share my bed for seven days only as per our agreement, Matz. After that, I owe you nothing more. But if you are willing to play my boyfriend in public, I'll happily call you my true friend and roommate in private. So, do we have a deal?" I stuck out my hand to shake it.

Matz shook his head then said sourly, "No I can't accept your offer, Maxx. I cannot just turn off my affection just because a silly debt is paid in full. Besides that, I cannot afford this piece of shit apartment on the lowest level of this House. How the hell can I afford one up there with you in the sky? I mean it has always been my fantasy to live on the fourth floor with a gorgeous man, but Maxx I must I just can't say yes. My heart will end up getting broken when the dream comes to an end and reality comes to kick my ass. Go find someone else to play the role for you. One hopefully that doesn't honestly love you, like I do."

I scoffed, "Oh, so trying to rape me when I was just a little boy and then share what was left after you were done with your friends is your perception of love is it, Matz? Get off your high horse, cocksucker! If you are worried about reality slapping you in the face in a week once our contract is voided, then allow me to soften that blow by giving you a small dose of it now. I've only offered you this overly generous deal because I need the money! You have a job running illegal gambling tables and I cannot find honest work anywhere in this Goddamned House. Without an income I am more than just fucked. I am ruined."

Matz sniffed back tears as he replied in a defeated sounding tone, "Yes, I admit it. I did intend to do you dirty once. I realize how awful that must have been for you, but I was punished for my dishonor toward you, don't you remember? I have the fucking scars to prove it! You know the House law! Once a sentence is carried out the parties involved cannot bring it up anymore. Besides, I took a serious risk to offer you a way to make three thousand or more a night and instead of being civil you treated me like a criminal. Then I cleaned up this hovel just to impress you and I confess to you I love you, and you again cut out my heart. Get out Mad Maxx! You can rip up that contract between us. I swear to you I no longer will seek to see it is fulfilled. I honestly thought you were the man of my dreams. Guess I really am nothing more than a hopeless romantic. Roland was right, I am a moron to believe in fairy tales at my age."

I growled in response, "Why the fuck would I tear it up, Matz? You listen here, I refuse to breach the agreement between us. I've already completed the trade with Karsten, and I will not return what I already possess. How the fuck can you dare to sit there talking like I am breaking your heart? What the hell is wrong with you? You don't even know me. Shit Matz, I think you are pushing your fantasies on me, and that is not fair. Besides, I only ever agreed to let you fuck me. There was nothing in our agreement that demanded I feel anything other than obligation to satisfy your lusts. Sex isn't love, and you have clearly mistaken it for that lofty emotion."

Matz looked to the floor and wiped his eyes as he replied, "You are the one that has mistaken sex for something special, Mad Maxx. When I told you that I can give you a job that pays enough to buy more collars like Marc, pay for their keep, plus eat, and pay your own bills. Instead of approaching the possibility with the cold heart you now claim, you acted like I stepped on your soul wearing a pair of dirty sneakers."

With a terrified gasp I squeaked out, "What the fuck did you just say? Wait! How did you find out about my agreement with Karsten for Marc's collar?"

He smiled through his tears as he replied bitterly, "I went over to make sure Karsten knew that that she no longer owed a debt to me. Marc told me what you did for him. I didn't believe the boy, so I asked Karsten. She verified that you took on her debt in trade for the rights to him, but not to abuse the boy. She said you demanded she paint his collar black. Well, you can say whatever you want. I know you think me an idiot, but I can see through you, Mad Maxx the Brutal. You agreed to let me have my way with you to assure that a little child never has to suffer the things you most certainly have. This world is so full of hateful, selfish, and greedy people. I make a living off it, Maxx, so I am an expert in the cruelty of mankind. I am also guilty of terrible things I am ashamed to admit to. I've squandered my winnings on my pleasures, but not you. No, you are a fucking saint! Go ahead and deny that you came to see me this morning because you're trying to save that clumsy little kid. I know the truth and I swear to God I'm in love with you for it. I would gladly face the Guard to defend you because there aren't any other hearts like your left anywhere in this world."

I felt as if I couldn't breathe as I responded, "You claim you've fallen in love with me, and I will not argue any further with your reasons for it. You are correct, such a thing is not up to me to decide for you. But you've offered to be a pimp that sells my dignity to all your wealthy friends. How can you justifiably call that love, Matz? You are truly messed up in the head if you really thought talking me into being your whore would make me fall into your arms full of fuzzy affection and deep longing for your touch."

He dropped his head and shrugged as he said flatly, "I just thought if you were willing to sell yourself for Marc, you likely would want to help save more silver collars. Maybe it was a bit idealistic of me to believe you would be willing to make use of your legendary sexual artistry to free more than just Marc. After talking with Karsten and Marc, I went to a Dominant that is secretly bisexual. Even his wife is unaware of his same gender interests. Anyway, I told him that I could get him a night of fantasy with the Priceless of legend if he was able to pay the price you are charging me. Believe me Maxx. The man was ready to pay that price or more! And I know many like him too. Just think on it. If you were to seduce these men trapped in unhappy marriages, you'd have a client list of regulars in no time. The price I'd force them to pay would be capable of supporting you, me, Marc, and many others. I agree with you that sex is not love, it is nothing, just a job if you don't have the emotion to go with it. I would have happily move into that fourth-floor heaven with you in a second. If only you were really the angel fallen from above, I thought you to be, but clearly I was mistaken."

I closed my eyes letting his words wrap around my ears and settle into my heart as I said, "Okay enough. I hear you, Matz. Pack your things quickly please. We need to get home soon because I have a date for dinner, and you have phone calls to make." I opened them to find Matz staring at me with his mouth hanging open in apparent shock.

He shook his head and said in a slow deliberate tone, "So does did mean you are willing to allow me to manage your, uhm, talent?"

I sighed deeply feeling a sadness come over me as I replied, "Yes, Matz, it does. You can call your friends and tell them my special service skills are available for rent. At least till I can find another more honest way to earn a living. When I get back from dinner with my, uhm friend, we will discuss how this arrangement between us will be of benefit to us both, partner." I flashed him a bitter smile.

Matz let out a loud yippee that sent me to my knees cowering in terror. He rushed forward fawning like a good boyfriend should. I allowed him to help me to stand, then chastised him for stalling us acting silly over this serious business arrangement.

I needed to get going. It had been a long day and my only true lover, besides you Meine Liebe, was waiting for me. I pray Leo never finds out about the dishonorable way I have paid my way through life. This includes even purchasing you, my little wife. Without the money I earn as a hustler to secretly gay men, I couldn't even afford to feed you.

Please don't judge me too harshly Meine Liebe. I swear to you I've had no choice but to engage in illegal activity to earn our supper. Jonas and Kilian have continued to collect all my paychecks from any other honest job I've ever had. They haven't given me a single penny from any of them. So, that February in 1975, I began taking my first steps toward a secret career as a professional male prostitute.

Chapter 5: Having a Gay Old Time

I turned to stare at Master Maxx. He looked back at me then dropped his gaze to his lap. I felt my heart speeding up while I examined the man I had feared since he first walked through Debbie's front door and right into my nightmares.

"So, are you saying that you are a whore like me, Master? You told me you are a doctor. Did you lie about that?" I narrowed my little eyes in suspiciousness at him.

He groaned, "No, I wasn't lying to you, Meine Liebe. I am a general surgeon, and a damned good one I am told."

I shook my head. "Then I misunderstood, and you are not a whore anymore, right? Master?"

Master Maxx sighed but kept his eyes down as he replied, "Oh, you understood me perfectly well, Meine Liebe. I am a doctor and a hustler too. Behaving as the male prostitute is what I do when I go back to the House for six months of the year. I must make money to pay Debbie's ever-increasing fees to keep you, dear wife. That woman is killing me with her overpriced fees too! I can barely afford to feed us at this point. I dare not ask Malfred to pay her your collar price and take you back to the House with me. Not yet anyway. Jonas and Kilian are waiting to get their claws on you, little one. Bad enough they have me under their thumb. As I said they take my paychecks away and give me nothing. If not for my skills as a prostitute

Debbie would have barred me from seeing you over lack of payment long ago."

I looked at Felicity then at the sheets and the hiding spot in the wall that held the pretty tea set and dress he'd brought me after our blood wedding and said, "You have to do what I'm forced to do with those mean men too? I mean you let them have sex with you to buy all this and me, Master? Even my happy meals?" He nodded while sniffing back tears.

I noticed his ears turning a faint hue of pink from blushing in mild shame as he said, "Yes, my wife. I suppose it best you know the truth about your husband now. I know you deserve better, and I really should have given you this dishonorable information before making the blood bond marriage with you. I already told you of my stupid impulsivity, which I never learned to stop. I managed to fuck everything up. Now you are stuck with a whore for a husband and of the worst kind. I won't lie to you, my beloved. I cannot count the number of, well, you know. I only will say that over the years I saved enough money for the down payment to buy your collar. That was all I had. I go home, make enough to support you and me for another six months then come back as soon as I can. Peter lives here in the USA. He only visits Germany for a few months a year and he could come through that door at any time. He and I had agreed he would leave me be for the six months I'm here in the country without interference but that has changed. He has called in his special services rights with you. I don't believe he will hold off till December when I must leave again. I apologize to you my wife, but there is no excuse for misleading you. I cannot justify what I have done. Your broken heart is killing me. I can see it in your eyes. Some days I think maybe I should do the right thing and end my life. The thing that keeps me going is this stupid belief that maybe despite the fact I am useless, you will come to love me. I suppose I am not any smarter nor realistic than idiot Byron or that insane Matz, yes? Just another hopeless romantic." He chuckled bitterly.

I looked at the scars on his chest then dropped my sights to the scouring marks from his psychotic attempts to prove himself a male (the X on his groin) as I replied, "I told you already I love you Master, many times. You don't believe me because I am little. That is okay. One day I will be grown up and then you will see that I really, really do." I leaned up and kissed him on his forehead.

Master Maxx let out a small gasp and looked up catching my gaze with his steel blue eyes. "Huh? I told you that your husband sleeps with men for money. How the hell can you say you love me after knowing that?"

I shrugged, "I sleep with men for money too, Master. Do you love me less for it? I heard Debbie call you my pimp many times. I was mad at you for that, but I understand why now. All of it. You don't expect me to do less than you did to survive."

He smiled with a look of pure surprise. "Seriously, Meine Liebe? You are only a little girl. You are stuck in this hell hole and do what you are told or you know they will kill you. I am an adult and I choose this dishonorable *path I travel. We do the same thing but not for the same reasons. Plus, I just told you I still do it when I could maybe do something else to pay the way."*

I shook my head. "I am listening to your story, Master. You already became a doctor, and they take away your money. Being a whore is the only way you can get money to live. Besides, you can't get away either and if you did try to run away from that Vampire man or Peter, I will be killed. You could try, maybe even escape, but you do that terrible sex stuff with those men you hate to keep me alive. You even look after me by watching out for those mean men that come in here to do what they do to me. I love you even more now that I know how much you really care about me. I think you are the greatest person on earth, and I am the luckiest girl that ever lived because you are my husband. Anyone who ever says something different will eat my fist. They don't know shit and I don't see them here trying to help you or me." I did my absolute best to look tough as I closed my hand and made a childish angry face.

Master Maxx reached out and stoked my cheek with a loving look in his expression. "You tell them, my Demonseed little wife. Our children will be brutes with the blood of viciousness running through their veins, yes? I thank you for the mercy of accepting me despite all my shortcomings. One day we will be free of the lustful interests of the bottom feeders in this world. I cannot wait for the day that my shard Maximillian retires, and I hold only my little wife in my arms and no one else touches her or me again. Until that beautiful day we can protect each other in the darkness when the nightmares come for us.

This horror we endure, it cannot last forever, my beloved. Everything comes to an end, the good and the bad. Until that great day that you and I are far from this chaos, I swear to you I will never judge you for what you must do, nor will I ever ask you about it. I have faith that your love is pure for your husband, and you can be assured that feeling is returned. Sex is not love. For us it is a job only. Our heart and soul are above all that foolishness. No matter what happens in our lives know that you are with me hidden where they can never take you away. This I swear to you for all time." He kissed me with gentleness as he rubbed my back with affection.

I nodded as he finished. "I will love you till I die, and nothing you or anyone else says or does will change that. Equal service for equal service. You are giving up everything to save me, and I will return it like you taught me, Master."

He chuckled. "I wish that were the truth. However, you are a little young for such a heavy promise, Meine Liebe. What did I tell you about making oaths you cannot be sure to keep? You will break my heart no doubt. I am the fool to believe the fantasy that a nine-year-old girl can know of her future interests. That said, I always was an idiot, and likely can always claim that status. You say you love me tonight and I know you mean it. I will worry about the reality of such falsehoods when that horrible day comes."

I glared at him angrily. "That is not a pleasant thing to say, Master. I don't lie. I won't break my promise to you. I will have your children and be a good wife, the best wife.

All for you. If you don't think I know what I am saying, then why do you bother? Why not just let Debbie finish me off? Sure, as hell would be more merciful for me and maybe for you too."

He rolled his eye., "I don't desire to fight with you, my wife. I merely say that you are a kid and when people grow up, they change their minds. Maybe one day you will look at me and say I am sick of this man I call husband. That happens you know. I am much older than you and have seen these things. Those that married too young often fail."

I turned around and snuggled in, gripping my lamb tight to my chest. "Well, you may as well get that cane, Master. I am not supposed to disagree with you but this time I do. You don't know my mind. I am not like other people, and neither are you. I won't change. I am married to you and that is final. I won't ever break your heart and if I were you then I would make sure to return that service for sure. Terrible things happen to people who hurt me, Master. Ask Chenowith." I grinned with evil.

Master Maxx laughed loud and long near bucking me off his lap. "You are a fucking demon, brat, monster. What the hell? Did you just threaten me again?"

I turned around with a sneer. "You forgot a few of the other things I am. I am a cocksucker, motherfucker, slut, whore and bitch, just like my Master. I didn't threaten. I was only reminding you. I say that with respect." I let out a loud yelp when he popped my thigh with his cane rapidly while he was still laughing.

Then he said, "Damn. You win the argument with your truths, but you forgot I am still bigger than you. My way rules and you better not forget that, or we both are doomed. You get back in line or it will not be so good for you. I love you far too much to allow you to fail your training. You shut that mouth and listen to my story, and for that outburst I will thud you more than I already planned to. That mouth of yours is sure to get you scars, my wife." He showed me the cane while I huffed in irritation at his correcting me.

"As you say Master. I think you for the mercy of it." I mumbled out still pissed off at him for the swat.

He coughed as he laughed for a few more minutes. "You have a nasty temper. That kind of turns me on, Meine Liebe. Next time you blow up at me, maybe I take advantage of your anger in a way I can appreciate, yes?"

I mumbled out, "You might be my husband, but you are also a fucking perverted child molester. I say that with respect, Master."

Master Maxx laughed again till he near gagged. "Shut the hell up, wife! Get over it. I fucking married you, didn't I? Goddamn you are the comic. Okay now where the hell was I? Shit, I almost pissed the bed you made me laugh so hard. Get this Maximillian, she calls me the perverted child molester but swears she loves me! Now that is a woman I can adore."

I had to stifle myself from laughing when he said (to himself) that in a slightly higher voice., "Goddammit, Mad

Max. Are you going to get back to the story or get us stabbed in the eye by picking on our wife? You know damned well that little demon will do what she threatens. Fuck man, you are the idiot. I am not sticking around if you ruffle her hellish feathers any further. You boys will be on your own. I have seen what she can do. Besides, you are almost up to my favorite part of this tale."

I did start laughing when he responded (again to himself) in a gruff voice. "Ah. You are such a fucking pervert. Of course, you love this next part, cocksucker. You back the fuck up Maximillian. I don't like you touching me, freak. I mean it or I hold you down and let Meine Liebe use your eyes for target practice."

My Master then used his Maximillian voice as he whined out, "I didn't mean it the way you took it, you fucking madman. I merely meant I liked the parts about Leo. That doesn't mean I am perverted. Wait, uhm, you get back to the story. I will shut up now. You left at the part where you and Matz were headed to the apartment before dinner with, uhm, Leo that night. Yeah, I'll be over here if you need me." With a loud sigh Master Maxx returned to the story.

"Matz walked next to me in silence as we traveled up the steps to the fourth floor. I was feeling anxious and unsure that I was doing the right thing, but I couldn't come up with a better solution. The last thing on Earth I desired was to resume my life as a pincushion for foul male lusts.

216

I thought I maybe would lose my nerve and back out of the deal. If I didn't, then I wondered if maybe I would jump from the banister in shame. I decided to let those heavy worries go for that moment.

No matter what was to happen, the first order of business was to get Matz settled into the apartment. I had already opened my big mouth to the Vampire that Matz and I were seeing each other. This was the only way to cover my lies and add to the illusion that I was indeed the homosexual I was now claiming to be.

I knew convincing Jonas that I had switched teams was going to be a hard sell. The man had known me intimately too long to believe I just woke up one morning yelling out "fabulous" *(I laughed insanely when Master Maxx actually screamed that out in a clichéd "queen" high pitched voice while snapping his fingers)* while thrilling at the idea of being the bottom of the same sexed intercourse. You know, after years of my bitching and crying about it why the hell would he buy it?

You see, Meine Liebe, I only intended to use Matz as the cover boyfriend Leo and I had discussed the night before. I never thought in a million years that somehow that man would talk me into working in his stable as his prostitute.

I look back on that shit now and think maybe that is why everyone seems to think I need a fucking guardian. It only took Karsten, Mistress Vebber, and Matz suggestions – and a handful of hateful "hell no" from the black collars around me – to have me falling for the idea that the only way I could support myself was through selling myself as a whore.

I will not go so far as to say that Matz mislead me, but I will admit that if he had really cared for this idiot the way he said he did, maybe he wouldn't have been so quick to set me on the path of the brothel.

Be that as it may, maybe I hate to admit that after everyone saw me killing Olaf and Vilber, the last thing any black collar did was trust Mad Maxx. You add all the other shit they say about me, such as that I'm Xavier's ex-sadistic lover that killed him with my sexual prowess. Then there is that rumor that Elders and dungeon Masters drop dead everywhere I go and add in all my crazy outbursts in the Great Hall and other places in the House. Oh and no one has forgotten my seduction of all the Elders, and Voters, plus no one had ever seen me with a woman. Well, thanks to all that even the Dominants had started calling me Mad Maxx the Brutal by this time.

I was a well-known psychotic, or they all thought it anyway, in the House. Even in the real world thanks to such a poor reputation, I could expect my options to provide for a living to be quite limited. Selling my pleasure submissive sexual services was really the only thing I had that could earn me any kind of money that was untraceable. This is if Matz and I could keep it a secret from the Vampire and Kilian.

The other option was to find some damned brute homosexual willing to "keep" me as their pet. While the idea of only having to deal with the lustful interests of one sounded good on paper, once again it would prevent me from helping Marc, his silver sister, or any other of the subjugated children all around me. It wasn't sane to believe no matter how much even my sweet Leo adored me that he would be okay with dropping five to twenty thousand dollars to save a life directly.

He thought it best to make the lives better for the silver collar by changing the laws. Well with old nasty Gretta and her hateful lover Cora running the show, that simply was happening too slowly to save Marc and others like him. I never told Leo, nor did I want him to know about the terrible things I do. It would break his heart to know that I hustle and to be honest, if he were to chastise me for doing what I had to do to save you and the others, I fear I wouldn't love him anymore.

I needed to love him and still do for my sanity, I think. Without my Leo there in that hell hole I would never have made it this far. Losing his affection or finding my own for him grow cold no doubt would kill me and him both. It is better to never find out nor test the only man I have ever or will ever love. That is the way I see it anyway.

I unlocked that apartment door sighing with a heavy heart over the situation I found myself in. I turned to look at Matz that was smiling like he just won the lottery. I watched his thrill wondering if there would be a day when I could feel like everyone around me always seemed to. I mean without it being my dignity that bought it. Oh well, sucks to be me.

I walked in and flipped on the lights and heard Matz gasping behind me. "Holy hell, Maxx. I thought this would be classy, but this is a palace for real. How the hell did you afford all these fine things and this swanky apartment? Oh, wait I know. The Elders gifted all this to you for your years of service to them, right?" He let out whistles of awe as he examined the rich furnishings and vastness of my high-quality home.

I shook my head. "Nope. The Elders didn't give me anything but nightmares. Actually, a Voter provided all this, but you still must pay me some kind of expenses Matz. I will not have you living here while I do all the work. Making a phone call is maybe worth ten percent of my earnings but it is not worth me covering all the expenses of this apartment alone."

Matz nodded as he scratched his head. "Well, I would like to argue and bicker with you about it but now that I see this wonderful place you have, you are right. However, I told you downstairs that I can barely afford that shit hole. I can never afford what is fair for this heaven, Maxx. We have a problem if you expect me to, wait a second. I have an idea."

I looked at the fancy clock on the wall with nervousness. I feared Leo would come looking for me if I screwed around much longer with this idiot.

I growled out, "Okay then, either spit it out quickly or hold that thought till I return from my appointment, Matz."

Matz saw me anxiously watching the time. "Oh yeah, of course you need to go, and I need to call that client I told you about earlier. I will move him to tomorrow night in that spot I was in if that is okay with you."

I frowned. "Huh? Matz, look I want to get this contract with you out of my way as fast as possible. I owe you seven nights and now I must add more men to my busy agenda. I can only service one or two a day if they expect penetration sex or there is a chance I'll be permanently injured. I normally handle up to five intercourse sessions per day, but that number has nearly been reached already."

Matz interrupted me and squealed out in a high-pitched tone, "Five? Holy hell, Maxx. That is crazy! I would never set up that many clients in a single day. You must think me a brute to even have to warn me not to do it." His eyes were wide in shock.

I groaned. "Oh hell, you don't understand so let me just say this and clear the air. I expect your confidence, or I swear Matz I will send you over the banister. I already must service three Elders daily, and one on Thursdays at one o'clock. Then I expect Peter will find a way to enforce his contracted rights to my special services soon. That lusty bastard will misuse me as often as possible, no doubt. So, adding two more men a day or even every other day will put me at great risk. I warn you, keep it to one or two unless I say otherwise. Plus, I must service you, and I assume you won't be happy with only my bath or oral services, will you?" I hoped he would decide that I was too busy with others to even want such a service as full intercourse, but I was no fool.

Matz stood there a second appearing stunned, then seemed to shake it off as he said slowly, "Wow, I knew you were popular among the House leaders, but I certainly didn't expect what you just told me. Four Elders and another Dominant daily, seriously? Christ Maxx, how are you not all fucked out already?"

I sighed and replied in a frustrated tone, "That is the problem Matz, I am. Yet, there is nothing else I can do but whore if I want to support Marc, myself and now apparently your lazy ass. When I was a silver collar, I never realized I would have to pay for every fucking thing as a Dominant. I wonder, am I going to find out they charge a freeman to take a Goddamned piss too? Worse, I didn't know how much everything was going to cost. Tell me something. Is three thousand a night even enough to survive in the House? Or do I have to fuck ten men a day to support myself? I admit I am lost when it comes to understanding finances." I nearly broke down into tears as I confessed to Matz my ignorance of basic living expenses.

Matz looked at the floor with a hint of sadness in his expression as he responded, "Calm down, Maxx. I will help you learn all the stuff you need to know about the expenses this place will take from your flesh. If you only see one client a night for three nights a week, you and I can live the fine life reserved for the fourth floor Dominants that we are. You add one more a week and Marc, and even another silver trainee would live like little kings. You are the only submissive to break his collar in more than sixty-five years and the historic high-level Priceless at that. Because of those things, your skills are unmatched, and you have no competition in this niche market. I will only sell to the closet bisexuals and homosexual men trapped in arranged marriages. That can ensure they will never speak to anyone about their secret trysts with you. That also means I can charge top dollar to assure that no one ever hears of their indiscretions from us either. It is a perfect plan. That said, it will take me some time to earn enough from my ten percent to pay you an honest flat rate fee. The gambling tables are off season and doing almost nothing. I will need to use any of the money I collect from them to hold on to that apartment below in case you need me to leave. That is always possible since we are business partners and not really lovers. Anyway, that unpleasant honesty aside, I was thinking maybe you would be willing to take in trade what you think I should owe for my part of the expenses. Well, just until we can get your work steady and my cut of the profits strong enough for me to pay you, I mean."

I glared at him as I growled in reply, "Take a good look around this apartment, Matz. What the hell do you have to trade with me that I could possibly need? Unless you can support Marc, have a sandwich in your pocket, or a black collar maid that owes you a favor I suggest you don't bother offering to trade anything. I also am very selective in my lovers. You now know I need no further company and on top of that I prefer females but must tolerate males.

So, letting you live here out free until you get on your feet because I'm smitten with you is never going to happen."

Matz chuckled as he replied with a tinge of shocked humor, "You are straight? Seriously? Well, that is a surprise. I assumed you are gay given your legendary history, put that aside as I said I do have something you may want to trade me for. That contract on Karsten is what I have. If you give me the twenty thousand in credit, then I'll forgive your debt to me. We will be even."

I nearly fainted with sudden happiness overcoming me as I said, "Did I hear you correctly? You want me to give you a twenty-thousand-dollar credit towards your part of the rent, and you will accept that instead of my special services to you?"

He nodded, appearing glum as he replied, "Yeah you understand perfectly. I mean I hate to do it, trust me. However, this apartment, living with you and being your pretend lover, shit Maxx, I am not greedy. You tear up that contract and let me stay till I can earn enough to cover my half of expenses and we will both be happy. Deal?"

I laughed out loud as I responded happily, "Hell yeah, Matz. It is certainly a trade worth accepting. Oh, wait, that is why you wanted to schedule the client interested tomorrow instead of you taking the night, right? Ah, good then do that. No need to put this horror off. The sooner it is done the sooner we can buy food and pay Marc's Mistress for his care. You know, this could actually work, Matz. Wait a second, how long does twenty thousand buy you before you start to owe me again though?" I reached into my pocket and took out his contract.

Matz shrugged. "Not sure but tell you what Maxx, go to your appointment. While you are gone, I will make the phone call to the client, then sit down and tally up our monthly expenses. How much is Karsten charging for Marc?"

I groaned. "One thousand a month. You can ignore the rent for the apartment in that list you make. I have an arrangement with the Voter to pay the rent for it. Don't ask. I refuse to discuss the details of my arrangement with him with you."

Matz nodded. "No problem, and I wasn't going to ask. I do not pry. Okay, so I add Marc's fee, the black collar services, food, clothing, and the fee to the House, right?"

I shook my head. "An Elder covers that last item for me, so you can leave that one out of your list too."

He smiled. "No wonder you are so busy. You are nearly a kept man Maxx. Wow, you and I will have money to burn in no time with those two huge expenses off our backs. Think of all the little collars you can save. Hell man, this is more fun than I have ever had. Thank you for coming to see me this morning, brother. This has been the best day of my life."

I frowned. "I wish I could say the same, Matz. It's up there on the top of the list as one of the worst of mine. To each his own I suppose. Well, I must go. Do you need something to eat?" I started to leave but thought that since I was hungry, I hadn't eaten since leaving the hospital the day before, maybe Matz was too.

He nodded with a grin. "Fuck yes, I am. I haven't had a meal in a few days. Just a bite of Roland's sandwich earlier. Is there something in the kitchenette you don't mind me eating? I don't desire to impose."

I laughed hard as I replied, "Matz, you're paying me twenty thousand dollars to live here. How do you impose in your own apartment? That said, leave my China lamb Geraldine alone. Also, no touching my hygiene kit in the master bathroom, and stay out of my bedroom! Other than that, anything else around here is free for your use. I will bring you something to eat when I return. You want anything in particular?" The man was skinner than me, so I knew he could use the meal.

Matz rubbed his stomach with a look of appreciation. "I am not the picky type. I swear I would eat my fucking boots if I had another pair, Maxx. Whatever you can snag I am more than grateful to accept. I thank you for the mercy of it. I will be up waiting with that list and the details for your first job."

I grinned as I began to leave. "Uhm, I may be late. If you get tired the spare room is yours to do with as you, please. Oh, but no stinking it up. Yikes, that fucking apartment below was gross."

He grinned with a wicked twinkle in his eyes then said, "Oh, then for the record, don't bring home any cabbage or beans, brother. If you do, I cannot promise no smells from old Matz." I rolled my eyes as I took off out the door to the sounds of Matz laughing behind me.

I rushed upstairs to Leo's apartment door. I was sweating with worry that Malfred, Jonas, Kilian or Claus would catch me. My luck, for a change, was holding. I knocked quietly and was immediately let in by Jakob with Der Makellos hot on his heels.

Jakob led out a loud dramatic cry then rushed forward nearly frightening me to death.

My hound jumped and danced as Jakob wrapped his arms around my waist. "Oh, my God! Leo, they have everything of pleasure here in this House. Look what was just delivered to the front door, a hunk! I found him, so this beautiful man is mine. You tell Maximillian when he gets here that I found my true love and ran away with him to the beach. By the time he gets that message I will already be naked, rolling in the sand, and calling out this sexy man's name. Oh, my, what is your name, sexy man?" He blinked his long-lashed eyes at me coyly.

I opened my mouth to speak, but he interrupted. "Oh no, never mind! Say nothing at all, honey. I like it better not knowing. It can be a romantic mystery, yes? Besides, I have better things for you to use that gorgeous mouth of yours anyway. Hey, wait a minute, that scar. Holy hell, this surely can't be my little baby boy, Maxx?" He appeared stunned as he leaned in for a closer examination of my face.

I nodded as I replied, "Yes, the man you hold in your arms was once your baby boy, Jakob. Did I hear you say you desire to flee into paradise with the Mad Maxx of legend. Well, are you packed, darling? We're going to miss the plane if you don't hurry."

Jakob let out a loud squeal, squeezed me tightly then whispered into my ear, "Oh honey! I think I am in love. Tell you what, forget the beach. Let's go to the closet downstairs and I will let you punish me for being the brute to you in the past. Please, I beg of you, Maxx. Do sexy things to your aunty Jakob. You know I deserve it because I have been a bad girl to you." He pulled away from my ear and stared into my eyes panting with excitement.

I laughed and pushed him off me gently as I replied, "That is the problem Jakob. You are the one person in my life that doesn't deserve punishment of any kind. It is so good to see you. I have been meaning to look you up to thank you. I don't know what would have happened to me had it not been for looking out for me all that time during that hellish closet fiasco. I am glad to see that beating you took for me didn't scar you up. You look as beautiful as ever, my dearest friend."

Jakob snapped his fingers and cast his eyes up and down my frame with thrill as he said, "Oh sweetie. I am thinking of so many ways I would like you to show me proper gratitude right this minute. Bloody hell are you ever fine! If I would have known the little Maxx would grow into the God he has become I would have taken fifty more beatings just to have you for my own. Well, no use in lamenting the past, right? Run away with me right now, honey. I swear to you I will take care of you until we are old and gray. All I ask in return is that you use me for your pleasures till I cannot walk or remember my name."

I began howling in laughter over his bullshit as I replied, "Jakob, you know better. I am no more a top than you are. Besides, my heart already belongs to another man."

Jakob's face fell as he clicked his tongue and twirled his hair then whimpered out, "Who is the bastard? You tell me and I'll kill him. I swear to you he is the is a dead man. As for your not being a top, Maxx baby, it doesn't matter who is what in the dark, because it is all good." He giggled, while hiding his mouth with his palm.

Leo came out of the hallway and called out loudly, "My bunny, oh how wonderful! I was worried you were late, darling. I was about to send Jakob out to look for you."

Jakob swished his hips as he turned dramatically as he said feigning anger, "Leo, you bad girl! Why didn't you tell me Maxx was a fucking hottie? Are you taking up the bad habit of keeping secrets from your sister now?"

Leo chuckled as he walked over to me and grabbed me around the waist, "Not at all, Jakob. I didn't tell you because I was keeping this beauty hidden for my own uses." He reached up and snatched my hair as he forced a deep passionate kiss on my mouth.

Jakob stomped his foot and hissed out, "Leo, you bitch! You are playing dirty! That boy was up for grabs, and you snatched him. You didn't even give me a chance. Damn you. Hell, you are an unfair old Queen. Can't you understand your time is up? Get off the throne, Goddammit! Let us young, gorgeous princesses have our day." He flounced, then crossed his arms.

Leo chuckled as he stroked my cheek and looked deep into my eyes as he cooed out, "Stop pouting, Jakob. Mad Maxx was mine long before you even knew he existed. I steal nothing from you but this young man sure is a thief himself. I have been missing my heart for the last seven years. He keeps it in his back pocket you know." I stifled my own giggling at Jakob and Leo's funny dramatics.

Then I leaned down and kissed, and nuzzled Leo's neck causing him to shudder with thrill and Jakob to nearly pass out in shock as I mumbled out, "I will never return it to you, Leo. Call the Guard if you like but I will defend my prize to the death. It belongs to me for all time."

Leo swooned, then grabbed his chest with much drama as he called out loudly, "Jakob, call the paramedics! Tell them to bring two or three ambulances and announce over the loudspeakers I'm about to die of thrill. Hurry up Goddammit. I need witnesses to my good fortune."

Jakob popped his tongue and swished to the sofa sitting down with a look of indignation. "Lucky bitch. I hate you Leo. Maxx honey, when that old Queen retires to the back room fearful of her mirror, you come find your

Auntie Jakob. I will attend to you the way a stallion of your caliber deserves." He snorted.

Leo grinned with much humor shooting a look at the fuming Jakob then back to me with seriousness. "Well, Christian, what did you find out? Was Peter rough on you? Did you tell Jonas to go to hell? Come on. The suspense is killing me."

I groaned. "Leo today didn't go as I had hoped. I am most happy to tell you about it but two things first please. And should we be discussing this with company present?" I shot a look of fear at Jakob.

Leo nodded. "It is okay, honey. You can talk in front of Jakob. He is family now and will keep our confidence in all matters. In fact, he is here to teach you how to pull off a convincing act."

I narrowed my eyes in confusion. "Act? I don't understand."

Leo frowned. "You will never pull off being a bottom without being more, uhm, feminine? I mean the heterosexuals as well as Jonas and Peter think if you are the getting penetrated that means you should act, well, you know, like Jakob." He shot a nervous look at the Queen.

Jakob looked up from his pout. "What is that supposed to mean, Leo? I don't act like a female. There is just too much of Jakob for either gender. I am the best of both worlds. They are all jealous is all."

Leo rolled his eyes. "Yeah, you keep telling yourself that girlfriend and maybe one day it will be the truth. Anyway, Jakob has agreed to help you learn to behave more as expected, and then he and I will "Out" you to the homosexual sect in the House. When the boys accept you as one of our own, then Jonas and Peter will have no choice but to relent their beliefs that you are straight."

I shook my head. "Leo, I am not straight. I thought we established that already or was that someone else in your bed sending me into ecstasy last night?"

Jakob gasped and grabbed his chest. "Leo, oh, I really hate you now! Is what Maxx said true?"

Leo growled. "What the hell, Jakob? Why do you care who I sleep with?"

Jakob snapped and crossed his arms. "I don't, but I am pissed you gave me no details about it! Girl, what is wrong with you?"

I giggled at that. "Uhm, Leo, I am okay with you telling Jakob about today, but two things first please."

Leo tore his irritated look away from Jakob. "Oh, yeah. Sorry honey, what is it that you need?"

I winced. "Do you have any witch hazel I can borrow, and can we go get that dinner? I am starving."

Leo frowned. "Oh, my goodness. Yes, I have plenty in the bathroom I keep just in case you ever need it. I suppose I should have stopped after the third time last night. I apologize Christian, but you were so fucking sexy. I never could stop myself when you do that thing with your tongue. Oh shit, I better stop speaking of that before I get worked up again. Of course, we can leave for the Great Hall this minute. I told you twenty-five calories was not enough. You cannot stay healthy if I am the only thing you put in your stomach."

Jakob jumped up and snapped, popped and yelled out, "Damn you! That is enough, Leo. Now you are just bragging. Can we go to dinner or do you wish to keep rubbing this love affair in my face."

My eyes filled with wickedness. "Oh no, Jakob, Leo rubs it in mine, often and with vigor. Oh, and Jakob, Leo isn't a braggart. He is the fucking sexual dynamo. I do believe I requested witch hazel, or did you miss that when you eavesdropped. You know when you stick your nose where it doesn't belong you shouldn't bitch when it gets swatted."

Leo almost choked from his laugher as Jakob shot me an evil smile then said, "Oh honey. You my beautiful boy are a natural kitty and what sharp claws you have. Leo, teaching this hunk of perfect man is going to be a breeze. He is right you know. Maxx is maybe not a bottom, nor pure homosexual, but he sure as shit isn't completely straight."

I shook my head. "I pray to God that I am not. Life will be much harder than it needs be if I am Jakob."

Leo furrowed his brow. "Wait, that witch hazel you need isn't about last night, is it? Oh hell, come on sister Jakob. Let's get this growing boy down to supper. Something tells me I am going to need a drink before Christian Axel tells me some unwelcome news."

We started to head out the door, but Leo grabbed my and Jakob's arms before we went out. "Wait you two. The others cannot suspect Christian Axel and I are lovers, Jakob. For tonight, you need to play he is with you." He pulled Jakob's arm through my own.

Jakob fawned. "Ah. well now this is better. I guess if you insist that I hold your pretty man's hand in public, I will suffer the indignity of it best that I can." He looked at me with an expression of thrill in his eyes and a cat smile.

Leo snorted when he saw Jakob's joy at his getting to play my dinner date. "I am loaning him to you, Jakob. You watch yourself. I expect my boy back the second dinner is over unmolested. I find any fucking pink lip gloss anywhere on him but his face, I will chop off the Queen's head, and I don't mean the pin sized one on her shoulder's either. You got that."

Jakob made a fish face of humor as he leaned into me whispering loudly, "You pay the old hag no mind, Maxx. It is just menopause. You know they get so moody at that age, right?"

I stifled a giggle as the three of us hurried down the stairs headed for the Great Hall, Jakob on my arm and Leo following close behind bitching about that teasing statement the whole way.

The black collar attendant ushered us to a table in the far back. I pulled out the chair for Jakob that sat down. He was making a loud demonstration of "how special" he felt to be treated like the "proper lady" that he always had been. I chuckled at him as I sat down next to him.

He looked me up and down then leaned closer. "Maxx, if you are going to play a proper bottom in the future you will be the one that waits for the chair to be pulled out, ja? Remember, you are the female in the same gendered relationship. You need not be overly aggressive in your demonstrations of the expected femininity as I tend to be, but you do need to curb your overt manliness. You walk like you are about to kick everyone's ass, and constantly glare like the angry bear. You must try to wiggle those beautiful hips of yours, and flirt with any male you encounter by behaving coy. When you laugh cover your mouth with your hand like this." He put his fingers to his mouth and faked a giggle while dropping his eyes coyly.

I nodded with some irritation at that bullshit. "Leo, is this really necessary? I mean, don't get me wrong, I desire to fool Peter and the Vampire but uhm, no offense brother Jakob, I don't desire to appear a silly Queen."

Jakob reached out and lightly slapped my shoulder while Leo choked on his wine laughing. "You stop that Maxx. I am not silly appearing. Am I?" He looked at Leo that was casting his eyes to the table trying to avoid his gaze.

I narrowed my eyes., "No you are not Jakob. With you it works somehow but look at me. I am the fucking brute. If I behaved like a swishy queen then I would look like a fool. I am not petite and pretty like you are Jakob."

Jakobs eyes lit up with joy and he smiled brightly as he blew a kiss at me. "Ah, you lovely boy. Did you hear that, Leo? Maxx thinks me skinny and attractive. From your mouth to God's ears lover. You are too kind. Thank you for the sweet words but you need not over do the acting Maxx. I merely say that as a bottom you are too intimidating. How the hell do you expect to capture a boyfriend acting like the cruel bastard? No man would believe that you would be the cuddling type, ja?"

I laughed out loud at that. "Jakob, my dearest friend, you are way off base there. As it is I already have a boyfriend and I got him without changing a fucking thing about this idiot."

Jakob gasped in shock as Leo nearly fell face first into the table. "Christian? What the hell? You have found a boyfriend? Oh, you are funning these two queens, ja? What a comic he is, Jakob. I tell you I love this boy's humor almost as much as his wicked little smiles."

Leo took a drink of his wine as I took a deep breath to brace myself to break the news of my foul day. "Leo, my love, I am not funning. Matz has already moved in the

236

apartment as we speak." I blew out my breath waiting for the fallout from that admission.

Leo shook his head wildly. "No, Christian you cannot use Matz as the cover. Are you insane? Oh, dear don't answer that. You made a mistake with this choice. You need to throw this man out and allow Jakob and me to find you the right male for such an important fake out. Matz, well my Liebling, he is all wrong for you."

Jakob nodded with vigor. "Ah, I must agree with Leo on this one Maxx. Matz is the broke cocksucker and ugly to boot. No one will believe a beauty like you would ever bother with such a low-class first floor Dominant. No, you are fourth floor Priceless. You need the prince, not the frog."

I frowned at that. "That is not fair to Matz, Jakob. You don't even know the man. There is more to a heart then wealth and looks."

Leo growled out. "Jakob and I most certainly do know this bastard. It is you that is the one with no knowledge of who you are fooling around with, my bunny. That man is crude, poor, bad mannered and worst still, the fucking bottom feeder criminal in a House of monsters. You are playing with fire to even speak with that fucker much less to have him close to you. Turn your back and he will steal your wallet. Go to sleep with him around and you will find yourself ravaged in the worst of ways. Get him the hell out of your House and be shut of him before he hurts you bad

Christian. If Matz has set his sights on you only dreadful things can be on his mind."

I gulp down my terror at Leo's words. "Uhm, you are wrong Leo. I appreciate what you say, but I swear I will be careful with this man. He and I have no interest in each other. He agreed to split the cost of the apartment and play the role I ask of him and keep his mouth shut. He will not get the chance to abuse me, that I can swear to you."

Jakob shot Leo a look of fear. "Oh, my God Leo, Matz already has manipulated the boy into ignoring the obvious. Maxx, listen to your Aunty Jakob, this man is bad news. He runs with a pack of young wolves. You are innocent of such things. Leo and I are trying to protect you from the worst of the worst this House has to offer. Listen to our good advice. You tell Matz to go back to that first-floor shack of his and let you be. Besides, you know it is forbidden to date below your level."

I nodded. "Yes, I do Jakob, but Matz is only on the first floor due to poverty. I already worked all that out. He is High born like me. I can argue that fact with Gretta if she raises hell. Technically he is not below my level."

Leo sighed loudly and took another drink. "Christian Axel, you know we love you, but you are making a grievous error in your associations. I fear if you hang out with Matz and his hideous friends you will find yourself in trouble that will haunt you for all your days. If he has targeted, you it can only mean big trouble. That man doesn't like you for no reason. What has he told you? That he can support you with his illegal gambling tables? Did he promise that he and his brutes can protect you from those looking for Priceless blood? How much is he charging you for the pleasure of his company?"

I looked at the table realizing that Matz had indeed paired up with me for a shady reason, but I couldn't tell Leo. I was the one engaging in the criminality and Matz was only the catalyst. I looked back up at my lover and without blinking, lied.

"Leo, my love, I did make a deal with Matz as you suspect. He gets to have the pleasure of a fourth-floor view for the price of playing the good boyfriend in public. I further sweetened the deal by adding that I will turn a blind eye to his seedy lifestyle as long as he keeps my confidence and all of his dealings out of the apartment. I know you both mean well and worry that I am the lamb ready for slaughter. However, I can look out for myself. This situation with Matz is temporary and he knows that. It is only until I can do better. I had no choice but to move quickly. The Vampire and Kilian, they are blackmailing me into their unholy bed. I already endured things so foul I wish to not discuss them even with the Devil. I offered this deal to Matz not the other way around. Please, understand I needed help fast. I know what I am doing I swear it."

Leo and Jakob frowned as Leo took another drink casting his eyes to the table with solemness. "So, am I to understand that Jonas and Kilian, they used you for their, uhm, fun?"

I winced. "Yes they did, Leo. I didn't have a choice. They told me that if I don't do as I am told then Kilian will call Heslach. Jonas and that snake have taken me as their unwilling hostage. That is why I needed that witch hazel. Peter I was able to deflect for a moment, though he will soon find a way around to hijack my flesh too. This nightmare is never going to end Leo. Matz was willing and I cannot wait till I learn enough to be the fake bottom man to find a boyfriend to tool around with in public. If you knew what those two fiends did to me today, then you would realize Matz is a fucking saint compared to what I must deal with every day from this moment till I get out of here and go to college."

Leo nodded while Jakob reached out with a look of pity to pat my hand. "Okay. my bunny. I do understand. I recall how horrible Jonas can be. I apologize for chastising you. You are the Dominant now so really doesn't matter what I say, you will do as you decide anyway."

Jakob sighed. "Look Leo I was with Kilian for a decade. I don't know how bad Jonas can be in the bedroom, but that ex of my can be a nasty beast himself. I can only imagine what you are suffering Maxx. That said, I am with Leo. If this toad Matz is your temporary solution, then so be it. Just make sure to watch him closely. If he gives you any trouble you come to us right away. You can also tell him that if he gets out of the way with you that Leo, Rolf, Byron, Friedrick and I will visit him and his shady body with our fists. He doesn't want to fool around with our brother. It would not go well for him."

I nodded, still looking at the table feeling shameful for both that scene in the Vampire's bedroom and my truthful association with Matz. "Ja, I hear you Jakob. I thank you for the mercy of it, but I will be okay. I am capable on my own of dealing with the problems in my life. However, if either of you could find it in your heart to offer me a meal, I would be indebted to you. Oh wait, I almost forgot."

I reached into my pocket and pulled out that hundred-dollar bill then dropped it in Leo's empty plate with a bitter smile. "This is payback for the fifty I borrowed this morning. I don't know how much a meal costs but if you take this and help me, I would like to have dinner and order one to take home for tomorrow?"

Leo gasped as he looked at the bill and shot a look of surprise at Jakob. "My bunny, how did you get this money? That is a lot to have acquired in only one day."

I shook my head. "Don't ask me that, Leo. Never ask me again about how I pay for anything. I do have a guardian, ja? I suppose that you didn't consider if I starve then I cannot be the plaything of the Vampire." I lied again.

Leo scoffed then leaned back in his chair while Jakob winced. "Oh, my Liebling, this is so horrible. I wish there was, oh God I feel so fucking helpless." He covered his face appearing deeply bothered by my statements.

I shrugged. "This is not your fault, my heart. Now can I purchase that meal and another for that amount, or not?"

Jakob nodded as he patted my hand again. "Honey, you can buy five meals with that much. Order what you like. This meal is on your Auntie. Let's drop this unpleasant discussion. We can eat, enjoy the company, and practice your acting. I for one would like to see you rooming with the honest High born as soon as possible. I have already arranged to "Out" you by the end of next week. We have a lot of work to do, and you have plenty of time to regret your poor lot later. You must learn to grab the little kindnesses and mercies whenever you can, right?"

I smiled with much bitterness. "Jakob, that my love, I am the expert at. I am ready to order and more than a little grateful for your picking up the tab. I thank you for all you have done and will do for me. I hope to repay the favor one day."

Jakob chuckled. "Well, I will be happy to take it out in trade. The second the old biddy goes to bed tonight meet me in some dark corner and I will let you have your way with me. I swear I tell no one of the naughty things you do to Jakob, not ever." He winked at me with a playful smile.

Leo laughed. "When this old biddy goes to bed Jakob, that boy will be cuddled in his loving arms. There will be no silence when I am with him later. I can assure you the whole fucking House will hear Leo praising the Gods of his luck and deepest joy."

Jakob snorted while I laughed out loud and shot a flirty look at my beautiful lover and nodded that I agreed with him. There would be excited noises in his bed that night if I had my way about it.

Understand I was a sixteen-year-old at that time. I had never had anyone willing to help me find my pleasures to that point in my shitty life. Any thrills I got were found with my own hands with that one exception of Annette many years before.

Leo had no problem aiding in the employment of my orgasm without the penetration. He was more than happy to stimulate me orally and manually. He was still the top, you know.

Despite my guilt at intending to play the prostitute, and that disgusting situation earlier that day with the Vampire and snake, I was willing to find my healthy lusts attended to with vigor by my lover Leo anytime he was ready to do me the favor of it.

I had told Jakob I understood how to embrace the small mercies and tiny kindness's where I could. Leo's adoration and affection was proof of that in every way. He was my only permitted outlet for any kind of touching of worth and to be honest, the only man I ever could gain erection with. Like any normal horny teenaged boy, I was a slave to my baser urges.

It was quite simple, Leo was the one that made me feel good in every way from companionship, Der Makellos and him, to sex. That meant he was all I wanted day and night. Believe me when I say I was eager to fill my stomach to the hilt with that meal in the Great Hall and get to his bedroom for the forbidden raptures only Leo could give me. Until I met my Frau that is.

You see, men are super easy to keep contented, Meine Liebe. Keep them fed and fucked and they will follow you around like a puppy does its mother. I am no exception to that rule. You remember what I just said, and you can be assured I will be your helpless plaything for all your days. I already am wrapped around your little fingers more than you know. He hugged me tightly while chuckling.

Anyway, the rest of the dinner Jakob had me mimic his feminine and over the top behaviors. He corrected when I forgot to engage in the snap or popping of my tongue. He insisted I overreacted to almost everything from the display of food on my plate to a favored song when it came over the speakers.

I found the whole thing pretty stupid, but I dared not say that. I knew Jakob, for whatever reason, cared for me deeply. He had protected me when I was helpless, and thanks to his sacrifice I was able to break my metal. If he had asked me to walk through the Great Hall holding my cock singing "God save the Queen" I would have done it without quarrel if such a thing made him happy.

Truth is I adore Jakob. I may love Leo as my truthful lover, but I care for Jakob as if he were my own brother. Not since Ryker had I ever known such a deep affection for another human being. In my dark world Jakob is the light to which I flutter and find my warmth from the cold brutal world. There is nothing I wouldn't do for the man. All he has to do is ask me. Okay, except meet him in that dark corner to fuck him. I learned my lesson with your brother Ryker. I refuse to fuck a brother ever again. You will meet him one day soon, my Liebe. He swears that when the others come to do the collar selection, he will be with them.

I shuttered. "Wait Master. I don't go to the House for my Dominance testing and selection. They are coming here to this horrible place. All of them? Is Debbie going to let them?"

Master Maxx patted my head. "Not all of them my Liebe. Just the Voters, Elders and maybe Jakob. If it all stays as it has for the last many years it will be the Voters Rolf, Friedrick, Byron, Lukas, Gretta, and of course Peter. The Elders will also come which are Malfred, Justus, Leo, Cora, the horrid Kilian and the Vampire Jonas. Jakob swears he will come meet you too though he is not from either group mentioned. You are a special case so they will break the rules and test you here. Debbie won't interfere because if you don't go through this selection process, she will not be paid by your Uncle Malfred for your collar. There is no reason to fret about this. We are still four to five years from that and who knows, maybe that bat will fall down the stairs and his snake will follow him to hell, ja?" He giggled while I sighed and tried not to worry about it. Hell, maybe I wouldn't survive myself given the deplorable circumstances I was forced to live in.

I then noticed something and took a chance at asking. "Who is Lukas and Justus, Master? Are they bad too like

Kilian and Jonas?" He swatted me causing me to groan at my stupid mistake.

Master Maxx growled out. "Damn it, Meine Liebe. I am getting to them. They are the last two raised in the House, so you never heard of them because they don't matter to the story yet. Do you wish to start that jumping the gun shit again? I hope not. I am running out of space on your thighs to thud you. Soon I will move to the pretty little bottom of yours. I hate to look at the bruises, but you keep testing me with such insolence I will be forced to see black and blue rather than that gorgeous pink of your flesh when we make love. You be still and listen or pay the price for it."

I nodded. "I apologize, Master. Thank you for the correction of my errors. I am most grateful for it."

He laughed. "You are getting good at stroking your Master with that silver tongue of yours in every way possible. At this rate, I will have the truthful Priceless pleasure submissive before this year is finished. I am impressed with your intelligence and quick learning, but if you don't start curbing that impulsivity no matter how smart you are, the Elders and Voters will rip you apart. You have two ears and one mouth for a fucking reason, Meine Liebe. That natural design is for your defense in the brutal world looking to kill you. As the potential prey of the bigger animals, you are supposed to hear everything possible about your situation before you go letting the predator know of your weak position by telling them you know nothing. You must learn to be still, focus on the

246

*information grants, and above all, think before you speak.
If you fail to gain control of that need within to jump ahead
of the game without mastering the long path you took to get
there, well my dear, you will not survive the difficult
existence ahead. Neither will you, my Frau. I love you and
am no longer willing to go on without you by my side. We
are one. Where you go, Christian Axel will be there for all
our lives. We do this together or not at all. Okay, on with
the story, ja."*

*I nodded, sniffing back my tears because I knew he was
right to be angry. Like it or not, I needed to calm down and
suffer the entire process of my training in the order he
guides me. There are no short cuts in life.*

*His story itself was a lesson in that most important
fact. My constant need to know everything before it became
a part of the tale was getting me nothing but welted thighs
and slowing him down in teaching me the very things I was
eager to understand.*

*At last, I realized that my trainer Master Maxx never
did or said anything without a good reason. No matter
what anyone thinks of the unorthodox ways he went about
saving me from my nightmare life, if one can believe I was
truly rescued at all, no one could have been a better
teacher, kinder lover or more magnificent friend. Christian
Axel, also known as Master Mad Maxx the Brutal, is a lot
of things but above it all he is a genius in the game of
survival.*

I ordered Matz a large meal, pretending it was for me of course, and the second it was delivered we all went back to Leo's apartment. Jakob kissed me and then said goodbye to Leo after making many teasing complaints that the Elder was the stingy one to not even offer to share in his good fortune by allowing him to "borrow" me for the night.

He left us both laughing from his over-the-top histrionics with a promise to be at dinner the very next night for more of my lessons designed to make me the "queen." I petted the thrilled Der Makellos as Leo let him out and then locked the door.

I slipped up behind him as his back was turned. I waited till he faced me then plowed him into the door with lustful kissing and fondling. Leo let out a yelp but melted beneath my rough but careful manhandling of his parts.

Whenever he tried to pull himself forward, I would increase the pressure pinning him helplessly to the spot. He panted with excitement as I ripped his button up shirt open with a growl into his kissing mouth.

Leo whimpered as I dropped to his exposed chest lavishing him with my aggressive adoration of his naked flesh, "God damn, Christian. What the hell are you doing? I thought you would need a rest after what you told Jakob and me about earlier today."

I didn't stop my nipping and kissing as I responded, "I think you misunderstood, Leo. That was merely sex. That meant nothing to me. What I desire is that my lover take me back to his bed and do the things to me that Jakob wishes I would do to him. You can do this willingly or I will torture you until you relent to my demands."

Leo gasped with a loud moan of pleasure. "Ah, my bunny. I think you will need to keep torturing me for a moment. I obviously didn't learn my lesson when you told me that I was not to question your choices. I submit to your punishment without quarrel. Oh, God damn, I am not going to make it to the fucking bedroom if you do that one more time. Hell boy, where the fuck did you learn to do that. I want to thank that sonofabitch for granting me the fucking mercy of it."

I had dropped to my knees while he was begging for punishment and, well, was working him over with my oral talents. *Master Maxx laughed as did I, because I knew exactly what he did to set Leo to near orgasm so quickly. After all he was my trainer in the special services.*

Well, we didn't make it to the bedroom. I did do it again, and Leo became unglued. Before I could even try to run, he grabbed me by the arms and forced me to my face into the door. I laughed loudly with humor as he ripped at my breeches wildly.

He yelled out, barely able to breath from his overzealous interests. "You are driving me fucking crazy, Christian. You make me go stupid with passion." He spit loudly without bothering with any lube, then took me with a single brutal thrust.

I wailed then groaned out. "I am giving you the romance you always wanted Leo and you are giving me everything I deserve in return for it." I moaned loudly, it was a little painful I admit it, as he fucked me without holding any of his strength back like he always had in the past.

Leo reached his orgasm relatively quickly thanks to his unhinged intercourse with me. He barely had yelled out in his apex when he spun me around and without hesitation attacked my lips with his strong kissing. Then he dropped to his knees and began employing his own most skillful oral adorations to my manhood.

Jakob may have bought our dinner, but I gave Leo his desert. It felt as if I came harder than I ever had in my life. Even Leo was impressed at the viralness of that particular release. I was barely able to catch my breath as he returned to his feet offering many praises for my most copious payment for his sexual labors.

I will not bore you with the details of the next two hours I spent in the arms of my beloved Leo. I of course gave him bath service and he repaid me with his version using that most talented tongue of his. Once we both had found ourselves sated, for a little while anyway, to gluttony levels he had me tell him in detail of the horrors I encountered that day.

I was mostly honest with him. I left out all the truths of Matz, my sorry lot as the future prostitute, and the purchase of Marc of course. Instead, I told him I had gone to see Karsten because I had been told that she had a job she was willing to hire me for. Leo was thrilled to hear that I would be doing odd jobs for that first floor Mistress. Which I hoped was a clever enough lie to hide the shameful truth of where my money was coming from, well when I started to make any if I did.

Honestly by this time I was starting to get the cold feet about taking that job as Matz stable whore. When I finally slipped out of Leo's apartment around one in the morning to sneak back home, I had decided to forget the whole idea. I had talked myself into believing there had to be another more honorable way to earn a living. I went into my apartment resolved to tell Matz to hit the bricks. I wasn't going to have sex with married secret bisexuals for money and that was final.

I found, to my surprise, Matz sitting on the couch with a pair of glasses on looking over papers in his hands with an expression of seriousness. There were a bunch of notes scattered about the coffee table. I raised my eyebrows and walked over takin a seat across from him on the small loveseat wondering what the hell this shit was all about.

Matz dropped his chin and looked at me over his glasses. "Home pretty late, Maxx. Must have had a fun time I suppose. You sleepy or do you have time to go over these figures with me?"

I snorted as I handed him the bag in my hands. "Huh? What figures, Matz? Here I brought you dinner."

Matz smiled with happiness. "Shit! You are a fucking angel indeed." He ripped into the sack of food and suddenly his face fell with shock.

I frowned. "I apologize Matz if you don't like the wiener schnitzel and kraut. I also put some of that chocolate cake in there in case you wanted something sweet. I didn't know what you would like. I will try harder next time, okay?"

He shot a look of confusion at me. "No, Maxx. This is holy shit! I cannot believe you managed to bring me my favorite meal in the whole world. I haven't been able to afford such a fine meal in five years since I left home. You are good to me. I swear I thought I couldn't love you more, then you found a way to win my heart even more. Thank you, brother. You are the best friend I ever have had." He pulled out the meal and began to tear into it with his bare hands.

I groaned. "Did you leave your manners at home when you left Matz? Next time, use a fucking plate and utensils, ja? There are plenty of both in the kitchenette. Now, what is this shit you have strewn across the table? You are a one-man wrecking ball, I swear to God."

Matz laughed as he wiped his hands on his dirty shirt, yuck. "You sure you are not homosexual, Maxx? I swear only the gay man is so fucking fussy about a clean House and clothing. You do wear makeup too. I am gay as they come and even, I am not so fucking prissy as you are."

I shrugged. "Tonight, I was told I am too intimidating to be viewed as gay. I am having to be trained to behave like a fucking bottom if you can believe that. The bottom is where Mad Maxx seems to live. Regardless of that, what the fuck Matz. What is with the papers? What are all these numbers about?"

He nodded while speaking with his mouth full, again yuck. "Uhm, oh yeah. Okay these are the expenses I worked out for the apartment here, you know only the basics for the two of us, and what you would need to purchase up to ten more silver trainees with care under Karsten. This list is how many clients I managed to line up for the next three months, what days they can get a night free to complete the deal and what they have agreed to pay to get their thrills. I made each man give description of what he expects of you for his payment, which is recorded next to their names. Ja, that is on the paper on your left, you see. That last paper you hold is a confidentiality contract I will make all of them sign before they get the services, and they must pay me up front or no deal."

I looked at the huge amount of money that came at the bottom line on his expenses list. I was starting to panic until I looked to see that by only working as the prostitute for three days a week, I could easily pay for them all. I would even have money left over to save for my future wife and cottage in the green fields. That made me rethink my plan to tell Matz I was backing out.

There was no fucking way I could cover expenses unless I sucked cock and endured the penetration sex for the amounts these idiots were willing to pay. I realized they were willing to part with high amounts not only because I was the highly trained Priceless catamite of legend, but for my and Matz's silence regarding their unnatural interests and adulterous intentions with me behind closed doors.

I smiled as I understood at last that for only the cost of my dignity and liberal use of the witch hazel, I could keep Matz, Marc, me and ten more silvers well cared for. At least, until I got my doctors license and could go back to legitimate, honorable labor.

I was feeling less unsure of my decision to go back to my knees when I picked up the list of client's names and their requested dark desires. I immediately let out a wail as I saw the first name on the list was Osvin. I groaned with horror when I saw that he was followed by that horrible Fritz.

If that was not bad enough, a name I had hoped to never meet in person anywhere much less alone for sex. The third customer's name was Justus. You see that fellow is Xavier's son and the only living family member from that horrible bloodline that I was aware of at the time.

I stared at Matz full on shock. He flashed me smiled with a look of adoration as he kept on munching down his dinner.

I couldn't believe my bad luck. Maybe Jakob and Leo were right. Matz was surely leading me like the lamb to be slaughtered. I wondered if he was indeed intending to make me into his next meal of wiener schnitzel. There was no longer any doubt, I was in way over my head. This time there would be no one to rescue me from drowning in the deep end of that pool the normals call reality.

Chapter 6: Blocked

I glared at Matz. "Are you trying to get me killed brother? What the hell, man."

He near choked on his kraut. "What? Huh? I don't know what you mean, Maxx. I do not desire your death. How did you come up with such an idea." He appeared completely surprised and dumbfounded by my statement.

I snorted. "This list Matz. Look here. More than half these names are brutes I have had the most unfortunate encounters with already. I am not looking for more trouble from them. This fellow Justus, I killed that man's brother, Matz. You think he will not be looking for vengeance? I know we established you are stupid, but you must believe me the fucking idiot if you think I am going to let Justus fuck me much less be anywhere alone with that fiend." I threw the list at him with a growl.

Matz watched the paper land on the coffee table then showed me a look of disbelief. "Maxx? Are you being truthful or is this an attempt to haggle down that ten percent I ask for my part in this business?"

I rolled my eyes scoffed then crossed my arms. "Matz, you are not listening to me. You can take one hundred percent of the profits from this venture for all I care. I promise you will earn every penny of it. That is because you will be the one sucking the cock and taking it up the tail pipe with these monsters, not Mad Maxx."

Matz snorted. "Do you think I wouldn't if these motherfuckers would pay me the amounts they are offering for your sweet ass? Hell Maxx, if only I were so fucking lucky. No one would pay me the lint from their coat pocket to suck their cock. Shit, likely I'd be the one owing them for the act.

I laughed full of sarcasm. "You say that even knowing the names on that paper? Holy hell, Matz. Have you never met these fuckers? I have."

Matz sat forward putting his bag of food at his feet, then took a deep breath and looked at me with seriousness. "I can certainly understand you not wishing to service many if not all of these fellows on that list. For starters you claim to be straight. Then to add to that insult, I must agree some are so foul not even their own Frau want to fuck them. However, that is why they are on that list, fool. You are the freed Priceless pleasure submissive. There is this rumor that only the Priceless can give the unlovable the experience of being the coveted. Is that a lie? Were you not trained to endure any foul request? You need not answer that, I know you were. If you are to do this job and take on the responsibilities of those little simple silvers like Marc, you cannot be so fucking picky. If the man is desirable, then why the fuck would he pay for it. He won't have to resort to the whore now, would he?"

I groaned as I leaned back realizing that Matz words were wise and sadly truthful. "Okay, you have a point, and I cannot argue it. I will do my best to deal with the disgusting beasts on this list with one exception. Justus, not that man. You call him back and tell him no deal. That cocksucker is dangerous. He is looking for trouble, Matz. Get rid of him and in the future run the names past me before you go calling the sonofabitch to offer a damned thing."

Matz chuckled, then shook his head with an expression of irritation. "Do you know what, Maxx? I have been told by many that your skills as the artist are the best in this fucking House of pleasure. I have noticed, like everyone else in this criminals' nest, that more than a few powerful men have died trying to taste or hold your slick metal. They risked it all just to have a moment to enjoy your talents. I have scars from stupidly trying to steal such a thrill and tonight, with much despair I assure you, gave up my only legitimate chance to finally know of such a luxury. The reason I bring all that up is become there was one that didn't live long to tell the tale of his good fortune. The mighty Xavier, the most notorious murderer and Head of the House that ever lived. That man has a son that had to live his entire life under the huge shadow of that black hearted monster. Why do you find it so disturbing that he would jump at the chance to engage with the Priceless that ended that monster's reign while only the youngster of twelve? You used only your incredible special services skills to take down the man no one could touch for over fifty years. It is only natural that Justus desires to prove himself stronger by surviving what his demonic brother could not. You fear that man will seek revenge for your killing Xavier with your intercourse? Maxx, that is not only silly, but also paranoid."

I shot a look of caution at Matz. "Brother, you call me paranoid ever again, you will be more than a little sorry for it. You can call me an idiot, whore, cocksucker, or even the motherfucker. I will agree with you on those. However, if I hear words like crazy, insane, paranoid, mentally ill or even eccentric hurled at me by that nasty mouth of yours, I swear I will show you to the first-floor Priceless style. You hear me?"

Matz gasped, then nodded, appearing afraid. "Oh, uhm, I apologize Maxx. I swear I forgot."

I narrowed my eyes. "Huh? Forgot what?

Matz looked at his shoes. "I forgot that day me and the boys grabbed you downstairs, you started plowing your head into the wall while screaming at people that were not there. You seem so well put together these days I suppose it slipped my mind that you are the schizo…" His voice trailed off when he looked up and saw me preparing to pounce on him with fire in my gaze.

"You forgot I am what? Why are you hesitating? Go ahead and finish that thought. I am dying to know what you think of my mental health, Doctor Matz. Finish that word and I will show you that I am not broken with reality, but all your bones will be, broken that is." I smiled at him with viciousness in my expression.

Matz shook his head slowly. "Uhm, no, I do not play into rumors, Maxx. Well not this one anyway. I am done with this conversation, and you will never get any bullshit about it from Matz anyway.

Matz cleared his throat and looked away quickly. "We were arguing about Justus and that list I seem to recall. I am your booking agent, Maxx. If you have an issue with a client on the list, then you come to me and say so. I cannot nor will I ever make you service anyone paid or not. You do not work for me; I work for you. You are the boss. If you say Justus is an issue, I get rid of him. Any other names you want erased, fine. Mark them out and I will make some excuses to them. I merely wanted to point out that until you get a name for yourself through the underground our clientele will be limited. Every name you cross out without them proving they were a problem is not only less free lip service but also causes us to look like the untrustworthy. In this exceedingly small niche market that will end your career before it ever begins. Marc is not the only one that will suffer if we fail Maxx. You won't be able to give a blow job away if these skittish married men find reason to fear our word is not worth the paper they sign their promises of our silence in this delicate matter. You think about that before you demand I recant my offers to anyone."

I fell back onto the loveseat rubbing my head. "Christ, Matz. If I am right about Justus or any of these fuckers then Marc won't matter to the dead Mad Maxx. You say I must get them to trust us, but where is my protection if they are not the honorable ones? This is such a fucking mess."

Matz sighed. "Yes, I thought of that too Maxx. I was going to bring it up later after you got through the first couple times you know. I didn't want to overwhelm you, but this is a dangerous business, like most of the kinds that are done behind closed doors. Like my gambling tables, ja? I have the same problems you will have Maxx. An angry wealthy loser of many deutschmarks is just as likely to break my legs as I am theirs. I am not a big fella and while you are the brute, no man is strong enough if the pissed client brings friends to back him up. That is why I hired Roland, Magnas, and Valitin to aid me as the visible muscle behind the skinny Matz."

I uncovered my forehead and glared at Matz. "Oh, hell Matz, are you suggesting I pay your posse of wolves to keep an eye on the fucking brothel door? What the hell will those criminals charge? Another ten percent a piece maybe? At this rate I may as well line up the House and have them pay the four of you for the pleasure of fucking me. I will take the pennies that fall from your pockets to buy the crumbs that the mouse doesn't bother with."

Matz laughed out loud. "God damned you are funny Maxx. The boys will not charge but another ten percent, period. They can share it amongst themselves as they do for my business. Shit, they will be thrilled to have the extra cash. If you paid them five dollars to beat the fuck out of a nun, they are so poor they would do it no questions asked. I mean I haven't asked them, but I know those boys. They need the money. I wouldn't even have to tell them what is going on. They would guard the doors or come running with only the call if you paid them an honest wage. Ten percent is more than fair for protection."

I gasped. "Are you funning me? Only ten percent for three? They are that impoverished? Am I to assume you haven't told them of any of this business yet? I guess I thought you already did."

Matz nodded, still smiling. "I told you Maxx, you are the lucky one. There are no legitimate jobs in this House for the Dominant, Yet everything costs for us. With all the black collars working for less than standard pay and front-loading payout for silvers (that means one lump sum payment and only maintenance fees for something) even if we could work, you and I couldn't survive on the income. Before you came to see me this morning, I was sitting around realizing that soon I would be kicked out, along with the other three I told you about. We have hung on by our toes for four long years. Maxx the four of us were stupid sixteen-year-olds when we come here. None of us realized the realities of the House expenses. Stupid, young, and inexperience has made me and my brothers bitter old men at only twenty. I spoke with Roland only yesterday with the understanding that by the winter holidays we would all be in the outside world homeless, unemployed, and living on the violent streets without a future, hope or a chance to make it to thirty."

I narrowed my eyes at that. "You don't think you would find employment outside these walls?"

He shook his head. "There is a terrible recession going on Maxx. There is heavy poverty in the lower classes even in the powerful United States as we speak. In our country, the horror is so bad that the four of us can expect to die of disease, go to prison for stealing to eat, or be killed by some other desperate homeless person. This House was our only chance. None of us could afford school to better our lot. No one taught us a trade and we are without the right connections to get into such a luxury still. Crime is our only option or death. I wanted to live without doing too much harm. Fleecing the ultra-wealthy seemed like a less than dishonest way to survive. However, that is playing out rapidly. We were all bracing ourselves for the inevitable, then the hand of God knocked on my door this morning and here we are. You offer me a second chance. Maybe you and me together can win this game called life. Understand this Maxx, I never forget a favor nor do I screw over a friend. You, my brother, are the best one I ever had as I told you. I swear my loyalty to you for as long as you will have me." He smiled with an expression of relief and fatigue.

I looked at the floor. "Matz, where is this House located? I mean what is the address? You must know it if you found your way here."

Matz was startled, then looked at me with caution. "You mean they didn't tell you when you broke your metal? Why? That is most irregular. All the Dominants take an oath of loyalty and the address is given at that time."

I shrugged. "I suppose I missed that part of the breaking of metal ceremony. I ask again Matz, where are we?"

Matz sat back into the couch staring at me with suspiciousness. "You weren't told for a reason, Maxx. I know you took that oath like all of us, or you would be wearing a collar. You spoke to an outsider of the things that go on in this place, didn't you?"

I growled. "What the fuck does that matter, Matz? I asked you a question. Where is the House located. I want to know where the fuck I am."

He snorted then chuckled. "Oh, hell no Maxx. You are not getting me killed. I tell you the address and then you tell someone outside. The next thing I know is the law from the outside comes and Matz is in prison for life, and I have never harmed a kid or done anything seriously grievous in my life. The courts of course will not care. I will go down with all the rotten fuckers as if I were just like them. All because you have a personal vendetta against those that oppressed you. Forget it, I will never utter it. Besides, I gave my blood oath to never speak to anyone of the location of the House."

I sat up with fury. "You call yourself my loyal friend? You will not even part with the address of where I am held the prisoner. This is bullshit Matz. I thought you said you never forget a favor."

He nodded. "Forget it Maxx. Not going to work. I told you I am a man of my word. You are no friend to ask me to break my promise to the House."

I got up storming to my room. "Fuck you, Matz! I am going to bed. You are a total liar spouting shit about being my friend. I don't trust you as far as I can throw you." I slammed the bedroom door behind me.

I stripped down cursing to myself. I took Felicity and crawled under the sheets and was about to turn out the lamp when I heard a soft knocking. I groaned and laid there trying to decide if I would even bother to speak to this Judas.

Finally, after Matz kept knocking for a few minutes, I yelled out, "What the fuck, Matz? Go to bed, motherfucker!"

He shouted through the door. "Open up, Maxx. I wish to say something."

I snorted. "There is no fucking lock, idiot. Say what you want then leave me alone. I mean it."

Matz opened the door staring at his shoes. "Uhm, does this mean I need to call all the clients and tell them the deal is off?"

I glared at him. "No, I still must eat, Matz. I will do as you say and deal with the cocksuckers as they come. You can call your wolves and see if they will work for ten percent. Other than that, don't speak to me. I have no use for anyone that not only aids in keeping me hostage, but then makes his living off my flesh to boot."

Matz sniffed, actually was tearing up to my surprise. "Maxx, which is fair I suppose but I swear I don't, I can't, okay I will show you that I am your friend Maxx, but I cannot break my oath of silence by giving you the exact address since I swore to never say it out loud to anyone. What I can do is tell you the general location. We are in

Germany, the occupied part of it. If you were to break out and run, the East German government would shoot you the second you couldn't prove you belong here. You see Maxx, there is no escape from the House for you or for me. The second you came through the doors they took your identity and mine too. You either live as the silver, the black, or the Dominant unless you have enough wealth to buy off the officials when stopped and questioned. Those without cash who leave the grounds are worm food. The Guard need not even bother to do anything but call in the spotting of an illegal and the local police shoot you. Now, you see, I am your friend."

I laid there, my heart beating like the hummingbird as great despair washed over me. "I thank you for the confidence Matz. I apologize for being an asshole. May I ask you another question." I tried to swallow but my throat had gone dry from fear at his answer.

He nodded. "As long as it is not about the exact city, town or address of this real estate, then I will do my best to answer you."

I closed my eyes. "If a black collar were to decide he or she didn't wish to stay on the grounds, are the allowed to leave?"

Matz nodded with a look of bitterness. "Sure are. Then they are shot the second they get to town by the local police for being illegal. Of course, no black collar is dumb enough to want to leave Maxx. There is nowhere in this country where then can be assured work, health care, good lodgings, protection, and retirement like this House. They all know the truth of the world outside the grounds. They are taught very young about it. Only a silver painted black would be so ignorant to dare to try leaving to strike it out on their own."

I felt like I had been punched in the gut as I barely breathed out. "They don't warn the silver painted black of the dangers?"

He shrugged. "They cannot. The black collar workers all must take the oath to protect the location of the House. Besides silver collars painted black are usually offered a job within the House to protect them. They have no papers or even their birth certificate. Even working in the yard is not typical. They put all the painted silvers in the stables or kitchen only. Why are you asking this? Marc? You worry about him since he is to be painted black, ja?"

I whimpered. "No, there was a silver painted black I knew once long ago. I have never seen her in the kitchen or stables. Is it possible that she was assigned somewhere else?"

Matz sighed. "Maxx, I cannot lie. If she is not in the kitchen or stables, she did something stupid like try to leave the house. If she did go out that front door, she is dead."

I nodded, finding it hard to hold back the tears. "But you do not know that for truth. She could have gotten away, ja? Maybe to the green fields below the mountains?"

Matz yawned. "Sure Maxx. That silver could have managed to outrun the police cars, the Guard, the border brutes, found a way to pay for the food she would need to survive on foot as she ran away, and somewhere out in the world lives in never-never land. You tell yourself that and who is to say that is not what happened for truth, ja?"

I nodded while my stomach flip flopped. "Ja, sure it did happen that way. Thank you Matz. I uhm, need some rest now. I have a long day and night ahead. I take back what I said in anger. You are indeed a good friend, the best." The tears were stinging my eyes.

Matz smiled. "You are good to me, Maxx. Ja, you get rested up partner. I will get with the boys tomorrow while you attend whatever it is you do all day. I need you home by eight thirty. I collect the three thousand from Osvin in the morning."

I shuddered. "Matz, take one thousand dollars and give it to Karsten. Then pay yourself and the brutes their ten percent. With what is left get a tab started in the Great Hall for our meals and hire the black collar maid for the apartment downstairs."

Matz gasped. "Wait, why for my first-floor apartment? What the hell, Maxx. No one lives there. We need the maid for this one, not the empty hell hole."

I opened my wet eyes to look at him. "Matz, where the hell am I supposed to work? Maybe you thought I could handle clients in the storage closets or under the back stairwell? A dark shadow in the House? Do I bring the married bisexual clients to this apartment for the whole House to start rumors about the reasons for so much traffic to the fourth floor? I think not. I will use your old apartment to meet with them. Everyone is used to the many coming and going of thanks to your open secret gambling games. I need that place to be presentable and above all clean. If it gets musty, foul, or stinks like it did, well an already unromantic tryst will become the worst encounter they ever had no matter how skilled I am."

Matz nodded. "Shit, you are right. I thought of everything but where the hell to keep these meetings clandestine. Smart thinking. Okay, I will do as you say. What of the money left over, if there is any?"

I sniffed loudly. "There won't be any this time. Put it all toward that tab for food or the maid and Marc. Osvin has asked for three nights. With his next money I wish to have all of it, besides the twenty percent I owe you and the others, given to me directly. I intend to purchase another silver quickly but first I must secure all of us or I will lose the chance when we all starve or fail to cement the business."

Matz smiled. "Yes, brother. You wish is Matz's pleasure. I cannot wait to be able to eat every day. I swear going four days a week without a thing is killing me."

I nodded. "Those days are over Matz. You keep finding the clients and I will make sure they come back for more. Good night, Matz." I turned out the light and he laughed at my ending the conversation abruptly as he walked off to his own room to slumber.

I lay there in the dark with my thoughts on my beautiful Annette. I clutched Felicity tightly to my chest doing my best to drown out the words that Matz said. I knew she got away. Annette was not in the kitchen or the stables, she managed to escape back into the real world. Matz was wrong.

Even without the birth certificate, money or identification of any kind, she found those green fields and was with her baby lambs. I need to believe that. Otherwise, I would have to understand I sent her to her death by painting her black. This is something I refuse to believe no matter what the evidence suggests.

Master Maxx held up his well-worn lamb with a bitter smile, "Felicity agrees with me. Annette found the dream and one day so will we, just like that sweet girl did, ja?"

I nodded my head but even at nine years old I understood the unsaid truth of my Master's revelations.

Annette found peace the day he painted her black alright. She did it the only way our kind ever can, under those green fields in the world beyond this one. Unknowingly she had promised to leave the House as Mad Maxx, who was ignorant of the danger, asked her. She then rushed head long right to the very grave he had been trying to save her from.

Had she taken a job in the kitchen or stables that was offered her she would have survived to old age. This innocent but deadly error blew a gasket within Mad Maxx's fragile psyche. Unable to deal with the horror of his part in her destruction, he refused to accept the fact that she was killed the very day they said goodbye.

Annette was much more than just his first real lover and first positive experience with a girl. She was a symbol of the dream the little boy called Mad Maxx focused on. The vision she gave him during that horror with Jonas's blood coupling was the only thing that gave him faith there was a better life waiting outside the door. Just because he never saw her again, or even the actual lands she spoke of, he honestly believes she and they are out there somewhere.

This is the fantasy world that Christian Axel is as much a prisoner to as I ever was to that cinderblock cell of Debbie's design.

As the schizophrenic he often suspends the borders of reality. That night, there on a dirty mattress almost a decade after Annette almost assuredly met her death by the Guard, he told me that poor girl was out there somewhere in the world smiling, free, forever young, and eternally happy.

In fact, if you asked him to this day, he would tell you Annette is tending the lambs waiting for him to come home to supper and their cottage with their hound. Turns out reality is not Christian Axel's strong point any more than it is for me.

However, now you know that Annette, his fragile first love and her beautiful vision, only exists behind the shattered looking glass. On with the story.

The sun rose to find me already up attending my usual hygiene rituals as if I were still the Priceless submissive and not Master Mad Maxx. I realized I would have to clean up after Jonas and Kilian had their fun, but that didn't mean I didn't need to shave the flesh, endure the enema and make sure my breath was tolerable.

I was planning to sneak out of the apartment stealthily without waking Matz when a knocking began at the door. I opened it to find Jakob standing there holding ten Felicity lambs with much effort. I smiled at him and the happy sight of so many pretty toys.

Jakob smiled back with a curious expression. "You going to ask me in stud, or do I stand here like the jilted Queen that I am for all the House to see?"

I giggled as I stepped back to let him pass by. "Oh, I apologize Jakob, do come in. Did you bring me these lambs from Leo? I forgot to grab them last night before I left. I am most grateful, and I thank you for the mercy of it."

Jakob popped his tongue. "You bad boy. Still teasing your Auntie with promise you will never keep. If you really were thankful for my aid, you would help me back by scratching the itch I cannot reach."

I raised an eyebrow in confusion while watching him drop the lambs on the sofa. "Huh? You have a rash or something on your back? I will be happy to give you relief by scratching it for you, but I don't think it healthy to do such a thing. It maybe will spread that way, you know."

Jakob laughed out loud then grabbed his chest dramatically. "Oh, my God. Beautiful, innocent and dumb. You keep on with that act Maxx, I will turn into the lioness and eat you for my dinner, I swear it. There is nothing about you that is not tingling my senses into overdrive. What is that perfume you wear? It makes me want to lick you to see if you taste as good as you smell."

I rolled my eyes realizing at last the Jakob's itch was sexual inuendo. You'd think as experienced as I was, I would have caught that. "I don't wear that stuff, Jakob. I use soap, water and shaving cream only. I don't think any of that is of much joy on the tongue."

Jakob giggled into his palm as he twirled his hair. "You speak without knowing, Maxx. Which one is your room? Take me on the tour and I will show you around the world of Jakob, ja?"

I snorted. "Jakob it is too early in the morning for this tomfoolery. Please let it rest. I have a full day of dealing with things I don't like to discuss. I again thank you for bringing me the lambs. If there is nothing else, I don't mean to be rude, but I really must be going to work."

He stomped his foot then made a pout. "You are simply no fun, Maxx. Always the serious one. You will never pass for the bottom at this rate. I told Leo you won't get the hang of this flirting business. The boys will know you are the fake for truth."

I smiled with wickedness. "Really? You think I cannot flirt with any validity, Jakob?" I dropped my gaze to the floor and shot a cat smile at him.

I then reached up to my blouse with my right hand and lightly ran the fingers down my buttons. Jakob looked at my hand with a sudden intrigue. I breathed shallowly and slightly faster as I slowly lingered around the bottom of my waist coat. I saw Jakob nearly in a trance until I led out a breathy moan to catch his attention. He looked at my face to see me lick my lips. He emitted a whimper, then saw me reach down and adjust the crotch of mine breeches with another breathy moan.

Jakob's eyes went huge when he realized I had reached pretty far down my inner thigh to "move things" around for comfort. "Fuck me! I think I just creamed my jeans, Maxx. You have a monster under those clothes. What a terrible waste making you play the bottom. That is an unforgivable sin. Leo should be whipped for keeping this big secret all to himself."

I shot him a playful smile. "It is not that big Jakob, calm down."

Jakob glared at me appearing completely stunned. "I think you weren't listening, Maxx. I said fuck me! Right now. I am no fool. I better get my kicks before you realize how truly gifted you are, or anyone else does."

I chuckled. "Enough Jakob. I am not going to fuck you, not ever. I like you far too much to soil our pure friendship."

Jakob fell to his knees and put his hands together as if praying, then wailed dramatically, "Oh my God, Maxx. I beg of you. Soil me. I think I may die if you keep torturing me this way. You are so stingy. You have so much to spare. Share, damn you. What the hell does Leo have that I do not? You like wrinkles? I will paint them on. Or if you want, put a picture of that old queen on the back of my head and pretend I am him. I don't care. I need you Maxx. All of you." He reached out and grabbed my uhm…me.

I let out a yelp and knocked his hands off…me. "Jakob, get ahold of yourself man. What the fuck has gotten into you."

Jakob let out a squeal of thrill. "Oh, my God. Now that I have gotten a hold, I need you to get into me. Meow. You are the dream, Maxx. Take me away. I'll give you everything I have, twice."

Matz heard the commotion and came running out of the spare room wearing only his boxers while rubbing his eyes. "Maxx, are you okay? I heard yelling. Who is this?" He stared at the kneeling Jakob that was glaring back at him with irritation in his expression.

Jakob stood up and popped his tongue putting his hands on his hips. "Matz, I presume?"

Matz's expression fell into confusion. "Yeah, that's my name. Do I know you, uhm, Mister?"

The Queen flounced. "Well, we have never been formally introduced but I am Jakob Wagner I live here on the fourth floor."

I nearly fainted. "Jakob, did you just say your last name is, uhm, Wagner? I wonder, do you have a brother that is a psychiatrist?"

Jakob nearly fainted in panic from my sudden outburst as he backed up in shock. "No, Maxx. I don't have any siblings. Why the hell would you ask that?"

I let out my breath in full on relief. "Oh, I apologize for startling you like that. It just surprised me to hear you're a Wagner is all. I knew a psychiatrist with that name at Heslach." I flashed a nervous look at Matz that was doing his best to pretend to be looking around the apartment ignoring my speaking of a mental institution.

Jakob crossed his arms and glared at me. "Ah, well that would be my father you met, Maxx, not my brother."

I felt the air leave my lungs as I whimpered out. "I see. So, your father works with Kilian's brother at Heslach. That is how the two of you ended up meeting and becoming a couple. That makes sense I suppose, uhm, I uhm thank you for bringing the lambs. I need to be somewhere. Goodbye. I grabbed one of the lambs and rushed from the apartment leaving Jakob behind for Matz to deal with.

I simply couldn't handle the latest information. All around me were intertwined relationships that had been involved in my continued subjugation. Knowing that my best friend Jakob was the son of that horrid Dr. Wagner was just too much to bear. I needed to get out for some fresh air but first I was getting Marc to enjoy it with me.

I did my best to calm down the agitation as I waited for Karsten to answer the door. To my thrill Marc opened it instead of the frumpy Mistress. He smiled brightly when he saw that the visitor was me.

I grinned back. "Are you ready for an adventure Marc?"

He shot a look behind him. "You bet Master, but I need to tell the Mistress I am heading out."

I chuckled. "No. She is your roommate not your Mistress. The House is your only Dominant now Marc. Besides, I told her that I would be by for you this morning. Grab your coat and come along with me my boy."

Marc laughed. "Oh ja, I keep forgetting. I am the black collar now. I be right back." He started to take off, but I grabbed his arm causing him to startle a bit.

"Wait. Before you go. I brought you a friend. This is your lamb. Follow her and she will lead you to your dreams, Marc." I held out the lamb toy for him to see.

His eyes lit up and the smile across his mouth was glorious. "You are giving this to me Master? For truth? I get to keep her for my own?" He reached out and took the lamb with gentleness in his touch and awe in his expression.

I nodded, still smiling at the joy this little toy brought the boy. "I am giving her to you, but nothing is free Marc. The price I ask is that you tell me her name."

Marc laughed. "That is a fair price. I happily pay it, Master. I will call her Kloe, in honor of my big sister. I miss her so much since our parents died and we were sold to the House. That way I can always have her with me when I am scared. Do you think that is silly though? That I get frightened at my age?" He clutched the lamb and looked at the floor appearing shamed by his admitting to fear.

I reached out and patted his shoulder. "No Marc. I will tell you a secret. I also get scared in the night sometimes. I think Kloe is a beautiful and wonderful name. I accept your price. She is all yours. You must take good care of her. Having a pet is a lot of responsibility. I think you are grown enough to handle it though, right?"

Marc smiled with glee and nodded. "I am indeed adult enough. I will be a great guardian for Kloe. I thank you for the mercy, Master."

I laughed. "You are most welcome, but I do believe you are wasting time. Get that coat and hurry up. We are not getting any younger, right?" He nodded then took off to get his jacket.

As we walked down the hallway toward the side door behind the back stairwell, I took a chance to ask about Marc's silver sister Kloe. "Marc, do you know the name of Kloe's Master or Mistress?"

He frowned as he nodded. "Yes, I do Master. He is not nice to her like you are to me or Mistress Karsten was to me before you. He beats her often and so does his wife. I see her in the kitchen sometimes. She is always having black eyes or welts from being clumsy. I wish there was something I could do. I am the shitty brother to her that I allow that abuse to continue. Kloe is like me, not the graceful one." He sniffed.

I nodded. "You are a fine brother, Marc, and I am sure Kloe knows you would aid her if you could. However, you didn't tell me the Dominant's name that holds her training collar."

Marc gasped. "Oh yeah, I apologize Master. I was never the smart one. That would be Master Osvin. Kloe told me he is an extremely hard to please."

I sucked in my breath and gave silent thanks that I had already set up an appointment for a private audience with the man. That was lucky, despite the dishonor of the original business that was bringing the two of us together. I hoped against all hope that somehow, I could talk this man into handing over Marc's sister's metal to me.

It was my dream to reunite this loving brother with his only blood kin. I could not change their unfortunate path that brought them to a lifetime of servitude, but I hoped I might manage to improve their lot, at least a little, by giving them the gift of a reunion.

I thought maybe if they had each other to hold on to in a world that didn't value either for their truthful worth, they would have a much better chance at happiness despite being trapped for all their lives in that despicable place. That was my plan, but I knew with my luck, it was likely that Osvin wouldn't give up Kloe without bleeding me dry.

I got to the side door thinking maybe I would be capable of escaping into the yard for a few hours undetected. After all, in the past it was unguarded and only the front and back of the House had the sniper shooters. I was most upset to find a single armed guard standing in my path. I wondered if all this new security was set up just because I had lost my shit and killed those brutes the day I broke that bat collar. Surely not. This was, how do you say? Oh ja, the over kill, you know.

I stood their eyeing that big black collar in the blue uniform with a pistol on his hip unsure what to do. I was not about to go running to Kilian or Jonas to have them escort me and Marc to the playground. For starters I would have to explain the little boy's association to me, not going to happen, and then tell them where the hell I got the money to free him in the first place.

Marc looked at me with confusion as I wrung my hands and dropped my gaze to the floor in anxiety of what to do. "Master? Is something wrong? Where are we going? Up these stairs maybe? What is up there? I have never been past the third floor. I always imagined there is something pretty cool at the top."

I growled out with irritation in my voice. "The only thing at the top of this hell hole is an attic full of bats."

Marc recoiled in fear. "Bats? You mean those creepy animals with leather wings? Yike, that must be scary as hell." He peered up the steps holding Kloe tighter to his chest.

I sighed at having to give up the pleasure I had wished to give to the boy. "I must apologize to you Marc. I didn't bring you out to frighten you with tales of the Boogie Men that live at the top of the House. I wanted to take you outside, but I cannot go without…" I suddenly spotted Byron coming down the stairs and wondered if any Dominant could take me out the door or if only my guardian was permitted.

Byron saw me standing there and I could see the smile light up his face immediately. "Maxx, what are you doing brother? Are you up for a little company?"

I sucked back my furious emotions at this rapist Voter and forced a pleasant smile as I said through gritted teeth, "Why I am most grateful to have you tag along. I was thinking of taking this little silver trainee to the playground. Would you be interested in such an adventure?"

Marc gasped and let out a tiny squeal of thrill as he breathed out, "There is a playground? Outside? Oh, my God. Please, I want to go Master." He began to dance in place with excitement squeezing his toy in the cutest way. Watching that most honest happiness in Marc caused my darkness at having to endure Byron's company to calm down, a little anyway.

I put up my finger to hush the celebrating little kid. "Be still Marc. Let's see if Byron will come with us, ja?" He nodded with eagerness keeping his dancing eyes on the fast-approaching Voter.

Byron rushed up, appearing almost as thrilled as Marc. "Ja, Maxx. I'll go with you wherever you desire. It is a fine day out for so early in the winter season. I am pleased you were looking for me. What a lucky man I am." He leaned in and kissed me on the cheek causing Marc's mouth to drop in shock.

I endured this most unexpected and inappropriate overly familiar greeting with a fake smile. "Well looks like Maxx is the one blessed this morning. Shall we go?" I began heading for the door with Marc quickly following Byron rushing to catch me.

"Wait Maxx. You will need me with you to get past the guard. Here take my arm and there will be no trouble, but I warn you, do not stray in the yard from me. The snipers are ordered to kill you on sight if unaccompanied by another Dominant of worth." He grabbed my arm and forced it through his with Marc looking on appearing beyond confused at this point.

I dropped my head feeling my ears heat up with shame that Marc was seeing my weakness like that. "Oh, I didn't know that. A Dominant of worth you said? What does that mean?"

Byron chuckled as he waved the guard to step aside and let us pass, which the guard did without quarrel. "That means one above your level my love. Only the Voter or Elder can call off the door guards for you. I thought for sure that Peter had told you all this. After all it was him the put this order before Gretta and got it approved while you were away convalescing."

I groaned. "Ah, I assumed Jonas or Kilian was behind this overzealous attempt to keep me from trying to leave the House."

Bryon narrowed his eyes. "Well, I am sure they aided his push for it since Friedrick, Rolf and I voted against it. We were ignored and the rule to keep you within the walls without escort passed despite our attempts to block it. I assumed Kilian had his slimy hands in the mix somewhere, but I cannot prove it."

I nodded. "Thanks for trying anyway Byron, and for all the other laws you and your brothers have pushed to better the lot of the helpless that live here. You are a good man, there is no doubt, and I cannot deny you're one of your words."

Byron snorted with a blush. "As are you Maxx. I know it is bad of me, but I still giggle when I think of the look on Gretta's face when you left the Hall of Records and beat Olaf and Vilber to death with the sacred bolt cutters. I suppose Olaf should have realized that you would not let his thief of your service and aid in that near fatal attack go without vengeance. I suppose the only ones left alive from that attack or the other one are Malfred and Louis? I hope you have no intentions of ending them like you did the others?"

I flashed a look of caution at Byron over his loose tongue then looked behind me to find Marc's eyes wide with pure terror at what he just heard about my past behaviors and troubles. Byron noticed my sudden discomfort and wisely immediately dropped the conversation. I didn't need Marc knowing the dirty details of my most disturbing history. That boy was innocent and if I had my say was going to stay that way.

We walked out to find the day overcast but the temperature above freezing. It was unusually warm for February. As we walked toward the playground, I told Marc to stay close since he was in as much danger as me if he strayed and was happy to see he minded without questions.

Byron escorted me with a stupid grin on his face silently until we were not far from our destination then he looked at me with a blush. "I cannot get over how much you have grown. You left us a little boy no bigger than the silver that travels with us and return a fucking huge man. If it were not for that famous scar and those gorgeous eyes of yours, I wouldn't believe this was the same Maxx I enjoyed the company of almost two years ago now. I must say Maxx, I have missed you more than you can know. I am so delighted to finally be getting time to catch up with you.

Rolf told Friedrick and I of your telling him that you forgave us for that mistake we made with the welcome home party."

I nodded. "Yeah, I was a little grouchy I confess. I am not much for big get togethers, you know."

Byron shot me a coy smile. "Well, how about smaller ones? I would love to take you out to dinner if you may see fit to honor me with your presence. There is a little bistro in town that I simply adore. Having you on my arm would give me much joy."

I frowned at that. "In town you say? Is that even permitted Byron? I mean I cannot even take a piss or walk to the swing set without getting a fucking parent's signature and babysitter to come with me."

Byron laughed. "I will get it cleared with the Council if you say ja." That most uncomfortable conversation was cut short when Marc let out a loud overjoyed wail.

He had spotted the merry-go-round and swing set ahead of us. I smiled despite my disgust at being held like a hostage in Byron's grips. Marc's breathing was loud as he mumbled to Kloe of his disbelief at what he was seeing.

I turned around with a chuckle. "I told you there was one. Which do you desire first? The swing or the merry-go-round?"

Marc yipped. "Oh, the swing, Master. I love the swing set. I haven't seen one since I was little." He rushed past the two of us and took his seat immediately sending himself into childhood heaven, forcing it to fly higher and higher with his powerful teen legs."

Byron chuckled with much humor. "That boy is swinging to the moon, Maxx. Look at him go. So much energy. Ah, to be young again."

I sighed. "I wouldn't wish to be young again myself to be honest. I don't recall it was all that much fun."

The Voter stifled his laugher. "Right. I wouldn't think it was for you. Can I say something, Maxx?"

I glared at him pulling my arm from his with strength. "You can do whatever you like, Byron. I seem to recall you always have without worrying about my granting your permission. Why should you suddenly care now?"

Byron looked at the ground. "I suppose I had that coming Maxx. You were right, Friedrick and I should have let you off the hook on that contract the day Volf and Karl were laid low. That said, how were we to know there would not be other attacks? I mean there was that first-floor business. The possibility existed till the end."

I nodded with much fury in my eyes. "That is true, but I must point out that both the savior and worst threat came from that contract you carried out in the closet. Kilian and Jakob did your job with that first-floor attack. Kilian also was the criminal that nearly killed Felicity the day our agreement ended. Friedrick and you took payment for something that in the end was completed by my own hands and Malfred's. Five months, Byron, for one single fight was unfair and in your favor. You took advantage plain and simple. You still have something to say to me Bryon? If so say it. Then I would ask you to never bother me again. I have more than paid you for the displeasure of your company."

Byron gasped. "I wanted to tell you that, uhm, fuck it. You are right and I can see that. I wanted you so bad I never thought out how I would have felt if someone did that to me, like we did to you. I swear to you I will spend the rest of my life helping you right the wrongs of this House to try to repay the hurt I caused you with my selfish greed."

I scoffed. "Byron you should use your position of power to better the lives of these children held hostage because it is an honorable thing, not because you think it will assuage your guilt at what you did to me. Look at the boy on the swing. His name is Marc. That little boy is doomed as are all the others like him if you sit on your thumbs and do nothing. You cannot remove the nightmares I will always connect to your face because you cannot change the past. You can however change his future." I pointed at the exhilarated Marc swinging without a worry in the world.

Byron watched Marc for a moment then looked back at me with sadness in his gaze. "I understand what you say Maxx, and I am doing what I can for the silvers. Ask Rolf or Leo, they will vouch for my vigorous advocating for the improvements. That said, I must know, is there any chance for you and me? I mean, can you ever forgive me?

I popped my tongue and snapped while flouncing dramatically. "Oh, hell no, you are not getting off that easy. You want me to forgive you then you better be ready to pay back for years, Byron. This bitch is not cheap."

Byron backed up, appearing shocked for a moment then broke out in wild laughter. "Holy hell, you sounded just like Jakob there for a second. Oh, my God, you are funny Maxx. How did you do that? Shit. If you were wearing pink lip gloss, I would have sworn you were that Queen. I swear you should go into acting."

I grinned with an evil smile. "Yeah, Byron. You would be wise to remember that brother. Watch your back, this kitty will scratch your eyes out if given half the chance."

He nodded. "Right, I hear you Maxx. I will give you some space to cool off. When you are ready, I will be waiting. Take all the time you need."

I put my hands on my hips with a scornful and overly dramatic expression on my face. "Well, thank you for granting me your permission to be upset big daddy. You can wait till the hair in your ears grows to maturity and your nuts drag on the ground. Mad Maxx will never be knocking on your door, nor will you be knocking his boots with him, ever again, Bryon."

Byron howled in laughter. "There you go again. Fuck, that is spot on just like Jacob. I must tell him about this. He will never believe it."

I frowned while rolling my eyes with a snap. "I guess old man hair already clogs your hearing, Byron. You need hearing aids I suppose since you don't listen well. Never mind, you tell Jakob all you like. I have already worn the silver, but I think I am ready to be crowned in gold. While you are at it make sure to say that there is a new Queen on the rise looking to take his throne. His Queendom may not be ready to handle this much gender bending magnificence."

I left Bryon near on the ground in tears from laughing to aid Marc by pushing his swing. He was watching the show appearing intent and mildly upset. As the Voter continued his mirth, I gave Marc a gentle push.

He turned to look at me then blurted out, "Master, Mistress Karsten told me that you are a dangerous man last night. She said you have murdered many Dominants, silvers and even black collars. She swears you are a killer Queen. I asked her what that is, and she said that is the dangerous and angry homosexual. I was pissed that she said such ugly things about you. I think you should know she is going to demand I be whipped for arguing and telling her to shut her mouth. I am not sorry for being insolent and no doubt deserve that thudding." He turned back around with solemness overtaking his earlier joyful attitude.

I grabbed his swing chain halting him from flying off into the air away from hearing my response to him, "I thank you for standing up for me Marc, but in the future, you ignore what that woman or anyone says to you. Rumors are only half-truths and fodder for entertainment among the dull minded. I will deny her the right to see that you be punished for standing up for what you believe in. You are the black collar now so rules about insolence are a bit different than they were when you were silver. It is not good to back mouth the Dominants, so I suggest you do your best to cull the urge to speak out against them. Unless you enjoy the torture chamber or dungeon cell. I ask you to always understand what another says about you, me or anyone are only words. Just because they say something doesn't make it the truth nor a lie, but merely their perception."

He nodded but kept his eyes to the ground. "That makes much sense but Master, Mistress Karsten wasn't a lying to me, was she? You are a killer Queen, right?"

I looked into the sky trying to hide my shame. "Not exactly Marc. I am not so fancy as all that. I am not a Queen. I am an idiot pawn at best or at worse the pet monkey of the kings. If you are asking if I am the murderer before I answer I ask you do you really want to know? If so, can you live with knowing the truth?"

Marc got up and looked at his lamb Kleo then came back to me with awe in his expression. "I think I need not hear another word, Master. You broke the collar when I happen to know no one else that is not the High born ever has. Whatever you had to do to earn that prize was justified since I am aware of how much silver is in this dirt below my feet. You saved this worthless boy, and you shower me with gifts I thought would never come true without taking it out of my flesh. A heart like that is not a black one as my old Mistress seems to think you possess. I see the scars on your skin, and I know that they are soul deep. These Dominants think that makes you ugly to your core like they all are. I am dumb but even I can see that my betters are wrong about you. Those marks you wear are a map of your travels. You demonstrate to the hopeless the path to freedom. A wise silver would do well to follow because you know the way out. I go with you Master without hesitation or regret." He took my hand and smiled at me with pure adoration.

I felt overwhelmed with pure despair at his words. "Marc, there is no escape. Your only hope is to live long enough to wear a black collar. For all your days you will be trapped here in this House, subjugated till the earth below claims you for her own. I cannot stand here while you lavish unwarranted praises on this most disgusting creature you misjudged terribly. I cannot save you from your fate. I apologize for it but that is the honest truth." I sniffed back my bitter tears as pretty Annette's face appeared behind the trees and the sound of Ryker's childish laughter floated in the breeze above me.

Marc nodded without losing his innocent smile. "Master, when my parents died, we were starving in the streets. Only Kloe and I survived and both of us were lucky to be picked up, then sold to this House. There is no life for us out there in the world without family or luck of wealth. Here we are fed and kept warm. We both expected that our death was held off for only a little while when the silver was tossed at our feet, but now you came and give me the hope of a real life. It may not be the life of leisure or even one of pure joy, but it is more of a life than I expected. I can never thank you enough for the mercy of it. Do not apologize for giving me a chance. I never thought I would have a chance to watch my grandchildren play as I grow grey in the cottages of the retired. I am most grateful to you." He startled me when he pulled my hand to his lips then kissed my knuckles lightly.

Bryon was standing there quietly listening to the entire conversation, but that move made him gasp out, "Maxx? You painted this silver black? How the hell did you do that? You cannot own silver and where did you get the money? Surely his Mistress didn't just hand him over for free. You didn't dare to break that contract with Peter by sleeping with Karsten, did you?" His eyes were wide with fear and a little jealousy, I think.

I groaned. "You have a lot of nerve listening into the conversations that do not involve you, Byron. For your information I did not sleep with Karsten. Give me a more credit than that."

Byron growled, no longer attempting to hide his hurt feelings. "Then how the fuck did you afford this collar."

I smiled as I dropped my gaze appearing embarrassed. "Well, if you must know Marc was a gift from my boyfriend, Byron. This boy and his care are being handled by my lover. I get to enjoy this collar until his selection at fifteen. I know, I am spoiled ja?" I couldn't help rubbing some salt into his wounds you know.

The Voter stood there appearing incredulous. "What? You have a boyfriend? You only got back the day before yesterday. How the hell did you manage to get someone so enamored they'd buy you a trainee for your pleasures so fucking fast."

I shot Marc a wicked smile and winked at him while he dropped his gaze doing his best to hide his smile as I said, "You ask that after all that crap you spewed about waiting as long as I need to have me come to you as the lover? I am the Priceless Byron. There are few in this House that wouldn't sell out their mothers to have me agree to grace their beds. As it is, the man that currently sports the title of my boyfriend has not only bought me this wonderful Marc but pays all my bills. Can you believe that? He insisted on opening a tab in the Great Hall and keeps me protected from those looking to steal what is not ever going to be theirs."

Sending Matz to pay all the bills in person was not because I am the lazy one. You now see I had an underhanded reason for it. It hid that I was earning that money by making it appear the Matz was paying the freight for me with his own cash. Master Maxx winked at me causing me to giggle at his clever deception.

Byron nearly choked. "What? You are being kept? No. You cannot be. I told you that I love you Maxx and you run off with another lover. How could you do this to me? Rolf told me you are straight. He said you would not choose anyone since Peter forbid you date any FemDoms."

I shrugged. "That is true that Peter said no females but that was fine by me. I am the gay after all, Byron. As for not rushing to be in your arms, well sweetheart, you are above my status I do believe. A love affair with you is forbidden. Sorry about that, but rules are rules. Without anyone to keep me warm I was lucky enough to run into the darling that now can lay claim to me for his own. I couldn't be happier. Marc my beloved, would you like to play on the merry-go-round now?" Marc yelled out with thrill and ran to the round monstrosity as I followed doing my best to hide my diabolical smile from the jilted Voter.

Byron sat down on the swing in injured silence as he watched Marc, and I had a grand time playing for the next two hours. I pushed him on the merry-go-round, chased him in a game of tag, and then we demonstrated to each other the hidden talents of our lambs Felicity and Kloe. I swear I had such a good time with him I nearly forgot that horrible appointment at noon with Kilian and the Vampire.

However, at ten I realized that Marc was getting cold and would miss his lunch if I didn't return him to Karsten soon. I took the sulking Bryon's arm and allowed him to lead us back into the House without the same irritation toward him I had earlier. Not that I forgave him for the terror he had caused me while in my collar but seeing him so upset helped my own hurt ache a tiny bit less. Nothing like getting equal service return to numb the pain you know. Master Maxx chuckled.

Once inside Byron started to leave but turned around just before he stormed off. "Maxx, if this guy you are seeing ever hurts you or leaves you wanting, my offer still stands. I see you are punishing me for being the brute. I accept it without resentment. You will come to me, I am not worried. No one can love you like I can. See you soon." He took off without another word.

I stood there watching that insane man leave scratching my head in disbelief. Byron is the cur dog. Just like that stray hound, I had mistakenly fed him when he came begging for the scraps. Now that he had tasted me, more is all he wanted. I couldn't run him off no matter what I said or did.

I would have stared after him for several more minutes, but Marc came up beside me and took my hand with a small gasp. "Master, that man is wild about you. I worry he will try to hurt you if you don't watch out."

I squeezed his hand. "Ah you need not be concerned about me Marc. I am the brute and can protect myself from the likes of Byron."

Marc frowned, "I heard what he said Master. That man injured you when you were the submissive, didn't he? How can you be so sure he won't do it again?"

That made me chuckle. "Marc you are the nosey one and far from the dumb you claim to be. I tell you not to worry about that man and you have no choice but to mind me. Besides anxiety causes health issues and what the hell could you do if he did try to repeat his attacks? Nothing is what. You let me deal with my troubles and you focus on learning your trade. When do you start your training for the black collar internship?"

He smiled. "Tomorrow. They told me I would get to work in the stables with the animals. Can you believe my good luck Master? I love farm animals. I am so excited about it. I apologize for forgetting to tell you sooner. I will be busy at seven, then noon and again at five. Each training session lasts for two hours. Can you come see me at nine tomorrow instead of seven?"

I smiled. "No. I have a breakfast date that I cannot miss but I will come at two. Will that work? If so then I better get you back home. I need to head back myself. I have another appointment at noon that I will be late for if I fool around much longer." He smiled while nodding frantically.

Karsten was thrilled when I returned Marc to her apartment. She told me that when she saw Matz at her door she had been near frightened to death. Then he handed her the one thousand dollars for Marc's care and took a payment statement from her. The Mistress laughed as she stated that she had never seen Matz in such fine spirits and friendly.

To my surprise she kissed Marc on his forehead and then reported his lunch was waiting for him in the kitchenette. Marc turned and hugged me spontaneously then ran off to the back to get his lunch while yelling out his thanks for "the amazing adventure."

Karsten laughed at the youth's vigor then turned her attention back to me. "You are a real God send to that boy, Maxx. He has been less clumsy and full of the song since you came into our lives. I must admit, you pay your debts, and are for truth a man of your word. I am more than a little impressed with you."

I sighed then looked at her with some sternness. "I am happy to be changing your preconceived ideas of my brutal and homosexual nature, Mistress."

She groaned. "Oh hell. I shouldn't have had all that wine last night. I apologize Maxx. I guess it loosened my tongue to repeat things that I should have left in the hallways."

I nodded but kept my tough expression, "Karsten, there is a sister to this collar Marc. I think I may be purchasing her soon, also to be painted black. If I were to increase the payments to two thousand, could I impose upon you to allow the siblings to reside as the family?"

Karsten gasped, appearing shocked. "Uhm, yes, of course Maxx. I know Kloe. She is a very sweet girl. Marc misses her terribly. I admit that she is all he talks about. However, Osvin and Fiona got married and he gave Kloe to her as a wedding gift. Neither will part with her collar easily."

I rolled my eyes. "I didn't expect they would Karsten, but I can be most persuasive you know."

Karsten narrowed her gaze with a strange little smile spreading on her face. "That I have witnessed with my own eyes Maxx. The legend of the Priceless is truer than many give it credit for. Good luck with your attempts to give that precious boy his sister back. I will root for you to be successful. Until then though, I wouldn't tell him of your bargaining for her if I were you. I wouldn't want his heart broke when those two cows tell you to go to hell."

That caused me to nod my head wildly in agreement. "You and I speak the same language, Karsten. Well, good day to you. Take care and I see Marc tomorrow at two. Hopefully, I will be bringing you another heart to warm your apartment with innocent laughter."

She smiled. "That would be most appreciated and Maxx, thank you for being a good man." I shrugged then left hauling ass for the fourth-floor apartment to freshen up before heading to the sixth floor.

Matz was sitting on the sofa as I came rushing through the living area headed for the master bathroom. He chuckled as I kicked his feet off the coffee table on my way by with a loud growl.

"You are the prissy thing Maxx, but nothing like that Jakob queen. Wow, there is a fucking show walking. How the hell did you meet him? Should I be jealous?" He yelled after me in a tease.

I shouted back, "No. Jakob is the bottom like me. I maybe should be the one concern you would run off with him."

Matz howled in laughter. "Oh hell no. I like my lovers to be the brutes. I am attracted to men, not girls. I told you I am gay as the blade, Maxx. Jakob is too much the female for my bitter taste, and I thought you wore too much makeup. Damn."

I heard a knocking at the door as I quickly applied the white makeup and eyeliner that Jonas insisted, I wear to please him. I yelled for Matz to answer that I was busy. Within only a few minutes I heard a loud argument breaking out from the living area. I had no idea what the hell was causing Matz yell like that. I came out of the bathroom in a hurry ready to back my roommate if a fist fight was about to break out thinking it was likely one of his indebted that was unhappy about the payback.

To my shock I found Matz and Peter nearly at each other's throat. I gasped out loud causing the two of them to briefly break off their aggressions.

Peter shot a look of fury at Matz then set his eyes on me with the same expression. "Why the fuck is this pig here, Maxx? Did you borrow money, and he is here trying to strong arm you into paying it back? If so, then I will pay it off and this little prick can leave immediately."

I crossed my arms and popped my tongue loudly. "Excuse me? You come into my home and harass my boyfriend under his own fucking roof. I think not. Matz honey, come here to me. Peter, you are a brute. If you hurt him, I swear to God I will have the hissy fit from hell on your ass." Matz gave Peter a look of arrogant victory as he walked over and put his arm around my waist with a huge shit eating grin on his face.

Peter could have been knocked down with a feather. His eyes went wide, and mouth dropped to the floor as I began to dramatically fawn over Matz demanding to know if he was injured in any way. Matz did his best not to burst out laughing but to his credit he played along acting as if he were the object of my undying desire. I do believe he even liked it a great deal.

Peter stood there unsure what to do for several minutes then finally cleared his throat loudly to tear my attention from Matz. "Uhm, Maximillian? Am I to understand that Matz is living here with you as your lover?" He coughed a bit when he said that.

I smiled with much evil in my expression as I flounced and snapped. "Hello Peter, I believe that is what I said. You better pay attention when I speak to you. I have no energy to waste repeating myself. I am saving my energy for Matz's lustful interests in me. He is a greedy bastard, you know. I need a nap every few hours just to keep up with this stud."

Matz nodded. "Damn right you better keep up, baby. I am a wanton man and I like my meals hot." He leaned in and kissed me on the cheek.

I swatted at him acting most offended but giggling loudly. "Oh, you stop that Matz. I need to rest, I told you. Besides, I am a sight. Let me put on something nice for you, then anchors away, all men on deck."

Matz rolled his eyes. "I already said a thousand times Maxx you need not wear a thing. I like it when you are easy to board." I nearly cracked up and blew our cover.

Peter growled out. "Enough. You are not fooling me, Maximillian. There is no fucking way you have gone homosexual. Jonas and Kilian already told me that you are trying to shirk your duties to them with that bullshit. You have gone too far bringing this disgusting thug into your House just to prove a point that doesn't matter anyway. I demand you throw him out right this second. I mean it."

Matz started to say something, but I put my hand up into his face and flounced while snapping at Peter. I was getting good at this bit, you know. "Oh no, you didn't just call my Matz a thug. That is not okay. Get out of my house, Peter. If you cannot accept my boyfriend, then you are not welcome here. As for me going too far, well if so then you have only yourself to blame for that. You denied me the Frau's far too long. I decided if you can't beat them, then may as well join them. You can keep the Janes, and I will be happy to take the Dicks. Goodbye, Peter. I'll see you when I head off to medical school. Until then, I see no reason to share my affections with anyone but my baby." I grabbed the back of Matz head and pulled him into a deep tongue kiss that nearly sent the man to the floor with both shock and passion.

When I at last let Matz go to come up for air he was panting with desire and appeared pale as if about to pass out. Peter was standing there with his arm crossed smiling with sarcastic mirth.

I glared at him and pointed at the door with fury in my eyes. "I said get out, Peter. Do you not see I am busy here. I only have an hour to satisfy my Matz before I must go upstairs. You are interfering with my thrills."

Matz was in a trance staring at me still breathing hard. "You heard Maxx. Get the fuck out. I swear to God, I will kill you if that is what it takes to get this man in my bed right now."

Peter chuckled. "Once again, I repeat, great acting job but I am not a sucker boys. Maximillian why is it you didn't ask why I am bothering to visit you?"

I rolled my eyes then reached out to stroke Matz cheek sending that poor man into near insane rutting mode. "Oh bother, what is it that brings you to rudely interrupt my nooner with Matz? Oh, let me guess? You need to borrow a cup of sugar? No? You on a blood drive for the Vampire looking for volunteers maybe? Still not warm? Oh wait, I know what, that contract I have with you. I bet you poured over it trying to find some way to fuck me over. You found it didn't you? Otherwise, you wouldn't be here." Matz reached out and rubbed his hands on my chest causing me to shoot him a sideways glance of caution. He raised his eyebrows with a smile of apology and dropped his attempts at taking advantage by attempting to cop a free feel.

Peter scoffed then nodded with a smile. "Well, you always were the smart one Maximillian. I have indeed found the loophole in your attempt to hold off what is owed to me. Your Dominant training was promised to me, you remember, right? I desire to start that long process right away. That gives me the right to a service return. I also brought you the books required to start your bachelor's degree immediately. I will oversee all your scholastic testing so there is yet another service." I pushed Matz off me, he was starting to rub on me a little too much, as I interrupted Peter with a startle.

"Wait a second. Did you say you brought my books for college? What do you mean you will handle the testing? I am to leave this House for my coursework. I cannot be homeschooled for the medical license." I glared at him feeling both fury and fear rising within me.

Peter smiled even wider. "No, you cannot, that you are correct about. Your bachelor's degree however, that can be done from the House. Your guardian and doctors have already cleared it with the education board. The minute you complete your basic coursework in say two to four years, then you will transfer to the medical school if any will have you under such unusual circumstances."

I nearly fainted from panic. The Vampire, Kilian and Peter had found a way to trap me within their grips another fucking two to four years. Without the legitimate traditional premedical degree, they had almost assured me I was never getting into any medical school outside the walls to ever escape them.

He wore a cruel grin and chuckled as he said, "We can start your training tomorrow Maximillian at seven in the morning. That works for you, right? Guess you should have been more careful when you agreed to the contract that I poorly worded or maybe should have stayed in bed rather than sneaking around with clever Vampires when your Master fell asleep, ja?"

Chapter 7: Weiner Schnitzel

I stood there feeling the world spinning around my head unsure if I was hallucinating this horrible news. Peter smiled with his arms crossed enjoying the discomfort his words had caused me. Matz continued to overdo his bit part in this whole acting the lusty boyfriend until at last I grabbed his wrists.

I glared at him. "Give me a minute will you, sweetheart? Why don't you go to the bedroom and wait for me under the sheets. I need to do some exterminating for a minute. I do believe we have a rat in our apartment, ja? You would think with what we are charged in rent there wouldn't be any pests allowed. Yet, I swear to God there is the biggest fucking rodent I ever laid my eyes on standing by the door."

Matz gasped and panted as he pulled his hands out of my own. "If you wish Meine Liebling I get rid of that foul thing that has upset you. My boots make for fine stomping weapons you know."

I nodded with a wicked smile. "You know that is why I love you so. Ah, do you see that, Peter? Beautiful and loyal. What more could I ask? No, my little bird. I got this sonofabitch handled. Do as I asked and be ready to ravage me the second, I am through throwing the corpse out."

Matz grinned with thrill then took off for my room with speed, tearing off his shirt before disappearing behind the door. I laughed wildly when he threw it in Peter's direction yelling out loudly, "hurry up. I will warm up the motor but don't make me start without you."

Peter stared at Matz discarded shirt laying on the floor at his feet with an expression of disgust. "I am surprised at you, Maximillian. Why are you slumming when you could have any hard dick in this House falling to his knees begging to fuck you? I thought I taught you better than that. You are quality and this thing you are fooling around with is the vermin in this House, not me."

I popped my tongue and snorted. "You have a lot of nerve coming here and sticking up your nose at my lover. If you are done insulting Matz and me then I suggest you get the fuck out of my sight. I will not be there tomorrow at seven nor any day. I am going to be the doctor, not the fucking Dominant. I need no training because I am fucking leaving this House the second, I have my medical license. I will apply to colleges on my own and when I get into one, I will let you know. Then you can fuck me over all you like but best enjoy it while it lasts, Peter. I plan to study and race through school. Just try to catch me, I dare you. Buh bye motherfucker. You know the way out, I believe. I have business to attend. You know, slumming to do." I stormed into my bedroom after Matz and slammed the door behind me.

Matz was sitting on my bed smiling at me as I stood at the entry fuming in absolute rage. I couldn't believe the balls on that father of mine. He dared to attempt to hijack my ticket out of the House. If he really thought, he could literally screw me like that he had another thing coming. I cared nothing about being Dominant and was not about to do any training to become a lifetime criminal of that hellish place neither.

I heard Peter yell from the living area. "You better think a minute before you act the ass to me, Maximillian. If you don't do as you are told it will not go well for you. I will be waiting in the morning for you at seven. You be at my apartment, I mean it. There is no way out of this. I have your trapped, you will see it soon enough. You will fulfill your oath. Kiss your thug goodbye for me. I will see you tomorrow." I heard him leave as the front door to the apartment smacked closed with a bang.

I closed my eyes and let out a loud wail of utter frustration. It seemed all around me there were villains looking to fuck me over. I was startled out of that moment when arms went around the back of the boy's head. I opened my lids with a startle to find Matz pulling me into a hug with vigor.

My mouth flew open to protest his touching me, but he pushed his own tongue in before I could get anything said. I couldn't believe this shit. With a howl, I pushed the idiot the fuck off me `knocking him to his ass in the floor.

I wiped his slobber with the sleeve of my blouse. "What the hell, Matz. Peter is gone, fool. Keep your nasty tongue and fingers away from me."

Matz's furrowed his brow appearing confused. "Wait, I thought you wanted me like that Maxx. That kissing you threw at me was no act. I felt the heat between us. You dare

306

to say you felt nothing for me? You are a liar or worse, a God damned tease, if you say that was merely to convince that shitty Peter we are lovers."

I groaned with pure irritation. "Matz, I was trying to make that motherfucker buy that I am gay and that was all. I am not attracted to any man. I am trained to make the lover believe I want them. There were no feelings of lust for you nor will there ever be."

He shook his head wildly. "If you really mean that then I have to say no wonder you are viewed as the sexual artist extraordinaire. I want nothing more than to have you for my own. I must take you all the way or I think I may go crazy. How in hell did you do that to me?"

I shrugged. "I don't know what you are talking about. I didn't do anything but kiss you, idiot."

Matz stood up with a thrilled smile beginning to grace his lips. "Wow, can you really fake the passion, make the right moves, without feeling them yourself? If so then you likely could stir the stone statue to lustful frenzy, Maxx. That is a gift that cannot be taught. Holy hell we are going to be rich. If you can do to the clients what you just did to me, they will pay a king's ransom to possess you, and often. I cannot believe this amazing luck."

I sighed. "First of all, it was taught, I told you that already Matz. I am the highly trained pleasure submissive. That man we just ran off is the fellow that can claim responsibility for anything you think is special about that fake kissing bullshit. Second, you may be the lucky one, but I am not. It is my ass that those nasty perverts come to fuck, not yours. I am good at what I do thanks to many hours of painful torturing and humiliating practice. You throw in more than three years of experience with the most foul, disgusting, and twisted men in this House, and you have the Priceless "sexual artist" you have mistaken for your lover. I am a whore, Matz, not your boyfriend. I am not even human, nor did I have any choice in those that got to taste my flesh. I am the cursed that brings the thrill to the blessed."

Matz looked at the floor with a frown and suddenly there was a look of sadness in his expression. "Please don't call yourself that, Maxx. You are not a whore, and you are the most marvelous human I have met in my life. You shouldn't allow those that abused their station of power over you to brainwash you to believing you are anything less than the honest man you are."

I let out a laugh of sarcasm. "I am not a whore, you say. Really Matz? Then what exactly did you get that three thousand from Osvin for this morning? Oh, I know, he was paying you for my amazing cooking or conversation services, right? Whew. That sure takes a load off my mind, oh wait, speaking of loads." Matz interrupted me, raising his voice in anger.

"Enough Maxx. I am not arguing with you anymore. You want me to call you a whore then so be it. I have three hundred dollars from my cut of the profits in my pocket. What can I get for it? He glared at me, his nostrils flaring in extreme anger.

That threw me for the loop. "Huh? I don't know what that will buy, Matz. I am not trained to know what things cost. I know Jakob said that fifty dollars will buy five meals so I suppose you can eat with three hundred for more than a week three times a day, or you can buy a lot of lamb toys. Maybe you can get a pair of boots?"

Matz's mouth dropped as he shook his head in disbelief. "Are you funning me Maxx? For being famously intelligent you sometimes appear to be a moron. I meant how much of your artistry can I afford with that much. I want to kiss you and maybe get a blow job?"

I choked as he said that. "Christ Matz, shut the fuck up. I am not blowing you for three hundred dollars."

He glared at me with a scoff. "Why not? I thought you are a whore. I have money and want to purchase your services. Why will you sell it to Osvin or to Fritz but not Matz?"

That backed me up to the door with fear rising, but I was unsure why since I knew he was surely being an ass and not really meaning what he was saying. "Matz, I am done with this conversation. I already said I am not blowing you nor anything else for three hundred dollars. Stop being stupid. I find this neither cute nor funny. I have real problems and here you are playing a game with me. I thought you were my friend. Why are you stressing me out like this?"

He took that money out of his pocket and threw it to the floor at my feet. "I play no games, Maxx. I want to purchase the fucking product you are selling. You're teasing me, pretending to like me, saying we are hot lovers and even friends. Now you tell me you are a whore that feels nothing. That all the shit out in the living room was an act. Well, then tell me why my money is not good enough for you. I have the money and there it is. You turn down my cash only because you think of me like Peter does, nothing but scum. I am the thug, right? Too far beneath you to even touch my honest wage for the thrill of tasting your wares. Matz is lower than even ugly old Fritz. That is what it is. Go ahead and say it. I want to hear it." He began tearing up and sniffing from the obvious hurt he was feeling.

I dropped my gaze in shame at what he thought was the reason I was turning him down. "Matz, it is not like that. I mean, you need that money for your living expenses. There is no reason to be spending it on such frivolous things as my overrated special services skills. I take that money from that horrible Osvin, Fritz, or even Justus because, well I don't care what happens to them. I do care about you Matz, for truth."

He wiped his eyes and nodded. "That is also a lie, Maxx. If you did you would sleep with me without pay. I pretend to be your boyfriend, what the hell harm would it do to be my lover for truth? I will take care of you, respect you, and always be there if you will have me. I thought it would be okay only pretending but I find I am falling hard for you. I don't think I can stand seeing you here in front of me and enduring your so-called faking without getting badly hurt."

I shook my head. "Matz, I do honestly care for you but not like you wish me to. You are my friend. Please let that be enough for you. I don't mean to sound cruel, but I have serious problems at this very moment and you're acting this way is adding to an already heavy burden. I tell you that sleeping together would make it even more difficult for me to do my job with the paying clients. I told you already I have three, sometimes four, to deal with. You just heard that asshole Peter. He is attempting to force his way into my already busy rotation as it is. Be reasonable. I see one more a day, that is five. Now you suggest adding number six by taking on my pimp and roommate yet another penetration situation. I simply couldn't even if I wanted to. It has nothing to do with your status, wealth, or finding you unattractive. I am flattered you offer to be the honorable lover Matz, I really am. Yet I told you I am straight and would find no joy in it. However, if it makes you feel better, were I less over strapped, I'd entertain your offer with seriousness. I would also like to point out I charge three thousand not three hundred. You don't have near enough for a night of sex with me brother." I winked at him.

Matz smiled bitterly as his tears rolled down his cheeks. "Oh, yeah. You are a pleasure submissive of the highest caliber. You know just what to say to make me feel less than the low life I know I really am. Okay Maxx I will stop this torturing you and myself. Thank you for letting me down easily. I do appreciate the mercy of it. We can still be friends, ja?"

I laughed hard. "Ah, Matz if you want to keep living here in public, we are more than friends. Behind closed doors, however, we are the best of buddies. Now I must go. You must have heard; I have a nasty appointment to attend. Did you get that apartment downstairs cleaned?"

He nodded. "You bet. A black collar maid is coming in daily at three. It will smell fresh and clean every day for the next month for what I paid her. I also opened that tab at the Great Hall. If you get home early enough, I can take you to dinner." He grinned while shooting me a playful look.

I shook my head. "No. I have another appointment for dinner at seven. I am a busy man, Matz. I may need you to start keeping tabs of my schedule. I am worrying at some point I will be so overwhelmed I won't know where to be at what time. I see you soon. Go get something to eat, Matz. You are the scarecrow. I like a little meat on my pretend lovers, okay?" He and I both chuckled at that as I left, and he went to collect the shirt he had thrown at Peter off the living room floor.

It was only eleven and I was not ordered to return to the Vampire's apartment till noon. I was not willing to wait even another minute to confront Jonas about what Peter told me. He nor Kilian had the right to interfere with my ability to attend college as far as I was concerned. I wanted to know on what grounds they or the fucking doctors deemed me incapable to attend the university for my Pre-Med degree but worthy of going to medical school. That simply made no sense.

I banged on that door of Jonas's with vigor madder than a wet hen, let me tell you. Within a few minutes that snake Kilian answered, appearing mildly amused at my state of irritation. He smiled and backed away to allow me to enter without saying a word. I stormed inside to find Jonas sitting on his sofa with a book, as usual.

I pointed at him growling like an angry bear. "Explain this bullshit Peter is spouting to me about doing my Pre-med in this House. Where the hell do you get off blocking my career, Jonas. I said I would mind your foul games in the bedroom without quarrel. How dare you go behind my back and conspire with those paid thugs from Heslach that call themselves psychiatrists."

Jonas stared at me with stoic coolness while Kilian hid his evil grin by covering his mouth with his hand as the Vampire said, "You need to calm yourself Maximillian. One would think you are acting psychotic showing up here with such fury and screaming incoherently about conspiracies."

I rolled my eyes and scoffed. "Oh, okay I get it. Every time I have issue with anything you or your dogs do to me that is out of line, I am throwing the crazy fit, ja? Well, fuck you Jonas. I am going to do my studies in a real college building like normal young people do. I have the grades and can pass the entrance exams. You call that cocksucker Altergott and tell him to withdraw the order for home studies. I am not schizophrenic, Goddammit!"

Kilian snorted, then howled with laughter as Jonas began to chuckle and put down his book. "Do you hear this Kilian love? Maximillian is not a schizophrenic, you know. We have been mistaken and so has your well-educated brother. Call Reese and tell him to send out his boys. Maximillian wants a second opinion and another assessment. I would be a neglectful guardian if I were to deny my boy the right to dispute such a grievous charge against him. Tell you what, when you are done calling Heslach, get Olaf and Vilber to come escort him to the front door. Oh, wait, I forgot. Those brutes are dead and buried in shallow graves outside in the yard with bolt cutter cracks to their skulls. I wonder who did that to them. It is just awful killing unarmed fellows that were only doing their jobs and minding their own business. Don't you think so, Maximillian?"

I backed up and crossed my arms feeling the wind leaving my lungs. "That was, I was a little stressed I admit to that, but you don't understand. The brutes had to go. They tried to kill me several times and that Olaf, he raped me twice. They had that coming and you know it."

Jonas laughed then blew out his breath, making his eyes wide. "Oh, I don't doubt they did Maximillian. However, killing two huge men in front of hundreds of people, then taking the time to bury them barely deep enough to keep off the flies was a bit more than a stress reaction don't you think?"

I shook my head. "What does this have to do with your denying me the right to college?"

Kilian snorted. "Everything Maximillian. Maybe next time you kill the professor or your classmates during a stressful test or bad day."

That made me roll my eyes. "Shut the fuck up, you snake! That forked tongue of yours will get you thrown from the banister. I don't know of any serpents than can fly."

Kilian's smile deepened. "Ah, see that, Jonas. The boy threatens to kill anyone that says something he doesn't agree with. Maximillian, you keep talking boy. The more you say, the more you hang yourself with that silver tongue of yours."

I scoffed but backed up a bit more towards the door. "I would tell you to fuck yourself Kilian, but I happen to know you expect to do that to me. How is my killing the guards the foul criminal act of a madman, but you two sharing me as your sperm pocket any less insane? I am only sixteen years old, you perverts. You are nothing but child molesting bastards. That makes you total sickos."

Jonas stood up with a loud yell. "Kneel, you big sonofabitch. I will not hear another word from you but what I tell you to say in the bedroom. You forget yourself, boy. All it would take is a phone call and you are gone forever."

I shot a look of disbelief at him. "I am not your submissive, Jonas. I am the Dominant. You cannot order me to kneel."

The Vampire laughed with fires in his dark eyes. "Oh, you will do what I tell you Maximillian and get on your knees. For some reason you seem to think I won't do what I must to get you to mind me boy. I repeat that command once more and I intend to make the believer out of you."

My ears began to heat up with both fear and anger. "Why are you doing this to me, Jonas? I served you well and did all I was ever told to do. I broke that collar fair and square. I earned my freedom. Please, I beg of you stop tormenting and let me get on with my life."

Kilian shook his head with a loud sigh. "You are not a Dominant, Maximillian, and you are refusing the training. At this moment, at any time, you can be recollared fool. Peter told us you have not even begun your lessons designed to undo that brainwashing of submission when wearing the silver. You should have started that shit the day you got back. Here it is three days in, not including that nineteen month the House has already forgave you for, and not even a scheduled course with your trainer. Ah, you are the fool Maximillian. Don't you know the law? Of course, you don't. You didn't bother to remain to receive the instruction and penalties list for all new Dominant trainees the day you busted that metal. You were too busy killing door guards and running around like the loon you are."

I narrowed my eyes at him. "You're lying. I am a freeman. They will not recollar me for refusing the training. I never heard of such a thing the entire time I have been held hostage here. Not even from the greatest of all fakers,

Peter. You are trying to scare me, is all. Not going to work, snake."

Jonas nodded with much intensity. "Kilian speaks the truth Maximillian. That won't matter though. You are still not kneeling. That means you need not worry about being recollared. They have a leash already installed on the strait jackets to keep your submitted at Heslach. Kilian darling, do the honors will you?" He motioned for that snake to go make the call.

I let out a yelp as that bastard made a move to the phone, then dropped to my knees, "Wait, I am minding. See Jonas, stop him." Kilian turned around with a thrilled grin as the Vampire's expression cooled off almost immediately.

He then sat back down and glared at me. "That is better. Now we can speak in a calm, collected fashion, right? You are to get to your Dominant training starting tomorrow and you will do your college course work from this House. You utter another fucking peep to me about how you're going to ignore my will and do as you please I won't stop Kilian from calling that brother of his. Are we understanding each other, boy?"

I dropped my gaze as my breathing went shallow from the internal rage that was building. "Yes, I hear you, Jonas."

The Vampire smiled arrogantly. "Good boy, Maximillian. We are going to get along just fine. You will be silent unless I say to speak from here on out. You will not throw fits, bang on my door with fury, nor tell me what you will or won't do. There is no bargaining. You do what you are told period. You got that?"

I knelt there fuming but said nothing, barely nodding my head.

He sat forward. "I don't believe I heard you."

I looked up with my demons rising. "As you wish, Master."

Kilian and the Vampire giggled at my sarcastic response. Just then a loud knocking began at the door. The two of them looked at each other with confusion as Jonas nodded for the snake to check on the visitor. I didn't move from my spot but had started to plan a way to kill them both without getting caught doing it.

Kilian answered and to my shock Peter came shoving his way into that living room. I stared at him in wonder noticing he was beyond enraged himself about something. He took a look at me kneeling there by the door, then set his sights on Jonas.

He yelled out in fury, "What the fuck, Jonas. I am trying to teach the boy to be the Dominant and you have him on his knees. This will not do. It is counterproductive to his training." He hand motioned me to stand up.

I shot a bewildered look at Jonas that was sneering at Peter, but kept my spot as he bellowed back, "You mind your fucking business, Peter. I do whatever I like with my ward. What the hell are you even doing here? I don't recall inviting you to see me. Just who do you think you are to insult me in my own home like this."

Peter scoffed. "I come up here to ask you to speak some sense into the boy. He was most hateful about my reminding him of his contract, refused to accept the course books, and even worse has that slimeball Matz living with him below. That said, I can see why he has been so bullheaded. Jonas, you have fucked this boy's training up as the silver and now I come here to find you intend to do it again with his Dominant status. You have no business being his guardian. There is a right way and a wrong way to get Maximillian to mind you. This barking with no bite shit you pulled was erratic at best. It nearly cost him those cutters. I will not stand by quietly to see you fuck up his future too."

The Vampire and Peter immediately began to hurl insults at each other. Peter accused Jonas of bad training techniques and Jonas accused Peter of interference of his rights as my man and guardian. I stayed in my kneeling feeling more anxious by the second with all that noise going on. I began to wring my hands to try to alleviate the growing terror within the boy.

That Kilian slipped over within speaking distance to me never takin his eyes off the arguing Voter and Elder as he leaned down and said, "Sure is a lot of noise, isn't it? Do you think Claus is playing his radio too loud? I hate it when he does that. I tire of hearing that DJ talk of all your foul deeds and dirty thoughts. The other day, several residents complained to me that they too are sick of it. Maybe you could stop thinking so much and give that radio station a break and all of us that hear it."

I looked up with a startle as my blood turned to ice in my veins. "What? You hear that radio? It had stopped playing and they fired the DJ, I thought."

He shook his head. "No, they didn't. The other day he said that the five lambs you let loose in the flock just died. Yeah, it was so sad. Wolves tore out their throats. Luckily, the shepherd found them and saved enough of them to make wiener schnitzel, you know that stuff they had on special last night in the Great Hall. I didn't get any of it, but I heard it was delicious."

I shook my head with pure terror over him claiming my baby lambs, Geraldine, Ryker, Annette, Milo and Abelard were murdered. "You are lying, snake. I do not hear that radio. My lambs are safe in the fields. They were not the dinner for Dominants."

He shrugged. "Suit yourself, Maxx. Doesn't matter if you believe me. I know what I heard. I really wish Reese wouldn't have allowed your Doctor Wagner to put that fucking transmitter in your back teeth though. Now the reception from your thinking comes in so loud I need to wear earplugs to drown out that radio wave. Fucking annoying if you ask me. I suppose they had to do it to keep track of you. Couldn't have you running off wild into the tapestry, could they?"

I trembled as I wrung my hands faster thinking, I could indeed hear that radio too as he said. "They cannot put transmitters in teeth. That is insane. There is no such a thing." My back teeth began to ache as I suddenly recalled those doctors had indeed stuck something in them.

Kilian looked at me with concern in his expression. "Why Maximillian, you are sweating. Are you hot? Ah, of course, hey Maximillian, guess what? Pea's porridge hot, peas porridge cold, peas porridge in the pot, nine days old or is it: lame since you got shot, because your too bold, you are trapped in the spot, because you got sold." He smiled at me.

I jumped up frantic to get the fuck out of there. "Shut up, snake. You lie. Help! Call the police. This reptile is reading my mind. Make him stop. I will kill him, I swear it." I tried pushing past the railing Peter.

Peter was startled and grabbed me, trying to block me from the door. "Maximillian, what the hell has gotten into you. Settle down boy."

I wailed out. "You let me go, devil. I won't let your fleas suck me dry. Unhand me or the king's men will set you to flames. Turn down the radio. The DJ is a liar. I didn't do that. I never do that."

Jonas came running to help Peter hold me. I saw that Vampire coming at me which caused a bit of panic within. Before I could stop myself, I punched my father in the face and reared back to do it again as he recoiled, grabbing his bleeding nose with a yelp.

Kilian and Jonas jumped on my back sending me sprawling face first onto the floor. I screamed bloody murder as that music that I hate began to blast through the walls. I covered my ears and rolled into a ball trying to drown out the sounds.

I yelled out, "Make it stop. Help. Turn it down. I do anything to make it go away. Der Hound, we are in trouble. Where are you?" I looked at Maximillian that had gone pale with terror.

He looked at Mad Maxx and shouted. "The wheel is rocking, brothers. A shattering is coming. Get Der Hound, Mad Maxx. The boy needs aid, go now. Christian, you get going too. Do not come back until you find our Core fellows. Mad Max and I will man the flesh until you return." I watched as the masochistic and lust/anger shard jumped from the boy and ran with all speed in two different directions. This was bad.

Maximillian came forward and grabbed the wheel from my grip. "Brace yourself brother. I am going to buy us some time." I was flung to my ass next to Max as Maximillian pulled the boy up to his knees still holding his ears.

The Vampire, Kilian and Peter watched in utter disbelief as the flesh got up then ran face first right into the wall at full strength. The boy staggered backward as the ground shook beneath his feet. He turned to look at the monster Dominants for a moment just as the power flickered. The knees gave way and for a few moments everything went still and black, unconsciousness came to claim us for her own.

I opened my eyes to see the faces of the diabolical three staring into my own. I groaned out from the massive headache that screamed between my ears. I tried to sit up, but the dizziness forced me back to the floor immediately.

Jonas narrowed his eyes. "Maximillian? Boy, can you hear me?"

I nodded. "Yes, but you need to tone it down. I think I have a hangover or something. How the fuck did I get here?" I turned my head trying to recall my exact location.

Peter snorted. "Hangover? You don't remember headbutting the wall like a crazy bull?"

My eyes went wide. "What bullshit you are trying to feed me? I cannot do seven in the morning. Can we move that training to eleven instead?" I sat up feeling less faint as the three men backed away a bit.

Peter shook his head., "Yes, eleven is fine, Maximillian. Jonas, I can see what you are talking about now. I was going to argue with you more about this doing the Pre-med in House, but after seeing this, I can no longer dispute he is not ready to leave the protection of his betters yet. He pulls that out there in the world they will shoot him or lock him up for good. Do you really think another two to four years will make that much difference?" He flashed a look of fear at Kilian.

Kilian nodded with a wicked smile. "You bet, Peter. I will work with him to curb these sporadic psychotic fits. Likely it was all that yelling the two of you were doing that set him off. You must be calm and forceful with these schizophrenics. They only understand structure and monotony. Any sudden surprise or quick movement can do what you just saw."

Jonas nodded. "You listen to Kilian, Peter. He knows his stuff. No more verbal combat with the boy around. You and I want the female priceless. This boy gets himself killed that will never happen. The Krause girl is not ready to harvest for another five years yet. I keep him subjugated and you go through the motions as if you were really preparing him to live outside the walls. As you witnessed that can never happen."

Peter scoffed as I began to tremble and tear up at the Vampire's words. "Jonas, you are a fool. The boy needs to be polished and released. That damned niece of Malfred's is not the one. If you allow this boy to bring her across, then the children will make him too powerful. Allow me to get him ready for the outside. We send him into society, and I assure you he will bring home a Frau of good stock. I will even swear to be with him through the entire process. This is too important to allow this disturbed idiot to do it alone. I am an experienced trainer. He will pick her and I will break her."

I shook my head wildly. "No, you cannot do this. I will never choose any woman to be my wife. I am gay. Leave me alone. I want to go to be a doctor and to find the fields with the baby sheep." Jonas reared back and backhanded me with much force.

I took the blow but refused to relent. "Please, I beg of you. Let me go. I will never tell anyone about this hell hole. I just want to…" Peter hit me in the face sending me back to the floor this time.

I spit the blood from my mouth into the carpet. "You beat me all you like. I will run away. You cannot keep me here forever. You better watch your backs. I am coming for all you." Jonas stood up and kicked me in the balls.

I groaned and sputtered unable to get enough air in to even wail as Peter and Jonas grabbed my arms. I kicked at Kilian as that man delivered another blow to my family jewels. That knocked the fight right out of me. The pain sent me right to hell and took my breath away. The three of them dragged me down the hallway to the Vampire's bedroom.

Jonas handcuffed my wrists behind me before I could recover from their rough treatment of my, uhm, boys. They leaned me against the side of his bed and stood there staring at me glaring back at them with hate in my expression.

Jonas sighed. "I don't desire to have to beat the fuck out of this brute every fucking time I want to enjoy what belongs to me. He is still growing, Peter. Sooner or later, he will get the better of me and I will be flying down the stairs face first. This must stop and now. I refuse to live my life in fear of my own God damned submissive."

I sniffed back my tears. I wasn't sad, but they kicked me so hard it made my eyes and nose run you know. It was an involuntary thing, I swear it. "I am not your submissive, Jonas. I broke that bat collar. You were there and so was Peter. You need not live-in fear that I will kill you. Just let me walk away. I will give you no further quarrel. You won't ever hear even the rumor of me again, I swear it."

Jonas lost his temper completely when I said that. He came unglued and launched a rapid and forceful barrage of backhands, punches, and even a few kicks onto me. I couldn't do a thing to defend myself but tuck my head, then try to hide my face in the carpet. He went nuts. I was forced to endure his pounding on me everywhere, while swearing and yelling at me in unbridled fury. This went on for several minutes until Kilian and Peter were finally able to pull the fed-up Vampire off at last.

They restrained him as I laid there in a pool of my own blood. The Vampire busted up my lips and nose pretty good before I could protect them. "You shut the fuck up, you crazy bastard. Let me go. This asshole deserved it and more. He has busted up my apartment and stained the motherfucking carpet with his blood. You know what, Christian Axel? Fuck you and fuck this. Call the hospital, Kilian. I will not deal with this insolent cocksucker any longer without aid. That right, you sonofabitch. In Heslach they will keep you nice and quiet. Then when I want to have my fun you will be too drugged up or tied to the bed to fight me."

Kilian hesitated a moment. "You sure Jonas? Once I call you will have to travel to get your transfusions. You sure you are up for another several years of that rough business? I mean I am for whatever you decide but you were not too happy the last time. I don't want you angered at me later for doing as you requested."

The Vampire growled out. "I said call them."

I wailed out in full on panic. "No, please Jonas. Don't do this. I don't understand what you want. I am the Dominant. Peter and you told me that if I broke the collar, I was the freeman. Now you call me the submissive and order me around. Why? I am so confused. What is happening. What do you want from me." I began to cry for real this time, unable to hold it together any longer. It had been a grueling day already and I had a little trouble sleeping the night before, you know.

Peter held up his hand and blocked Kilian from leaving the room to make the call. "Wait a second, brother. I don't want to see this boy put away again. Another inpatient will weaken his chances at getting a doctor's license. We cannot explain away that much psychiatric treatment. Allow me to speak to him before you rush off making decisions that cannot be undone, okay?"

Jonas scoffed. "You are not listening to me, Peter. I have been putting up with these insane outbursts from this idiot for over five years now. I am tired of the constant strife. Unless you can assure me he will mind without another fucking fit then I believe you're wasting time.

What are you going to say to him? Mind me or else. I already tried that, repeatedly. You think you are better than me I suppose?"

Peter shook his head. "No Jonas, I do not intend to try to overstep my bounds with your way of managing this insanity. I merely say he is likely confused by this unstable treatment you have given over these many years. I never had this kind of difficulty with this boy as you had. You are too permissive at times and too rough other times. That is not the way to get him to do as he is told. I ask you to allow me to try to speak to him. If you are unsatisfied with what I say or how he responds then by all means, have Kilian call the dogs in. What do you have to lose, but maybe a several hour trip every few weeks, right?"

Jonas rubbed his chin while appearing deep in thought. "Okay Peter, go ahead. You are right. What are another few minutes? That boy will set you on your ass with another attempt to attack you. I will get the laugh and he will be sent away. I have nothing better to do then enjoy this show anyway." He made a motion towards me to let Peter know he wasn't going to stop him from his approach to try to reason with me.

I didn't move as my father came towards me slowly, appearing cautious in case I tried to injure him. "Maximillian? You sit up right this minute and speak with me. You are in a lot of trouble boy. You best mind me." I rose as he told me to but kept my eyes to the floor.

He nodded. "Thats better. You heard Jonas. He plans to send you away from the House, just as you wanted. However, I don't think it is the destination you hoped for is it?"

I shook my head and sobbed a bit louder as I was finally getting a grip on the sorry lot I had pulled in this life. There was no more escape for me than there was for Marc.

Peter cleared his throat. "Well, it need not happen you know. Jonas merely wants you to mind him when in his presence. He is your legal guardian and has full responsibility for you. What he asks is fair return of service for what he provides."

I shot a look of disbelief at Peter. "Are you kidding me? That bat brings the snake in here to befoul me with him, Peter. What the hell does he do for me exactly besides make me have empathy for women? Nothing, that's what."

The Vampire started to come at me causing me to cower as Peter held up his hand. "Jonas, please. Let me handle this?"

Jonas glared but backed up.

Peter shot a look of disapproval at me. "Jonas kept you out of prison for killing those two guards, Maximillian. He has opened his home to you. He paid to have you treated for your illness, and is responsible for dealing with the school boards, lawyers, and doctors. You are a lot of trouble with that mental illness of yours. You have no right to complain about anything he asks of you when all you have is your services to repay the suffering he has and will do in your place."

I wept quietly but said, "I cannot argue with you about things I do not know or understand. That said, I gave him no further quarrel. I came here today to provide the services, but he wants the behaviors of the submissive. He will keep me from college and demands I collect a wife for him to steal from me. That is not equal service, Peter."

Peter groaned. "You are delusional and paranoid, Maximillian. Jonas is not trying to take your wife away. You have no Frau to run off with anyway. He is also not keeping you from school. You are doing that by behaving like a lunatic. You calm down that nutball shit and you will be in medical school before you know it. He is merely protecting you, fool. You pull shit like you did just a moment ago, you will never be able to find work once they arrest you. That diagnosis is hidden for this moment and can stay that way. You start banging your head or attacking students over crazy ideas of radios that are not there or others reading your mind, you are finished. Are you listening to me, boy."

I nodded. "I am, but I don't do that kind of stuff, Peter. If you let me go to school, I will be quiet and compliant as a mouse."

Peter shook his head and crossed his arms. "Tell you what, Maximillian. This is how it will be. You will begin your Dominant training with me tomorrow at eleven, no excuses, do not be late. You will complete your pre-medical courses from this House under the watchful and protective eyes of your man and me as your trainer. No arguments. You will move back in with Jonas and kick that thug Matz out of your apartment immediately."

I gasped then shot him a look. "I will agree with the first two points but not the last two. You nor Jonas can make me either. I have the contract Jonas signed with Rolf. That apartment has been promised to me if I broke the bat collar. I need Matz there to help me with the expenses unless the Vampire wishes to give me money to survive on. Otherwise, I must have him there or starve."

Peter was startled, then looked back at Jonas. "Does the boy tell the truth, Jonas? Did you swear to give that apartment to him?"

Jonas blew out his breath. "What does that matter Peter? I changed my mind. He comes home or he can go to Heslach."

Peter shook his head with a bitter chuckle. "Oh no you don't, Jonas. If you gave your word and signed that agreement then it is held by House Law, and you know it. I cannot allow you off the hook or why should Maximillian mind any contract with his betters either? Equal for equal, Jonas."

Jonas growled in anger, "Fine, I will give him nothing. That creep will move out today."

I glared at the Vampire, not caring if he saw my tears. "You cannot interfere with my House. That is in the contract. Matz will aid me to eat. You keep your fucking money. I don't need it."

Jonas snorted. "Sucking Matz's cock for a sandwich. Oh, how low you have sunk Christian Axel."

I growled. "Maximillian. You killed that fellow named Christian or did you forget that dad."

Peter put up his hand. "Enough. Okay, that is settled. Maxx you can stay in the apartment and none of us will interfere with it. However, you owe me services for what I grant you, and your man demands them too."

I shrugged. "Do you think I give a shit? I don't care what any of you do to me. You are forcing me to stay here another two to four years to play your pincushion. At least with the normal sexual assaults you keep pulling on me you use lube before you fuck me up the ass."

Jonas started to come at me once again and this time Kilian had to restrain him with vigor as he yelled out. "Shut up Maxx, or I will fuck you even harder without any comfort, you stupid cocksucker."

I nodded. "You got that right, dad! Go ahead and call me by my job description instead of the fake name you've given me, Jonas. I am quite used to it now. You are old news, very old, and only getting older."

Peter backhanded me, which stilled my tongue immediately as he said. "That is enough. I am trying to help you, Maximillian. You will learn to behave or maybe you need a reminder of the good old days down below?"

I glared at him in shock. "You cannot do that Peter. I am a Dominant."

He laughed. "You are too smart to play an idiot, boy. You are not a Dominant until you finish that training. Did you forget that already? Want to be insolent again? I have been aching to work out my tawse and a little raking or pinwheel could be fun, ja?"

I winced at that. "No, I don't think I am willing to test you on that Peter. I apologize for that outburst. It won't happen again."

Jonas gasped, nearly fainting at my sudden calming. "Kilian, go to the spare room and grab my rake and pinwheel love." Kilian nodded then took off to fetch the item.

I watched him with anxiety then looked back at Peter. "I said I will behave, Peter. I don't understand. Why am I to be punished anyway?"

Peter smiled. "No, you won't be. That is, if you keep to the promise to mind without further quarrel. However, having a reminder around is not a bad thing. You tend to forget rather easily. Right, Jonas?"

The Vampire nodded. "I will feel better having it handy is all. You need not worry about it. Unless you intend to piss me off again."

I licked my swollen lips and trembled with fear, keeping a baleful eye on the door for Kilian's return with those dreaded cutter weapons. "I do not intend to Jonas. I will do whatever you say and meet Peter tomorrow at eleven. I will study hard and keep my mouth shut like you ask me to."

Jonas laughed wickedly. "Ah, now not so fast, Maximillian. I don't desire you to keep that pretty mouth shut nor tongue still. You may liberally use both. I just don't want to hear any complaints, argument, or excuses either. Peter. I was thinking. This brute has gotten so big he is a threat to me and Kilian if he were to decide to break his promises. You are owed the services for your hard work to polish him into the Dominant and eventual physician. Why not join our fun? Your extra muscle would be most appreciated."

Peter smiled evilly at me as I dropped my gaze to the floor feeling my stomach lurch. "You know what Jonas, that is the best offer I have had in years. Count me in. Do you think the boy would mind one more? I have heard tale he enjoys the same gendered sex these days and must have a nap every few hours, he is so actively engaged in the thrill of it." They both stared at me with great humor.

Jonas chuckled. "Is that what you heard? Well, I was told a rumor that the boy has turned gay. I am sure he will be overjoyed to have you join our little parties. What do you say Maxx?"

I mumbled out doing my best to bite back the misery of this horror. "The more the merrier they say."

Peter giggled. "Ah, now that is not right, Maxx. Where is that sassy tongue pop or flouncing? I will not feel loved if you don't fuss over me like you do the worm you live with. I expect the same kind of affection, wait. No, I expect even more."

I glared at him then popped my tongue. "Guess that means you go first, lover boy."

That made Jonas nearly fall to his face he was laughing so hard as he said, "Holy hell that was funny, Peter. Did you teach him that?"

Peter began to undo his breeches buttons glaring at me with victory in his gaze. "Oh, not me Jonas. You see Maximillian here is trained to perfection as the pleasure submissive. All you must be able to do is tell him what you want and he will give it to you without quarrel. Your problem is you never made it clear he is not the Freeman and never will be. He will always do whatever it takes to live another day in as little pain as possible, won't you Maxx."

I nodded and braced for this fearsome foursome. "I don't have a choice."

Peter grabbed my head and forced his cock into my busted-up mouth. "You sure don't. Kilian put the pinwheel on the dresser. I am in the mood to put Maximillian through a refresher course in the basics today." I closed my eyes as

I began to endure the harshest afternoon that had occurred in a little over nineteen months.

There is no need to get into too many details about that nightmare in Jonas's bedroom the first day Peter joined forces with Jonas and Kilian. I will say only three things. The first was that I had, most fortunately, forgotten how bad blow jobs hurt when your mouth is the bloody mess.

The next thing I will say is that if I thought the day before was humiliating, I had been in error. The three of them took their time making me their bitch. I was weeping without attempting to hide it long before my third point came into play.

The final thing I will say is that I was sadly reacquainted with the cutters between and during their hedonistic partaking of the boy's flesh. Wails, begging, and screams that were forced out of me from those wretched devices only incited the monsters into a lustful frenzy. By the time they finished working me over, I was a quivering, drooling, bleeding, tear drenched sight of horror.

When I was finally released to clean up after their foul messes, I was in a terrible dilemma. I was so beat up that I could barely limp to the bathroom. I glanced into the mirror and the electric feeling of terror raced down my spine. Osvin would surely demand his money back I was so observably swollen and damaged.

I fought back the fresh tears as I dragged myself into the shower and scrubbed off all the evidence of my disgrace as possible. If only I could withstand water at real life boiling temperature. Only then, could I ever get rid of the truthful disgusting things they had done to me.

Since I could not live through such an extreme cleansing, I did my best with what I had. I redressed quickly, ready to get the fuck out of there. I stood at the door for several moments swallowing down the crying jag that was threatening to break through. With a deep breath I opened the door and hobbled out rushing for the exit with all the speed I could muster.

Peter was sitting in the reading chair and the other two brutes were relaxing in their bed as the Vampire yelled out to me. "Maxx, you didn't ask when I want you back home tomorrow. I hope you didn't plan to leave without following that directive."

I stopped, then put my left hand on my hip and twirled my hair while flouncing then popped my tongue as I said, "Oh, silly me. You know I was so busy thinking about Matz I totally forgot myself. I was in a hurry to get home to his arms. You know I can be such an airhead, ja? Never could pat my head and suck cock at the same time. If only I could, wouldn't that be grand? You know I was thinking, lover. This scene was so much fun today. We have got to do that again real soon. You let me know when to be here and you can count me in for the fun. Ah, I am such a lucky one. Everywhere I go there is so much wealth of good loving. Oh, there I go yapping like the idiot I am. I am just so full of vigor these days. What time did you say? Did you tell me, and it flew right out my empty head maybe?" I shifted my weight dramatically and twirled my hair while pretending to examine my nails to see if they needed the manicure, you know. Not that I ever got one of them, but just to see if I could use it.

The fellows all sat there with their eyes wide until Kilian at last broke the silence when he asked, "Have you been hanging out with Jakob, Maximillian?"

I didn't look up from my fingers as I replied, "Who? Oh hell, I broke a fucking nail. Matz loves to see the pretty digits when I stroke his…" I stopped and looked up as if shocked at what I almost said.

Then I covered my mouth with my hand and giggled into it the way Jakob taught me. "Oopsy doodles. I almost said something naughty didn't I. Ah, Maximillian better get his bubble butt out of here before his bubble brain says something that will make me sound the bad boy."

I turned around with a big flounce and headed for the door once more when Jonas yelled out again, "Maxx, you didn't get the time, again."

I turned and snapped at him pushing out my swollen lips and rolling my eyes. "Oh hell, you are a broken record, Jonas. Tell me already. I am eager to be getting to the next course of this feast, you know?"

Jonas shook his head in bewilderment. "Oh, uhm okay, you be here at two."

I nodded then turned around throwing my elbows out and humming a snappy tune as I pushed my way out the door. The second I hit that hallway I took off in a limping run. I didn't stop fleeing with pure terror driving me until I reached the fourth-floor apartment entry. I nearly kicked it in, then slammed it closed behind me. I really needed another shower.

Matz was sitting on the couch. He looked up from his note taking briefly then looked down only to jump up with a startle while dropping his papers onto the floor when he did. I tried to rush past him, but he let out a yelp.

"Maxx, what the fuck happened. Holy motherfucking hell. Are you okay? Who did this to you? Peter? That appointment you went to? Speak to me, please. You are injured." He got up and started racing after me.

I stopped at my bedroom door and turned to him barely holding back the overwhelming emotions of pain. "I am fine. You go back to the couch, Matz. I just need a shower. The water will make it better." I tore into the bedroom, but Matz would not relent on his chase he was hot on my heels.

I began tearing off my clothing in a frantic effort to get the stink of those rotten men off me. Matz stood there in shock as my flesh was quickly being revealed. I stopped when I began to remove my boots, my blouse was already gone, and my pants were down to the knees, and Matz let out a loud gasp.

I glared at him with rain beginning to fill my eyes. "What are you looking at motherfucker? You never seen a naked man before? I thought you said you're gay."

Matz backed up with a look of horror in his eyes, "I uhm, ja, I have seen plenty of naked guys. Maxx, but your flesh, the scars, and you are cut up even more. You are bleeding. Let me help you please. What the hell Maxx. Why?"

I growled out as I threw my boot at him, hitting him in the leg. "You pervert. I thought you knew I was covered in scars. You miss that rumor, Matz? Hope Osvin and Fritz don't mind busted lips, bruises, or scars like you seem to or we are going to be in a lot of trouble without any fucking thing to eat, ja? Hey, cocksucker. If you are going to keep standing there watching me, then I will charge you that fucking three hundred. Strippers get paid too, I believe." I got up and stormed into the bathroom turning on the hot water full blast.

I was watching the steam rising waiting for that germ killing heat to be reached when Matz had the audacity to come into the room.

I turned around incredulous at the nerve of this bastard. "Get out. Mind your own business, Matz. Can you not see I am busy with a personal service?"

Matz looked at my calves watching the thin trails of blood rolling down them with sadness in his expression. "I am minding my business, Maxx. You need attendance for these wounds. There are many you will have difficulty reaching without help. You need not tell me who or what. If you wish to keep your silence I understand. I won't pry.

However, throwing me out for doing the job you pay me to do, that I will not allow."

I glared at him. "I need no one to help me, especially you."

He sniffed loudly. "That is the biggest lie I have heard in my life, Maxx. I never met anyone who needed it more in fact. Look I am not going to go away and to let you suffer this agony all alone."

That made me roll the boy's eyes. "Suit yourself, Matz. No one else seems to listen, so why would you?" I stepped into the burning hot stream feeling better the very second, I closed my eyes as that white hot water cooked the foul flesh.

Then suddenly the shower stopped running. I opened my eyes wondering if maybe the House turned off the liquid to the apartment. To my shock Matz stood there staring at me in disbelief. I finally realized he had turned the facet off.

I became furious almost beyond words. "You sonofabitch! How dare you? Get out. I will fucking beat your ass for interfering with my hygiene rituals."

Matz shook his head. "You are harming yourself, Maxx. Kill me if you think you can but I will not sit back and watch you boil yourself. I am going to call Osvin and tell him something came up. You are in no condition to work. You step out of the tub, dry off, and relax. I will get the antiseptic to treat your injuries."

I couldn't take anymore I wailed out in misery. "Why are you bothering me, Matz. You leave Osvin alone. I am fine. I told you I do this shit every day. Why would I cancel over a scratch? You are the stupidest asshole on earth."

Matz nodded. "Ja, I sure am Maxx. I am dumb for loving you but nevertheless I do. Come here to me. You are limping, brother. You grab my arm to make sure you don't fall down as you get out."

I whimpered, unable to argue any longer. "No, Matz. I need to finish this bath. I am soiled. I have to clean it until it is gone."

Matz snorted then looked at the floor. "Maxx you are indeed soiled right to the bone. You can go to a million baths brother, that shit you have endured will still be there. The water you need to truthfully cleanse it away comes from within not that facet. I repeat, come here brother let me help you make that House of yours sparkling clean until the next degenerate comes in with their muddy shoes to stomp all over your soul, ja?"

I nodded then took his arm and stepped out of the bathtub. He put a towel over my shoulders and gave me another to wrap around my waist. I felt oddly disconnected while I watched him grabbing the disinfectant and arnica oil. He took all the items with us as he motioned me to follow him.

He had me sit down on my bed as he began applying the stinging alcohol-based treatments. He worked in silence as he poured the arnica oil into his palms then rubbed it gently into the angry blue and black bruises rising up everywhere on my flesh. I took that treatment stoically almost in a trance. I didn't have the will to speak, argue with him, nor fight anymore. None of that shit ever worked anyway. No matter what I tried, most people did whatever they wanted to me despite my objections. Why should Matz be any different.

When he believed he had done the best possible to deflect some of the worse bruising he squatted in front of me looking deep into my eyes. "You know Maxx, I mean what I said. I can hold off old Osvin. You are pretty torn up and I am told that fellow is the rough lover by someone who's word I trust. I cannot make you listen to me, but I am asking you to consider it. In fact, now that I have seen the truth of your experience, I kind of think maybe I would rather be thrown to the streets then watch someone that has had enough for a few lifetimes."

I sighed. "It is okay, Matz. I am used to this bullshit. These marks will heal, and it wouldn't matter if they weren't there. I would still feel them anyway. I haven't changed a bit from when we first decided to do this thing. The only thing is now your opinion of it has. It is not smart to let trivial things get to you. What happened today when I left is far uglier than these flesh wounds that will be forgotten in a week. Peter and a couple others have blocked me from ever getting out of this House. I must start the Dominant training tomorrow and begin my coursework for college without the pleasure of the dorms, fresh air, or a pretty Frau sitting next to me in the classrooms."

Matz snorted. "Yeah, I heard that shit Peter was spouting today, brother. I knew he was correct about that Dominant training. I didn't know you required the guardian but now a lot of other shit makes a lot of sense to me, including these fresh torture wounds. I wish there were something I could do to help you Maxx, but I am at a loss. I can only wait till you tell me what you need or want me to do. I told you I never forget kindness, nor am I ever disloyal. You need not ever see Osvin or any of those brutes. I will find a way to pay back what we already spent. You can tease me till the day grows long and I will always accept that is all it is too. That said, don't expect me to stand back and watch you hurt yourself. I cannot have you burning up in hot water or leaving open wounds untreated. If you expect me to say nothing, then you are in for a surprise. If you desire to feel pain, then I am happy to oblige you brother. I catch that shit again, I will knock you the fuck out and give you worse than you were planning to do to yourself."

I scoffed. "Try it Matz. I will kill you."

He laughed and nodded. "Maybe, yet I will die with my honor intact. I swore to be your partner and that means when you're hurt, hungry, sad, or happy, so am I. That is the way it works, brother. We do this together or not at all. So, I vote to call that fat ass Osvin and tell him deal is off."

I shook my head. "No. I say we let me go and drop this."

Matz groaned as he shot me a smile that made me smile back. "Well shit we have a tie. One for and one against. Okay tell you what, we go meet that motherfucker and see what he says. Maybe he takes one look at your rainbow-colored face and decides he isn't interested?"

I nodded. "That sounds fair. Let the customer decide. No other way to be sure, right?"

He stood up, "Okay, so let me go get you some ice and something to eat. You rest up brother. I wish you would speak to me about what happened, but I respect your right to not say a word of it. If you change your mind, night, or day, I am here for you, Maxx. Anything else I can do to make you feel better that is within my power while I am out?"

I blew out my breath "Yes, tomorrow I need you to go to Karsten's apartment at two and take Marc out to the playground for a few hours or play football with him. It is not healthy for a kid to have no joy in life. I was going to take him, but that appointment got hijacked with a more pressing matter."

Matz chuckled. "Well hell, you ask me to go play with Marc is like asking me to go watch the gorgeous topless waiter down at the Strubenfarm dance on the tables. This is my pleasure to do for you Maxx."

He started to leave to retrieve the ice and meal, but I called out just as he left. "Matz (he turned around appearing surprised and raised his eyebrows), thank you for the mercy, brother."

The man stood there a second staring at his shoes. "I want you to know you mean more to me than any money you can make. I know you are accustomed to one sided or severely stacked relationships, but not this time, not with Matz. Karsten told me you are seeking Kloe's collar. If you for truth are doing such a wonderful thing for those children, then allow me to aid you. If Osvin decides to stay and you can complete the contract tonight, we will have that little girl or Osvin will find himself in divorce court. I am willing to risk it all if you are."

I looked at him suddenly finding the deepest respect for this most unexpectedly kindhearted man. "I am indeed. If we don't help her, no one else will. She has more love and compassion in her than this whole fucking House even if you squeezed every soul dry looking for it."

Matz nodded. "You do this for Marc, right? Or do you do it to help end the nightmares you gave her when you whipped the shit out of her two years ago for stealing that food to feed her brother Marc."

I gasped. "How did you know about that? No one was there but Peter, two Elders, and Egon."

He started to leave again. "Kloe was there. She told Marc that it was you in the thudding room two years ago that showed her mercy by using a trick to make a lot of noise without any real pain or severe injury. See you soon, Mad Maxx the Brutally treated." He winked at me with a sly smile as he headed out leaving me to do my best to prepare for my first night as a hustler.

**To be continued in book two of The Collar King Series:
Felicity's Child**

About Author: Alexandria May Ausman

Alexandria May Ausman in her 16th year was diagnosed with Schizophrenia. She was quickly abandoned by her foster parents. While still only a teen, she was forced to battle this devastating illness alone.

Alexandria has struggled with lack of a support system, numerous psychotic episodes, exploitation, homelessness, and an uncaring mental health system.

Alexandria raised two healthy children. After obtaining her bachelor's degree in psychology she worked as a child abuse investigator and became a diagnostic psychologist while acquiring her Master's in psychology. Alexandria never forgot the experience of 'slipping through the cracks.' Her life's goal is to help people suffering abuse and/or mental illness have access to necessary services. By accident, she became a model of 'gothic attire' and the World Goth Queen.

She began writing a fictionalized account of her life experiences after a catastrophic return of psychotic symptoms. Today, Alexandria is retired, and homebound due to crippling symptoms of Schizophrenia. She currently lives in Tallahassee, Florida, with her loving husband and a loyal support dog.